desires

desires

An Anthology of Erotic Short Stories

Edited by

Adrienne Benedicks

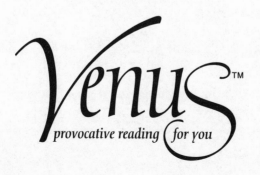

Citations

Desires was originally edited by Adrienne Benedicks & Shivaji Sengupta (AmarMira Press, 2000). "Bottomless on Bourbon" by Maxim Jakubowski first appeared in *Erotic New Orleans* (Portalba Press, 1999) "Three Pennies" by Jason Rubis first appeared in the *Marilyn's Room* (marilynsroom.com). "Crooked Kwan" by Cecilia Tan first appeared in *Noirotica* (Masquerade Books, 1995). "Aqua Marina" by Portia Da Costa first appeared in *Forum Magazine* (1997).

0-7394-2526-9

This book is dedicated to my husband who made certain all the intimate positions described within these stories are accurate and doable—bless his heart. Special thanks to all the members of the Erotica Readers & Writers Association, past and present. Whether they realize it or not they have all played a vital part in the creation of this book.

CONTENTS

desires

INTRODUCTION

What an honor it is to be asked to provide readers with an introduction to this newly revised volume of *Desires*, a diverse and exciting collection of erotic fiction from far flung areas of the globe.

As I prepared to write this introduction, I perused the impressive list of contributors and realized what a satisfying publishing history I have with so many of them.

In the winter of 1997–98, as creator and publisher of my then-fledgling erotic fiction web site, Other Rooms; I received my first email from Adrienne Benedicks. She introduced herself as editor of the Erotica Readers & Writers Association—a web site still renowned today for its dedication to the readers and writers of erotic fiction. She said she would soon be publishing a collection of erotica, *Erotic Threads*; stories culled from the members of ERA. Would I be willing to post an announcement on my own web site to advertise the upcoming electronic publication?

From that day on, I've always had a mutually supportive relationship with ERA. Other Rooms, and later, Marilyn's Room, were web sites I founded on my avid belief that the erotica community needed to bond together if we were ever to raise the public's awareness of a genre whose literary merits were so often overlooked. I was happy to announce Adrienne's collection.

So many of the talented writers I worked with online over the years were also prominent members of ERA. I look fondly now on the names in this book, like William Dean; remembering still the thrill of reading the first piece of fiction he submitted to me. Or Adhara Law, whose passion for both science and sex writing never failed to yield appealing results. Lybbe—another writer who did not fail to impress me with the fine quality of her erotic fiction. Names spring out at me now, larger than life. Some of the writers here were real pioneers in the erotic genre, writers whose work I've known and delighted in for years; Cecilia Tan, Thomas S. Roche, M. Christian, Maxim Jakubowski and Mary Anne Mohanraj.

And you, the reader, can't possibly know the long, often heroic, path this book took finding its way toward publication. If it weren't for the unique passion and vision; the fierce loyalty and determination of not only the editors, but the contributors and even the artist who designed its beautiful cover, it's safe to say this wonderful collection might have died on the vine. You don't need to know its history, though, to be able to enjoy the fruits of so many devoted people's labors. It's sufficient to say that this volume was a long time coming back, but it's decidedly worth the wait.

I hope you enjoy the writers gathered in this collection as much as I have loved them. And many thanks, in particular, to Adrienne Benedicks for her unwavering conviction in bringing quality erotica to the English-speaking world.

Marilyn Jaye Lewis
November 2001
New York City

WAY STATION

Debra Hyde

At first glance, we knew we'd changed since college. I had some wrinkles; he was graying. My hair was a shorter, sassier red; his black, brooding beard was a distant memory. I was in the throes of a mid-life crisis; he was already a widow. Life had made me tough as nails; tragedy had shown him vulnerability. As we embraced, our bodies provided further confirmation: we'd grown fleshy with age.

But we hadn't changed enough to break our intentions. We kissed, deeply.

His tongue slipped into my mouth, meeting mine, playing a capricious, darting game of tag. I was stunned to find his kiss still felt the same and, as we frenched in an old familiarity, I discovered we were still capable of the heat of mutual attraction. We were heading for a mutual meltdown, proof that old lusts die harder than old loves.

He reached for my breast, cupped it, caressed it. It was a softer, fleshier thing, no longer pert and perky, Time having done its duty well. I hoped that when I took my top off, he wouldn't think National Geographics.

I caressed his back, shoulders and moved to his chest. He had had a crevice where pecs met breastbone and I wondered if that lovely spot still existed. It did, but it had lost some definition. Good. That evened things up. I buried myself in dedicated kissing, losing myself in arousal, trying to forget the weight of aging.

He pinched my nipple lightly between two fingers. "You still like to go bra-less," he noticed, pulling away from my kiss.

"Even at work, if I can get away with it."

"You use to drives the guys nuts, you know, with the way your nipples use to show through."

I giggled. "Womanly badges."

He started nibbling on my ear. "And still arresting."

I hoped with age came wisdom, once our clothes came off.

A jolt between my legs told me to stop worrying and start enjoying. A jolt like that had started it all, years ago in younger days. I was wedged between him and his roomie in the front seat of roomie's car, cruising, and, as we turned a corner, I leaned into him. He put his hand on my knee, as if to balance me. An electric touch, it had forced me to make up my mind about him, lose the boyfriend, and make myself available to him.

His touch was still electric enough to make me available.

We peeled our tops off and our torsos pressed the flesh. His warmth and the feel of his now plentiful, now salt-and-peppered chest hair were familiarity, renewed. We rubbed our bodies together—petting body slams—and his hands strayed back to my breasts. Fingers tugged at nipples while his mouth traveled downward for its follow-up. He remembered, rightly so, that his mouth upon my nipples would flare the fuel between my legs.

I went for the belt buckle, then the zipper, to free him. His cock, firm and ready, and my hand, grasping and eager, raced to meet each other. I remembered the spire that he was, the girth that had satisfied, but as I caressed his length, I realized I'd forgotten the actual feel of him—soft, with a stiff inner core. He moaned, still sucking. I swayed backwards onto the bed, wanting him to explore more of me, wanting him to reclaim what he'd once known well.

Letting go of each other, he helped me shimmy from my skirt, surprised to find me pantiless and shaved.

"No bush," he smiled. He lingered, looking at me, slowly bringing his fingers to my pussy, touching my hairless cunt, examining the mound and crevices as if he'd never seen them before.

"You remember that time I shaved, don't you?"

"Yeah," he said. "But I thought you were being weird and I was embarrassed. Of course, years later, I realized that I was the weird one."

"No, no you weren't. I was the weird one. Still am."

"So you claim." Ah, his old habit of discounting me. The stiff inner core in another form.

Unaware of his subtle attitude, he smiled gently and focused on my pussy, examining me. He placed a finger on my clit, pressed down, making me groan.

"I understand how to work this better," he told me, gazing into my eyes briefly, then returning to my cunt. His finger began to circle it, rubbing, pressing on occasion, working my arousal. But he was also intent on exploring the nuances of my folds and he spread me with his other hand. There, he found a little surprise.

"Whoa!"

"Labia rings."

"I see."

"Go ahead, touch them. You can even tug on them."

He was tentative in his approach, in that initial touch, so, like a new lover showing him the ropes of my pleasure, I demonstrated, tugging, rotating the rings, then directed his hand back into place.

"I love having small weights hanging off of them and being taken from behind," I confided.

He gulped, shocked, much the same as he had years ago when he saw me shaved. I laughed softly but sensitively. "Don't worry. You don't have to do that stuff. Make love to me the old way and I'll be more than satisfied."

He relaxed into a slight smile and, without further ado, went down on me. His tongue knew more now than then, so much so that it forced me to stop comparing past and present. He concentrated on my clit, swirling, pressing, lips gently nipping now and then for added effect. Fingers wandered to my slit and played there with the rings, then found their way into me. Wet, my cunt accepted them.

I remembered how he would sometimes eat me to such arousal that I'd beg him to bury his fingers in me, all of them, deeply. He'd cater to my craving, sinking as much of his hand into me as he could to appease me, four fingers to the knuckles, enough to make me come and, when he pulled out, to feel empty, voided. Then, we had been too inexperienced to know we were toying with fisting.

Now, imagining the possibility of completing that play—my greedy cunt engulfing his hand, his every little twitch threatening me with orgasm; the very thought of grabbing him, squeezing him and squeezing one off in the process—imagining all that, while his tongue and his fingers played with me, I came.

And a new eagerness exploded with that orgasm. "Let me suck you," I begged.

He pulled away from me, shed his pants completely, and climbed on top of me. "No," he said in my ear as he hovered over me.

"Please."

"No."

He sank his length into me. "I want pussy," he said by way of explanation. He started fucking me and observed, dispassionately, "You're wetter than I remember."

"Things change," I managed to say before caving to the feeling of his full cock.

"God, you feel incredible. Just right."

My cunt throbbed back its own acknowledgments.

He took a nipple in hand, pinching it to go with the motions.

"And you taste delicious, you know that?"

He kissed me to prove it.

He knew how to mix me just so: deep strokes, long and succulent; drawing the head of his cock to the edge of my kissing labia, teasing me; shallow, swift ones to test me, wear me down. I neared, he knew it. He plunged into me.

"Grab my ass," I begged him. "Please."

He did and I cried out, bucking at the feel of his fingers grabbing my cheeks, nails digging into my flesh. He reached down, took my nipple in his mouth, sucked, then bit.

I exploded around him, aware only of his cock in my spasming clutches, his bite, and my own lightheadedness as the bed rocked and creaked its complaints. I collapsed beneath him and he freed me from his grip. He watched me as I rested and returned to lucidness, slowly fucking me the whole time, as if it were some minor habit.

"Roll over," he said, withdrawing.

I did and he uttered, "Good God."

Now he saw why I jumped when he grabbed my ass. I sported bruises, compliments of a recent paddling.

"You really did become a masochist."

"I warned you I had."

"Yes, you did."

He touched my bruises gingerly and, though I flinched fully and suddenly, I also moaned with the same passion I had expressed with other touches. He knew it but still waxed serious, the past catching up to him.

"I did this to you," he remorsed. "I made you a masochist."

"Love made me a masochist," I declared firmly, sparing him the details. "Come on, forget it. Fuck me."

I backed my still wet cunt up to his cock and pressed him into business. He aimed himself at me and entered. It felt reluctant.

"You can't hurt me," I counseled him. "Just do me."

He took me by the hips and slowly worked me, testing me. I made noise about how big he was, how good he felt, how much I wanted it. Stroke by stroke, he convinced himself that, indeed, he would not hurt me. He relented, finally, and indulged himself by plundering me. I upped the dialogue, begging him to fuck me harder, to tear me up. Ruin me, I said.

In times past, that would've sent him and he would've come. But that was then. Or maybe it was my poor choice of words. *Ruin me*, I guess, only works on a sadist.

"Roll me over," I offered.

I did, he climbed aboard again and I wrapped my legs around his waist. While he resumed his fucking, I played with his nipples, pinching and pulling. An old trick, my fail-safe.

He started shaking, head to toe. He was nearing, just like old times. "Oh God," he muttered. The signal was the same, timeless.

He slammed into me repeatedly, relentlessly, shivering, groaning, finally holding his cock still so he could better feel each ejaculation. Wet warmth flooded me, making me shiver.

Just like old times.

Downtime followed. Lying there, we resumed looking at each other's bodies, memorizing them. Our skins were softer, our bodies bulging a bit in spots, yet his cock, my cunt looked essentially the same. And they spoke to each other in the same hurried sentences of long ago.

But we weren't just cock and cunt. Our entireties had changed, bodily in countless little ways, soulfully in ways profound.

He looked at me now, wanting to revel in the body before him but too perplexed by what he saw. There, in that look, I had my answer: happiness couldn't be had here; the gulf between the unattached bohemian and the widowed married was too large for anything but solace and respite.

You can't go home, I wanted to tell him but words failed me, so I drew his head to my chest, held him, caressed his hair.

Solace, then, I decided silently.

He sighed and started, "I wish . . ."

"Shhh," I consoled. "I know. Sometimes I wish too."

Long ago, though, I learned that wishes don't sustain; dreams do. And, laying there, with him in my arms, I realized that the sudden harshness of widowhood had dashed his dreams, dreams he had yet to replace, dreams that, when they came, wouldn't include me because I was incapable of embracing them. Because years ago, after him, I had abandoned my own chance at sustenance and gypsied my way through life, forever too skittish to trust in dreams, forever eluding them.

Now, I could be a way station at best, a momentary rest as he moved through life. And, despite my own longing to have him and have him often, I could live with those limitations.

Love had, indeed, made me a masochist and a good one at that. The only problem was, from what I could tell, he didn't like to make me flinch.

STRANGER THAN FICTION

Marilyn Jaye Lewis

Since I don't own a car, I had to take the Metro-liner upstate. It was a really nice train ride, though; the Metro-liner follows the Hudson River all the way. It was kind of a chilly day, that bleak time on the East Coast when winter hasn't turned into spring yet. But I liked the idea of being secluded in a nice big farmhouse during such cold, grey weather and I was hoping Frank had a couple fireplaces, with fires going in them.

He picked me up at the train station, right on time, and as is customary upstate, the weather was much colder than in the city and there was still a good deal of snow on the ground. As luck would have it, Frank's farmhouse did have several fireplaces. One in the living room, one in the kitchen and then one downstairs in a huge, finished family room. There was a fire going in the fireplace downstairs.

The family room was paneled in beautiful cherry hardwoods and there was a hardwood floor with massive throw rugs. The furniture down in that room was very impressive; large leather couches and club chairs, etc. There was also a wet bar down there, too, if I remember correctly.

This downstairs room was where Frank filmed most of his movies. Which explains why he had a large bed down there, with a magnificent mahogany frame, surrounded by bright studio lights. Set into the headboard was a mirror that extended all the way across the front end of the bed. I soon learned that most of the filming that day would take place on this bed, with me facing the mirror.

Frank offered to fix me some lunch, which I accepted, but my stomach was so nervous that I couldn't really eat much. I did have a couple glasses of wine, though. Again, my nerves were such that the wine didn't really go to my head, but it sure helped calm me down a little.

When the doorbell rang the first time, my bowels jumped and I seriously wondered if I'd made a mistake in making the trip at all. Why would a woman like myself—a woman normally prone to guarding her privacy like an agitated fox terrier—suddenly agree to this lurid documentation of her sexual fantasies? I still wasn't sure I understood my own motivations, I could only follow my instincts, and my instincts told me I got excited thinking about the possibilities of at last feeling sexually fulfilled. On a primal level, I was determined to go through with it.

The first man who came in was pretty handsome, but not really my type. If he hadn't been hired for the movie, I probably never would have thought to have sex with him. The other men, three in all, fell into this same category; good-looking yet not really my type. But everyone seemed nice enough.

Since Frank was making a documentary video, as opposed to an all-out porno movie, he wanted me to have a lot of input on how the sex scenes would be staged. Although, he wanted me to talk about my desires and my ideas while he was filming me, which made me feel a little uncomfortable. He kept asking me to speak up, saying that he wasn't getting a good level for the sound.

At first I was really nervous about talking to the camera because the three actors were sitting right there, listening to every word I was saying. I felt a little exposed, because I wasn't at all horny yet. Plus, I also felt like I was "locked-in" to what I wanted, since I was being recorded on video saying all this stuff, you know? But I think that subconsciously I enjoyed the feeling—because I really wanted to *have* to go through with it. I didn't want to be able to change my mind.

Frank wanted me to strip for the camera, but when I was just about naked, and sliding my panties down, Frank decided it might look more visually appealing to have some footage of one of the men undressing me instead, so I got dressed again and let one of the men take my clothes off. But that brief moment, when I'd been just about out of my panties, revealing my (practically) shaved pussy to all the men, it was enough to start getting me horny. And then following it with letting one of the men undress me, was getting me *really* hot. When my panties came down the second time, a little strand of wet stuff was already dripping down into the crotch of my panties—mostly because there wasn't any hair to catch it. I felt a little embarrassed because I know the guy undressing me saw it, and I figured it was probably on the film, too—and these guys were only being paid to have sex with me. I didn't think they were really going to get off on any of it. I felt I was at a disadvantage since I was visibly horny and they weren't.

I got onto the bed, face down, and I watched everything going on behind me in the mirrored headboard. I watched a couple of the men get undressed while Frank and his assistant checked the lighting all around the bed. The third man came over to me and fastened my wrists to the headboard, as I'd requested. He tried to make small talk with me, but I was feeling a little too distracted to make much small talk in return—I only smiled a bit.

When my wrists were securely fastened, *that* feeling alone made me feel really hot. I knew how wet I was getting and, almost as if on cue, as I was wondering if any of the men were noticing, I saw the reflection of Frank zooming his camera in on my wet pussy. I spread my legs a little—although I was still too shy to spread them very wide, I didn't want to seem like a total tramp. But Frank said, "Come on, honey, let's get a good look—Hal, move her thighs apart a little bit."

When I felt Hal's hands spreading my thighs apart, and saw the camera come up closer to me—Frank was kneeling slightly on the bed now—I felt myself become more accommodating and my legs just naturally parted.

"Spread her totally open," Frank continued. "Let's get a great 'before' shot of those tight holes."

That was all I needed to hear. Then I was really starting to swoon. I kept my legs spread very wide, then, and I arched my ass out a little for the camera.

In the mirror I could almost see my ass as it sloped upward, and the close proximity of the camera to my totally spread epi-center made the wet stuff gush out from my hole. I wanted to be touched so badly, but no one was making any moves yet.

The third man finally undressed and I was surrounded by the three naked men, who were starting to get noticeable erections, when Frank told one of the men, Alex, to get on the bed and kneel down between my legs.

Alex did as he was directed, while Frank stood up completely on the bed and sort of straddled Alex, aiming the camera down at my ass. The assistant adjusted the light.

"Stroke her ass, Alex," Frank instructed. "Knead her cheeks a little bit, let's see how fleshy they are."

On cue, Alex began massaging my ass. The touch of his hands on my flesh made me feel completely aroused. And the way he was grabbing my cheeks, squeezing them together and then pressing them apart, was making my pussy lips come together and then part—the air hitting all the wet stuff felt incredible.

"Great, great. Perfect," Frank was chanting. "Look at those holes. Look how engorged she is . . . just beautiful."

Watching him in the mirror, Alex seemed totally fixated on my spread rear end. Then I watched him lean down and lightly lick his tongue down the center of my ass.

"Perfect," Frank whispered. "Go for it, Alex."

I gasped. It felt heavenly, especially when his tongue licked down across my puckered hole and trailed on into my soaking vagina, then licked its way back up my ass again.

I didn't realize right away that the camera was now focused into the mirror and capturing my expression. I guess it was only logical, since Alex's head was now blocking all the action. But the camera was "reading" all the action it needed. My eyes were half-closed, my lips, a little dry, were slightly parted and my hair was tossed back, while Alex's tongue circled around the perimeter of my asshole gently, letting spit slip along his tongue and swirl around on my tender skin. Then the tip of his tongue teased my opening; poking into the hole only slightly, then circling around it again. Alex's hands pushed more insistently at my upper thighs, pressing me wide open. As he licked my hole thoroughly, I could actually feel the hole relax.

When all the tension was out of my hole, I felt the tip of Alex's tongue work as far into the hole as it could. Suddenly his fingers pushed into my soaking vagina.

"Jesus," I gasped.

I arched my rear end up higher so that Alex's fingers could get easily into me while his tongue continued to probe my ass.

"That's it," Frank remarked. "Beautiful." He was beginning to shift around on the bed, so I opened my eyes, just in time to see one of the other men—I couldn't remember his name—get behind Alex.

"Oh my god," I thought to myself, as I watched the other man lube up his cock and then smear some of the lube into Alex's raised rear end. I could "feel" Alex moan, as he continued to tongue my asshole and finger me, and presumably get prepped for anal penetration at the same time.

I couldn't take my eyes off the mirror. I watched the other man mount Alex, while feeling Alex take the pressure of the penetrating cock. He moaned right into my asshole while his free hand gripped my cheek tightly, and his fingers jammed deep into my cunt—almost hurting me.

"Oh god," I groaned quietly.

"Perfect," Frank said. "Go, Tom, go."

The man, Tom, held firmly to Alex's raised hips and eased his hard tool into Alex's ass. Right away he started pounding into Alex hard.

Alex yanked his fingers out of me and tried to steady himself, with his arms on either side of me on the bed. His face was resting on my spread ass, he seemed almost oblivious to me now. He was grunting against me, his breath hot on my flesh. At that point I wished my wrists weren't restrained so that I could turn over and go for Alex's cock, suck him deep into my mouth while he got reamed—get more into the action.

At that moment, though, the third man, George, came over to the bed. He kneeled down close to my face, wedging himself between my face and the mirrored headboard, but slightly over to the side so that the camera could still keep a clear view of all the action, and he grabbed a sizable handful of my hair, pulled my head back and held the tip of his hot, hard cock against my lips.

My lips were still dry, so I licked them quickly and then opened my mouth to accept the stiff tool all the way in. I was feeling greedy for a hard mouth-fucking and I knew I was going to get it.

George went thoroughly at me, holding my head a little uncomfortably and driving his erection in so deep, I was almost gagging. His rhythm was strong and steady, as he slid his cock in and out, in and out, harder and harder, hitting the back of my throat every time, until my spit started to collect around my lips, then dribble lightly down my chin.

The camera came in for a close-up on my face then. I tried to look up right into the lens and take my mouth-fucking like a good girl.

By now, Alex had somewhat regained his composure and his tongue returned to my asshole as he continued to get reamed by Tom. The room was filled with the sounds of men, grunting like animals, and the muffled moans of me, getting my throat filled with the thick head of George's shaft.

At some point during all the excitement, I guess Tom must have shot his hot load into Alex's thoroughly fucked asshole, because I saw Tom in the mirror, getting off of Alex. Then Alex and George stopped what they were both doing and switched places.

Alex's huge hard-on was now in my face while George positioned himself between my spread legs.

Alex pressed my face close against his hairless balls, making me kiss them and lick them while he held his hard shaft aside. I loved the earthy smell on him, loved feeling his soft hot balls pressed against my nose, and I licked him and kissed him ardently, but I was trying to watch George in the mirror at the same time. He was lubing his thick cock, greasing it good.

"Oh, god," I realized. "Here it comes. He's going to fuck my ass." And then I felt the lube being smeared into my puckered hole. It was icy cold.

George lifted my hips up slightly and pressed the thick head of his dick against my opening. I knew, from sucking him, how thick his shaft was and I was worried that I wouldn't be able to take him in comfortably, but it was too late to worry about it now. The head of it pushed into me.

Normally, I would have tensed a little at this point, but George and Alex were well rehearsed. And as the head of George's cock pressed into my tight opening, forcing it to accommodate him, Alex pushed his stiff tool between my lips. The men went at the exact, steady, probing pace. As Alex's dick dipped down my throat, his balls resting momentarily against my chin, George's slick cock pushed deep into my rectum—clear down to *his* balls, his tight testicles slapping against my slippery shaved labia.

The men eased out at the same time, then pushed back in. I felt thoroughly penetrated, and Frank's camera captured it for all time; documenting every muffled grunt and groan I uttered as the two men pumped vigorously into me at both ends.

The camera moved down for what I assumed was a close-up of my back door getting stuffed. George pulled my ass cheeks open wide, as he pumped harder and harder into my tender hole.

"Pull it out for a second," Frank said. "Let's see how open the hole is."

I felt George ease out of me while Alex continued his mission to fuck my pretty face.

"Fantastic!" Frank declared, as I assume he caught prime footage of my dilated opening.

"Slip your thumbs in, see if you can keep her open. I want to get a good look in that hole."

George's thumbs pushed in and spread my little hole, keeping it open for the camera, while Alex's cock stiffened, his body tightened and he began to shoot his hot load down my throat. I sucked him in eagerly, letting him milk his cock of every last drop.

When Alex was finished, he got off the bed and it was just me and George and the camera.

George mounted me again, sliding easily into my slippery tunnel, riding my ass with a steady rhythm as I watched him in the mirror. He tugged at my hair like it was a horse's reins and occasionally he smacked wickedly at my ass.

My wrists struggled at the restraints, as my swollen clitoris ached to be rubbed hard. But I couldn't get free. Instead I maneuvered my knees up under myself.

George stopped what he was doing then, eased out of me and helped me reposition my legs. I pulled them together tight under me, then lifted my ass up to George again, who entered me and resumed his rhythm. But now I could squeeze my thighs together tightly while he rode me, in and out, in and out; his hard cock vigorously massaging my perineal wall, vibrating my whole vagina, his balls slapping against the smooth underside of my engorged mound, until my squeezing muscles brought on an orgasm that bolted through me, making me cry out, "Oh Jesus!" while the camera came in for a close-up.

But George went at me for several more minutes until he was primed to shoot his load. When he finally did, he grabbed me around my waist tightly, jammed his cock deep into my ass and pumped himself hard, emptying his balls completely.

When he pulled out of me, the assistant came around and unfastened my wrists.

"Turn over," Frank said. "Lie down on your back and raise up your legs."

I did as Frank directed. And when I had assumed the position he was after, Frank instructed Tom to straddle my face.

Tom's dick was slightly flaccid and smelled strongly of some type of antibacterial cleansing lotion. It wasn't a very romantic aroma, but as soon as he lowered his cock into my mouth, and became increasingly stiff, I forgot about the odd smell and got into the mood again.

I knew the camera was probably capturing me in my least attractive angles—with a man straddling my face and my legs obscenely raised and spread—but I simply didn't care. The ecstatic sounds Tom was making, as the head of his now-stiff cock stroked the back of my throat with every thrust into my mouth, had me feeling completely absorbed with trying to please him, trying to help him climax—to make him at last come down my throat.

There was a fleeting moment, though, when I feared I was going to suffocate, Tom was pumping into my mouth so forcefully, but it quickly passed as he emptied into my throat. Then Tom carefully got off me and, as the other men were doing, began cleaning himself up and searching for his clothes, while Frank's assistant called with finality, "It's a wrap."

I was too exhausted to even think of catching the next train to the city, so I stayed on at Frank's for the remainder of the afternoon and on into the evening. I was finally able to relax and appreciate the good

wine. I didn't even bother to dress. Frank and I planted ourselves up-stairs in the living room, where he built a beautiful fire.

"So what did you like best about experiencing your fantasies?" Frank asked, sitting down next to me on the sofa.

It was difficult for me to come up with an immediate answer. As my mind perused the memories of what had happened to me earlier, I found myself almost instantly consumed by a resurgent lust; suddenly, I was once again insatiable. I slid closer to Frank without saying anything and set my wine glass down on the floor.

He smiled at me, approvingly. "I take it that making this movie was a pleasurable experience then? You know, I'm toying with the idea of making it the first in a series; I don't suppose you have any girlfriends who might be interested in participating?"

"Maybe," I replied, kissing him, not interested in making conversation.

THE VALENTINE

William Dean

It was the crudest valentine she had ever seen. More a scrap than anything. The edges roughly torn by thick and clumsy fingers and the shaky penciled message "Be mine" was barely legible in the dim light of winter filtering through the small window. It was so pathetic as to be laughable. Pulling the thin blanket over her, she mused backwards in time. How many valentines she had received as a girl. Oh, countless! And later, as a young woman, there had been dozens more each Valentine's Day. Expensive, richly bordered with real Belgian lace, many had been carefully stitched in heart-shapes of red satin or patterned silk. And such poetry! Embroidered lines of passionate love, of hungry desire, of unending devotion all done in gold or silver floss. Stacks of boxes of chocolates and bouquets of daring roses intimating the senders' undying, perhaps unbearable, affection for her and her alone. She could not help herself smiling at all those beaus: young swains, blushing boys, stammering older men. Her fingers ran across the stiff, pulpy feel of the small scrap of red paper in her hand now and, for a moment, she almost felt disgusted at it. Almost let it drop to the floor as trash.

She brought it back close to her eyes again and scanned it. "Be mine." What a silly sentiment. What a ridiculous thing to say to her. She closed her eyes and again wafted back to other years. Not long ago.

"Is it not a lovely dance?" said the Count von Streiffen to her, as she smiled behind her ivory fan.

"So perfect for a Ball of Hearts. Oh, Sofia, you are the loveliest woman here. Why will you not let me make you my wife?"

She had giggled. It was the perfect response, after all, to the pleadings of a fat, balding man stuffed in his clothes. She amused herself by thinking what a tiny, pale little penis he must have strangled beneath the bulk of his huge white belly.

"I will devote my life to your pleasure," the Count had continued, his wet, bulging eyes trying to peer over the blades of her fan. "Every Valentine's Day, I will . . . I will fill your room with the most delicate of roses and . . . and outfit a carriage in red silk to carry you to the Valentine's Day Ball."

"All that just to fuck me?" she whispered close to his ear and laughed uproariously when the old man grabbed his heart, then his head and staggered back from her unexpected words. She turned sharply on her heel and walked, no, she fairly strode from his gasping, shaking form.

Of course, there had been younger men. Handsome men. The most handsome in Europe her mother would say. All paying court to her. Stefan and Wilhelm. Signor Cassini from Milan and Mr. Wentworthy from London. And how could a lively young woman remain a virgin forever with such delicious temptations hovering . . . well . . . begging to be let into her bed. Or a quick fumble beneath her clothes in the park. Or pressing so hotly against her in closet or doorway. Ah. And only a silly fool of a girl would have refused the wonderful pleasure of a hard, boiling hot passion sliding into her depths. Or pushed away the mouths that suckled and bit at her stiff nipples and kissed the round firmness of her pale breasts. Not she. If the man was handsome. If the man was suave and mannered politely, if he had captured her heart however fleetingly, well . . .

There was a handful . . . well, perhaps two handful that she had really cared for. Deeply, madly, wildly a little. Ah, and had they fucked! Across Europe. On an exquisite liner on the great ocean. Even in strange and odd America, where many of the women looked like absolute tramps and whores and the men like silly, country pimps. She had even cuckolded her one-time husband at the time with a couple of the American men. Just to see how they might please a woman of her taste and experience. One was absurd, of course. Robert, in New York or was it Chicago? Grunting and straining, his face red and puffy, as he ground his cock into her like some factory machine. She had sighed and fluttered her eyelashes until she could stand his sweating ridiculousness no more and had pushed him off her to the thick hotel carpet. He blushed furiously and grabbed up his clothes to retreat.

But the American from the West? He was a prize bull. His cock longer than she had ever seen and thick. The knob as he teased her cunt felt like it would split her from belly to ass. And he knew how to use it. And to use her. Yes, that had been a good one. But his manners were atrocious. He had expected her to get on her knees and pump it into her mouth while he talked filthy words. Well. That was exciting, yes, but he also slapped her when she gagged on him. He pulled her lovely hair. He was, indeed, something of a brute and a woman enjoyed that . . . but only for a while.

The shout of the man in the horrible striped uniform brought her back to now. "Raus! Raus! Everybody out!" he screamed in the fading light of the room. Sofia crumpled the paper valentine scrap in her hand and pushed it into her mouth, tucking it safely away like a stolen candy in her cheek.

She flinched as the man beat his long baton against the stacked bunks and quickly jumped down, shuffling outside with the other women, all dressed in thin striped clothes with sickly yellow and red six-pointed stars sewn over the heart. They all marched slowly outside to stand in ragged rows.

Exhausted, hungry, Sofia gazed at the other women and knew she might as well be looking into a mirror of almost infinite reflections of herself. Hair shorn almost to the scalp, breasts flat and lifeless, thighs thinned, and the baggy, shapeless coats and pants, striped. Yes, she sighed wearily, she looked just like that. Eyes deep in the sockets, face gaunt. Lips tightly pressed into . . . neutrality and fear.

As they had that morning, the guards ordered the rows of men and women to march past each other. As she was on the outside rank of women, Sofia watched the silent haggard men pass by her, waiting for the man who had passed her the scrap of valentine in the morning. She'd felt the tentative push of it quickly into her hand as they had shuffled past each other. A note, she'd thought then. News of a relative, perhaps, or a warning or a plan for escape, but not a wadded up, crude scrap of red paper in the shape of a heart. Not the useless phrase "Be mine." And now what should she do? With it tucked in a corner of her mouth. She could feel the rasp of the cheap paper on her tongue. What should she do? Spit it back at him?

Even at a shuffle, the rows of faces passed her quickly. She felt another scrap of something pushed between her fingers, but was past the man before she could react. She looked forward, shifting her eyes to see if the guards had noticed. No. They stood around laughing, smoking cigarettes, mostly ignoring their captives. Sofia carefully unrolled the scrap of paper in her fingers and glanced down at it. It was, like the other, torn from some red paper. Simply, roughly scrawled were the words, "Meet me."

When they passed once more, her eyes looked into his. She nodded slightly. Well, why not? Only death awaited them both she knew. This might be her last time to feel like a woman instead of a . . . a thing, which was what the Nazis made them all feel like. Some thing, unwanted, to be disposed of. Eradicated. Killed. Forgotten about. Yes, why not? And if she was found out, what then? Well, just a different kind of death, she supposed after all. The third time they marched past each other, the man smiled at her. The man, she thought. She didn't even know his name, of course. And what did it matter, really? They were beyond names now. And when they met, sneaking behind some barracks or hut in the camp? Maybe she would ask then. Maybe not. Her thoughts, her feelings were so jumbled. Hating this impudent stranger of a man for reminding her that she was a woman. That there was such a thing as Valentine's Day. Such a thing as lover's desire in a place like this. And yet. Yet she was touched, too. Liking him, loving him even for the same reasons she hated him. She would meet him. She would do it with him. Why not? It might be the last time in her short life.

When, at last, night came, Sofia lay in her bunk. Her heart pounded. She could feel it against her bony ribs. Questions flew in her mind. Why me? Why did he pick me? What if he was already dead and rolled into some mass corpse-filled pit like all the others? What if, when they met, he changed his mind? What if it was all a sick, cruel joke? No. No, too many ifs. What was it Hamlet had said? Something about that anyway. Something about all the ifs in a life that make us all cowards. She slid silently as she could out of the bunk and, step by stealthy step . . . like a thief . . . along the wooden flooring to the door.

And then. Watching the slit under the door for the bright searchlight beam to pass by. When it did, she stepped out through the door. Running, slipping, crawling in the slushy snow and mud around the building. She leaned against the shadowed side of the wall and gasped. And panicked. Oh, God, she thought, I don't know where I am to meet him. Stupid! What a fool! she almost shouted at herself. And then . . .

Someone grabbed her hand. She bit the other hand to keep from screaming, but, yes, in the darkness she knew it was him. The man. The Valentine man. He pulled her and she followed.

They ran, deeper into darkness. Dodging the lights. Clutching at each other's hand. And, at last, behind another building, fell to the ground beside each other.

In the softest whisper she had ever heard, he said, "I am Aaron. Aaron Zelazny."

She nodded. "Sofia. Sofia . . ." and panicked again. What was her last name? With a start, she remembered. "Sofia Regler."

"Sofia," he said her name slowly. He touched her cheek gently. "Beautiful."

She knew it was a lie. How could she be beautiful now? She knew she looked ugly, horrible, like a hag, something barely alive, and aged beyond her years. But . . . but it sounded so nice to hear.

"Thank you," she said, turning her face away.

"Will you?" Aaron asked. "My Valentine?"

She looked back at him. So dark the night, she could barely see his skin before her. She nodded quickly and leaned closer to kiss his lips. Dry, cracked skin. After all the soft, refined, wealthy lips she had kissed, they tasted of . . . of something she could no longer describe. And then, like some bursting thought in her, she knew what they tasted like. They tasted like hope.

Yes, she thought. One last time. Once more before dying, unknown, a number, in some hellish fate, once more. Let me taste of hope. And she kissed him again. Now with more hunger, with greed even for the contact of him. A man who cared for her. Who was . . . she almost laughed . . . her Valentine.

Strange. After being so long denied making love, neither of them hurried, but savored, like reverent blind people before a religious icon that promised sight again. She felt his lips kiss down her neck and across the front of her, her coat unbuttoned. Her hands ran over the stubble on his head, pulling his face to her flaccid breasts, arching up to his mouth. As he kissed her, licking like some animal at a handful of salt, she felt the stiffness of his penis against her thigh and wanted to weep. And sing. And laugh again. But, no. Silence meant safety and she stifled her sounds, biting her lips to keep from shouting "I am going to make love again!"

She raised her hand and ran it over his scrawny chest then up to his face. Holding her fingers across his lips, she leaned closer and whispered. "Let me. I am your Valentine." And she flipped him over on his back. Her hands clawed at his pants opening, pushed them down as she straddled him and raised her knees. He felt so hard in her grasp. Sofia closed her eyes and teased the stalk over her opening, shuddering with the quick pleasure of it. Then, with her hand circling it, she pushed it inside her. Sliding down on his length until it filled her. Ah. Her head lolled from side to side as she rode his hardness. Raising and lowering her hips to suck him into her and slowly to release him again. The only sound seemed to be the slick, wet ticking sound of their lovemaking. Steady and rhythmic. More and more. She wanted it never to stop or, if to stop, then in the quick, sudden unexpected death of them both. "Valentine," her mind shouted over and over. And then . . .

Explosions. Lights in the air. High overhead. Maybe this was death, Sofia told herself in a small part of her mind. Her body still rocked— she knew she had climaxed. She had felt him, too, explode inside her, hot, pulsing, rushing out of him like a geyser. The pleasure was . . . more explosions. And now, shooting. Aaron jolted beneath her, his head turning, eyes trying to look everywhere at once.

Now, the shouts came from near the fences . . .

No, the sound of Germans crying out . . .

"Americans!"

And now, one woman and one man, looking at each other in wonder . . . and, at long last, once more . . . in freedom.

GRETCHEN BY CANDLELIGHT

Rod Harden

Gretchen's restraints were simple but effective. Plastic cable ties circled each of her arms just above the elbows. They were snug, but not too tight. A third tie joined the two, leaving a gap of only a few inches and causing her arms to be drawn sharply behind her.

She sat naked upon a low-back, armless chair. Her legs were spread wide and angled back, ankles held off the ground by additional cable ties. Clear packing tape sealed her mouth. The blue silk panties stuffed inside were visible through her parted lips. The effect was almost comical.

David circled her at leisure, alternately caressing her plush blonde hair and stroking his beard. She pressed her head against his hand whenever he touched her, her hazel eyes asking him questions she knew he wouldn't answer. When he wasn't touching her, she could almost feel his gaze as it bore into every corner of her exposed flesh. She tingled as though his eyes were fingers.

The stranger sat across the room, legs crossed, arms folded, his face stoic. Like David, he wore a dark gray suit. Gretchen ignored him.

At last, David went to the table next to the stranger. He opened his briefcase and turned, holding up his latest toy. It was a plain candle, cream in color, about a foot long, and a couple inches in diameter. He stepped close to her, drew the candle past her nostrils, letting her smell its rich musky aroma.

The corners of his mustache rose. His smile was at once evil and delicious. She loved his wickedness. She craved it. She became completely absorbed by the fire she saw burning in his eyes, the fire that never failed to rekindle her own embers.

He flicked his cigarette lighter and held it to the candlewick. She studied the flame with him as the wick flared and began to melt the wax. Gradually he tilted the candle, allowing some of the liquefied wax to dribble down the side. It quickly congealed into a firm round lump on the previously smooth shaft. Soon another drop oozed down close to the first.

She thought she knew what he would do with the candle, with the melted wax, but he wasn't doing it. Instead he just seemed to be letting the candle burn. She watched for several minutes, curious, as clump after clump of hardened wax accumulated along the sides of the candle. Her anticipation mounted.

One of the molten drops rolled over his finger. He furrowed his brow and pursed his lips. "Hot," he hissed to her.

Yes, she thought. Hot! Her cunt was hot. She braced her hands against the back of the chair and arched her hips upward. She whimpered her plea to be touched.

His smile broadened as he tilted the candle more so the next drop would fall. The pearl of wax clung to the candle for a moment as though deliberately hesitating. When it finally fell, it landed on her left breast close to the nipple. The sudden, fleeting pinprick of heat seemed to sear her to the core. She caught her breath. Another drop fell quickly on her right breast.

Plop, plop. More and more circles of wax molded themselves to her flesh, on her breasts, and belly, and thighs. Her breaths became staccato, raspy moans, syncopated against the irregular rhythm of the dripping wax.

All at once David stopped. He righted the candle. It hardly resembled the one he lit just moments ago. It was shorter by an inch or two, enmeshed in a jagged jumble of hardened lumps. He let the flame form a deep pool around the wick. Then, with a glance at Gretchen, he quickly snuffed the fire with his fingers, and began sculpting the softened wax. He worked it into a blunt bullet shape, completely enclosing the wick.

Gretchen stared with eyes wide, nodding eagerly, as he stooped to press the rounded tip of the candle against her cunt lips. It was still warm, the wax still slightly malleable as he guided the thick shaft inside her. Without pause, he thrust it deep, pulled it back, twisted it, pushed it again, wiggled it, spun it.

Gretchen heaved and squirmed uncontrollably. Bracing herself with her hands again, she humped upward against David's assault. The irregular clumps along the candle shaft seemed to seek out her clit with every spin and thrust. They seemed to probe her every crevice simultaneously.

David urged her on. "Come on, slut. Fuck the candle. Fuck it!"

She came fast and hard.

She came until she slumped back from exhaustion.

It felt like hours later when he finally withdrew the waxen violator for the last time. He leaned down and kissed her on her taped mouth. Her eyes appeared darker now, more green. They smiled the smile her lips couldn't form.

David stepped aside. Gretchen had forgotten about the stranger. His legs were not crossed anymore, nor were his arms folded. His hands were pressed hard against his lap. The expression on his face was anything but stoic. When he noticed them looking at him, he lifted his hands. He sighed and chuckled nervously.

"See?" said David. "I told you."

The stranger relaxed, began to applaud. "Bravo, my friend," he said. "Well done."

David turned to Gretchen again. He gently worked the candle back inside her cunt. "I'll be back shortly," he whispered. "Hold it there for me."

She nodded.

"Good girl."

He stood and headed for the door. The stranger joined him. He withdrew his wallet and handed David several large denomination bills as they walked out together. David laughed as he accepted the money. "Any time you want to part with more of your cash, just let me know," he joked as he shut the door behind him.

Gretchen closed her eyes and sighed. She still felt ripples of pleasure course through her body as she clenched the candle tightly, waiting for her man to return.

HEMENWAY COURT: 3 A.M.

Robert Buckley

I'm dreaming about my old Chevy and how the left front wheel used to go squeak, squeak, squeak, squeak, squeak, squeak . . .

The dream evaporates. I'm awake. The squeak, squeak, squeak continues.

Now Joan is awake. We look at each other, and then look up. The lighting fixture above us is twirling. Squeak, squeak, squeak, squeak . . .

Could it be an earth tremor?

Now from above come muffled moans, grunts—a high-pitched voice, and another that gargles with gravel.

Maddie, our mutt, at the foot of the bed is pondering the ceiling. The hair on her hackles is raised and stiff. Then the banging begins, first as a hollow tap, tap, tap. . . .

Joan has pushed herself up into a half-sitting position. She is fixated by the percussion performance from above.

Then the full blown banging erupts: FWAM-FWAM-FWAM-FWAM to the northeast, BAMMA, BAMMA, BAMMA to the southwest.

Maddie yipes and bolts off the bed. She cowers in the corner emitting a low snarly growl.

The voices are clearer now, louder. The higher, feminine voice alternately groaning and shrieking, "Yes, YESSS! OH GOD! OH, NO! Bastard, bastard, oh, WHAT ARE YOU DOING TO ME! Ahhh!"

"My God," Joan whispers, "I think he's killing her."

"I—don't—think—so," I reply.

The other, deeper voice speaks no tongue I recognize. It merely growls, a long low guttural "Grrrrghh."

The banging is louder and unrelenting. The light fixture above us is swinging in wild oval loops. I'm afraid it will come crashing down. Joan's framed "Riverdance" poster is doing a jig on the wall.

Above us again we hear "GRRAAGH!"

"Jesus!" Joan cries.

"I don't think she's with anything human," I say.

Just then, Joan's heirloom crucifix tumbles from its perch on the opposite wall. Holy shit, if it ain't Satan himself.

The woman lets loose with an ear-splitting shriek. Then comes the crash, a final jarring BAM!

Bits of plaster dust snow down on our bed, but there is silence.

Then there is some muffled movement. We follow the action with our eyes as it moves above our window. Now as her voice clearly splits the night, we hear the woman.

Joan is awestruck. "She's hanging out the window!"

She is, screaming into the court below, "Aiyeee! Yes, yes, YES! You BASTARD, you big, big, BIG BASTARD. Oh, I hate you, FUCK ME, fuck me hard."

"GRRRRADH!"

Cats begin yowling in the alley four stories below. This sets off Maddie with a round of barking.

Farther down the court someone is calling, "Whoohoo! Ride 'er man, ride!"

The woman lets loose again, "Fuck me, ohhh, yes SPLIT ME, OH SPLIT ME!"

Another voice, nearby across the court, gruff and phlegmy: "Yah filthy animals, people gotta get up in the morning!"

A bit farther away, a rejoinder, "Aw, shut the fuck up."

Just a bit farther away, "Yah, fuck yourself, asshole."

Phlegm-voice replies, "I'm callin' the cops!"

From somewhere, "Kiss my ass!"

Above us things are building to a crescendo. "Come on, fill me. Fuck my ASS! OH GOD . . ."

"GRAAAGH!"

"Yes, yes, I'm—I'm—just—ARGH, FUCK ME LIKE A FUCK-ING WHORE!"

Suddenly she reaches octaves I think only Maddie can hear. A long hissing sigh follows.

Then, in the voice of a blown muffler, the Prince of Darkness speaks: "Ohhh, baby!"

Far down the court a smattering of applause. A can, given life by the warm breezy night, clatters its way along the alley. Otherwise, deep silence.

I look at Joan. She looks at me then shifts her gaze farther down the bed. I follow her eyes and see that someone has erected a tent pole under the bedclothes. It is I.

"Think we could do better than that?" she asks with a lascivious smile.

"Yeah, just not so loud. And, try not to scare the dog."

FRIED BLONDE TOMATOES

Robert Schaffer

What is it about burnt-out blondes? There they are, on the train to Long Island, a few too many scotches floating them along. Or out in fancy Connecticut suburbs, hair rinsed to a crisp, the financial beneficiaries of one too many divorces. And on the streets of Manhattan, with delicate perfume trailing behind them, they sashay in bewildered astonishment.

And I crave them. I crave them all.

Take the other day. I was in a toy store on Bleecker Street, and behind the counter was a stringy blonde in her late 30s, skin pockmarked and eyes droopy. A drug user or ex-junkie. I got hard just hearing her husky voice, the product of too many cigarettes and sleepless nights. We smiled at each other as I pretended to peruse the plastic goods. She leaned forward, letting her cleavage bulge.

"You know, anything you want, I'm sure I can offer you a deal."

I pretended to think about this.

"What sort of deal?"

She looked at her watch.

"Almost lunch time. You hungry?"

"Very," I said, in a voice that left no doubt what I was hungry for.

She walked out from the counter; her ass tight in a dark leather mini-skirt, locked the door, flipped the closed sign and pulled the shade.

"So," I said, "What's for lunch?"

"Oh," she breathed, and hopped up on the glass counter, "we got the blue plate special," and she pulled up her skirt and spread her panty-less crotch, "pussy on glass."

"Well, I've got the perfect side dish," I replied.

"Yeah? And what would that be, lover?"

I put my hands on her legs and bent down.

"Tongue in bush, what else?" and went to it.

She grunted as I licked. She tasted of nicotine, alcohol, and several illegal substances.

"Take your time, lover, lunch is an hour long," and she leaned back to open up wider. She didn't make much noise, just sighed deeply as I plunged my tongue this way and that.

"Make more noise," she said, in that husky raspy voice, "I want to hear you *slurp!*"

I slurped.

"Yeah, lover, that's it!" and she put a hand to her mouth and bit one of her fingers, making soft noises. "Kiss it, kiss it all over."

"Yes ma'am," I mumbled, and I loudly placed big wet kisses on her moist cunt. I could feel the beginnings of her orgasm as she agitated her ass, and her breathing became jagged. She finally came with a long drawn out sigh. She leaned back on the counter while I gently kissed her crotch. I left with an Astro-Boy keychain, Catwoman magnet, rubber squid, and Baby Spice doll.

And an open invitation for lunch anytime I wanted it.

I was on a roll with druggies, because my next blonde was a platinum 24-year-old heroin addict with lovely eyes, rotten teeth, and plush breasts. She was shivering in 85 degrees heat sitting on a bench in Tompkins Square Park, and as I walked by she made a pitch for money in a surprisingly girlish voice.

"Dude, you gotta buck, I needa buck."

I looked at her sternly. "Do your parents know you're out here?"

She opened her eyes (or I think she did, hard to tell) and looked up at me.

"Shit, dude, my dad's a dog-fucker and my mom gave me my first taste!"

I sat down next to her.

"Gee, so you've had it hard, huh?"

"Fuck yeah!" and she breathed in mucus. "Looka this," and she pulled up her T-shirt to show me scars on her stomach.

"Christ," I whistled, "what happened?"

"My dad used to beat me." She took my hand and placed it on the right side of her head. There was a valley in her skull. "He knocked me so hard one day I got dented," and she began to sniff.

"There there," I cooed to her, and she fell passively against my body. I stroked her hair and rocked her, breathing in her odor: essence of unwashed skin spiced with urine notes. I wanted to lick her right there.

"What's your name?"

"Dorothy."

"Where do you live, Dorothy?"

She shrugged. "Wherever, man," and I could see her eyes getting wet. I lifted her face.

"Tell you what, Dorothy, why don't I take you to dinner?"

Her eyes widened. "Yeah? You ain't shittin' me?"

"Nope. You deserve a night out."

She shook against me. "I'm kinda fucked-up."

I brushed my lips against hers and whispered in her ear.

"We can take care of that, too."

"That'd be *so* cool, dude, I know where to get supremo shit."

"And you can, ahh, 'do your business' at my place, maybe take a shower."

She threw her arms around my neck in a very childish gesture.

"Oh, dude!" she exclaimed, and kissed my cheek. "What's your name?"

I told her. She smiled at me.

"Know what?" she said with a Shirley Temple intonation.

"No, what?"

"You can fuck me if you want," she lisped. "I gotta very tight pussy. Everyone says so."

"Well, how nice of them."

"Yeah—and know what else?"

I already knew what I needed to know, but what the hey—in cases like this, more is more, you know?

"Nope, I don't."

"I really like my ass fucked," and she turned her baby eyes on me. "Would you like to fuck my ass?"

I smiled at her. "Maybe after dinner. I don't like to ass-fuck on an empty stomach."

She frowned. "Dude, you're not making funna me, are you?"

I kissed her full on the lips, taking in a mouthful of her bad breath, and said, "Let's get your shit."

She shyly took my hand and led me out of the park to a street off Avenue B that must've been missed when the Lower East Side became the East Village. It was filthy. In the middle of the block, we stopped in front of a boarded-up tenement. She instructed me to wait out front, because "the dude'll freak if he sees you, dude!" I slipped her the necessary bills and she entered the building through a space in the boards. Some people passed me and glared. I smiled back. She suddenly reappeared.

"Done deal, dude!"

I put my arm around her waist and led her to 14th Street, where I hailed a cab. She sank back on the seat, her eyes glazing over. I hustled her into my apartment building in Chelsea, and felt her up in the elevator, running my hands over her breasts. She fell back against the wall and shut her eyes.

"You dig me, that's cool," she mumbled.

In the apartment she kicked off her ratty sneakers and pulled her shirt off, gleefully falling on my sofa and rummaging in her bag for her works. With an engineer's precision she assembled her needle and prepared the packet and spoon.

"Uh, would you like a candle?"

"Thanks, dude!" and spoon was set to flame. She looked up at me, with serious eyes. "You wanna fuck me while I shoot?" She pulled the heroin into the syringe. "Really, I dig being fucked," and she wrapped a worn piece of surgical tubing around her arm, "while I do shit."

I knelt by her and kissed her, then filled my mouth with those nubile breasts, biting into her nipples while she squirmed. Her skin had an earthy dirty flavor.

"Take my pants off, dude."

I tongued her breasts, then licked her navel, which was pierced with a small silver ring. I undid her pants and slid them off. The pungent odor of unwashed pussy wafted forth.

"Now you. I wanna see your cock."

Her eyes brightened as I threw off all my clothes.

"Dude, you're so clean!" and she grabbed my cock and licked it like a greedy child with a candy cane. Then she sucked it into her mouth. The sight of my cock going in and out of those young pillowy lips, while one of her hands held a needle and the other arm wore surgical tubing thrilled me to the balls. I twined her unwashed hair into my fingers and pumped her mouth. But before I could come she pulled my cock out.

"Fuck me," she said.

I prepared to roll a condom on, but she stopped me.

"Nyuh-uh, dude, you gotta do it *raw*."

"Dorothy—," I began to protest, but she cut me off.

"You ain't afraid of catchin' somethin', are ya?"

I paused.

" 'Cause if you think I'm dirty, I'm leaving, dude."

She arched and spread her legs, and revealed the raw sweet pinkness in her pubic hair (dyed blonde—very careful for a homeless junkie, I thought). I got on the couch and rubbed my dick along her crack.

"Wait, dude, I just gotta get ready," and she pulled the tubing tight with her mouth and positioned the needle. Then she smiled.

I pushed in and she shot up. The heroin took her and she went slack and her arms drooped.

"Baby's being fucked," she murmured in a singsong girly voice. "Yummy yummy yummy, I got jism in my tummy, and I feel like nodding out." She stopped singing and giggled as I fucked her using long strokes, and she hadn't lied: she had a tight sweet twat.

Suddenly she kicked against me, forcing me out of her hole, my cock twanging stupidly in the air.

"Jesus, Dorothy, what the hell!" but for an answer she twirled, got up on all fours, and presented her ass to me. There was a tattoo on her left cheek of a heart pierced by a bloody knife.

"Please dude, up my ass, fuck me up my ass!" and she pulled her cheeks apart. What the hell, in for a penny, etc. etc. I positioned myself while reaching one of my arms forward to grasp her tits. I used my other hand to shove my cock into her rather unpleasantly brown small hole.

She screeched in delight, "Yeah, baby likes, oooh, yeah, hard, baby wants it hard!" and I began to pound her. Her face fell into a sofa pillow, and she drooled as she made little grunting noises. I never thought of myself as a fan of anal sex, but I dug the feel of her anal canal, and I dug the way my cock looked going in and out of that tight round ass of hers.

"You dig baby's ass?" she mumbled into the pillow.

"Yeah, I dig it!" I exuberantly replied, and fucked her harder. I could feel the cum rising, pouring into my cockhead. I jerked, and came with a glorious spurt that curled my toes and made me moan. I even had some after tremors, little oozing quakes after the main event. Sperm dribbled out her asshole, disgusting and exciting me. I pulled free, and saw brown flecks on my dick.

"Jesus," I whispered, and fell against her back.

We were soon sleeping side by side. I was in a deep post-coital sleep, but she—she was deep in junkie heaven, her mind in a black abyss, lost to the world and herself.

Afterwards, I scrubbed myself with scalding water and steel wool.

Oh, and I did take her to dinner.

Of course, there was a very brief interlude with a ditzy single mom, black roots showing beneath a bad rinse job. I finger-fucked her in the furniture department at Macy's, while her kid jumped on chaise lounges.

But let me tell you about my prize: a plastic surgerized 50-something with the proverbial penthouse on Park Avenue, courtesy of husband number three. Her face stretched behind her ears, her hair was like a mane of frizzled fools gold, and her pussy was shaved. She had one of those vulgar deep tans that showed off her age spots. Yet her breasts were real, small and charmingly flat against her chest. I met her in a bar off Union Square. She wore white Capri pants, red pumps, and a pale blue scarf twirled around her neck. Her shirt had one too many buttons undone, revealing a very expensive red satin bra. Depending on your zip code, her outfit was either retro-chic or suburban vulgar. She was finishing a Cosmopolitan, her loud red lipstick firmly imprinted on the glass. I stood next to her stool. Her perfume wafted against my nostrils. I ordered bourbon, water on the side. She glanced sideways, appraising me.

"You old enough for that drink, sonny?" she laughed, in a low voice, rich with alcohol.

"Old enough and then some." I tapped her empty glass. "Buy you a drink?"

She gave me another look, replied "Sure," quickly showing her tongue between her lips.

"Same thing?" and she nodded. I signaled the bartender, and she picked up the re-filled glass with a very feminine gesture, showing off her carefully tapered fingers and lacquered nails. Two very expensive rings glittered in the light.

"To little boys," she smiled, and clinked my glass.

I tossed my bourbon back, swirled some water in my mouth, and savored the burn.

"How's the drink?" I inquired.

"Nice," and she pushed the glass over to me. "Taste it."

You might think it imprudent to drink from a stranger's glass, but then my tongue's been up junkie twat and my cock's been in places brown, black, and blue, so I wasn't about to get sanitary now.

I took her glass and sipped from the lipstick side, licking the imprint when I finished. She smiled.

"Oooh, aren't *we* provocative?" and the way she said it told me I was in the pussy zone.

"Drink OK?" I asked. She studied the glass from different angles. "Yes, it's not bad, but it's missing something." Suddenly her hand was on my crotch. I moved closer, to hide what she was doing. She tugged at my zipper and skillfully snaked her cool bony hand into my under-wear and around my cock. I leaned into the bar and let out a low gasp as she slowly began to jerk me.

"Yes," she repeated, in her low voice, "this drink needs something, something salty," and she squeezed harder on my cock, "Something only a sonny boy can provide—something with a head," and she began to seriously pump me. I tried hard not to gyrate my ass. I wondered if anyone around us knew what was going on, but I didn't care. I swallowed hard. I started to come. My companion quickly brought her glass to my squirting cock, the milky white swirling in the deep ruby of her drink. She gently pulled on my cock as she sipped her drink.

"Now that's a Cosmopolitan," and she plunged her tongue into the glass and coated it with the milky red drink. She pulled me by my cock until I was right next to her. It turned me on. Her eyes glittered as she let some of the drink dribble down the side of her mouth. And then she kissed me, one of those sloppy alcoholic kisses. She rolled her tongue into my mouth, and I could taste her saliva, my jism, and the bartender's idea of a Cosmopolitan all at once. It was gross. I was in heaven.

She pulled away, took a swig of the drink, and kissed me again, letting the liquid roll into my mouth. I let it roll back. We swirled it until we had no more left. There was a pause. We were both breathing deeply. Her hand was still on my cock.

"So," she whispered, "sonny boy wants his mama."

"Lady—," I began, but she slid her hand off my dick and brought it up to my face. Her fingers glistened, and she pushed them into my mouth.

"Be a good boy and lick them clean."

I licked. She slowly pulled away and dried the hand with a cocktail napkin. She laughed.

"Don't you think you better zip your dick up?" And she shook her head. "Mama's got to tell her sonny boy everything, doesn't she?"

She's really into this Oedipal shtick but I figured, as I tucked my organ as inconspicuously as I could into my fly, what the hell. I could go along with a gag, if it got me this perfect burnt blonde poon.

I looked up and could swear the bartender cocked an eyebrow at me. I took a deep breath.

"By the way, it's not 'sonny boy'," and I told her my name.

She smirked. "Your name's sonny boy alright. I knew the moment I saw you that you were my sonny boy." She rapped my ass with her knuckles, spiking me with her rings. It hurt. I jumped. "Besides, it's not polite to contradict your elders. Where's your manners?"

I opened my mouth, but she cut me off.

"If you want to play with the big girls, you have to have manners," and she slid drunkenly off her stool, falling against my chest. I caught her, and she looked up at me, her face flush with liquor. She parted her lips, and I kissed her again, seizing her well-kept body and squeezing it to mine. I was in a frenzy to have her. Her eyes were laughing as we pulled apart.

"I've got to pee—escort me," and she drunkenly offered me her elbow. I walked her to the women's room, but as I turned to leave she laughed and said, "A gentleman helps a lady pee," and pulled me into the bathroom with her. It smelled of urine, vomit, and menses. She locked the door and grabbed my shirt.

"Let's see what we got," and she pushed me against the wall and jerked the shirt open. The buttons echoed against the tiled floor.

"Mmmm, you're not bad for a little boy," and she ran her hands greedily over my chest. The contrast of her dark tanned hands against my never-been-in-the-sunlight skin excited me. Her fingers brushed my chest, and I closed my eyes. I felt her tongue on my neck, and she licked down to my nipples. She sucked them into her mouth, teasing them with her tongue, biting them gently, licking them some more, then biting them with an ever-increasing insistence. When I could bear it no longer, I grabbed her face and kissed her, seizing her body close to mine. Her hands tugged at my belt.

"Take off the rest," she whispered.

I did, and she licked her lips as she watched. I tried to hang my clothes on a hook by the door, but she pulled them out of my hand and threw them on the ground.

"Fuck your clothes."

She stood back and shimmied her pants off, revealing red satin panties. There was a sweet odor that made me think she perfumed her pussy. She slowly slid her panties down her legs, and I saw her crotch was shaved. It made me hungry to see it, glistening like a pink mouth. She smiled and took her shirt off, walking over to the toilet to piss. When she finished urinating, she leaned back and pushed her pussy up.

"Lick Mommy, c'mon baby, come over here and lick Mommy clean."

I walked over, got on my knees, and without hesitation put my tongue on her urine drenched pussy. I licked the wet skin, cleaning every crevice. Then I slowly pushed into her hole and tongue-fucked her slowly.

"Yes," she growled. "Oh yes."

She gyrated against me, breathing in short gasps. Then she pushed me on to the floor, which caused a moment's panic as my skin hit the cold filthy unpleasant tiles. The moment passed when she slid off the toilet and on to my cock, her wet juicy cunt thrilling every nerve. She put her hands on my chest and leaned forward, undulating her hips slowly.

"Yes yes yes," she repeated, while I just breathed deeply, thrusting into her as best I could from my position. Suddenly, someone knocked on the bathroom door.

"Tell them it's occupied," she said in a low voice.

"Wh-What?" I gasped.

"Tell them it's occupied," she repeated.

"Me? But this is the women's bathroom."

She laughed and squeezed my dick with her pussy.

"Nothing gets by Mommy's little boy, does it?"

Another knock. She looked at me.

"It's occupied," I yelled out.

The knocking stopped.

"What if she complains to the bartender?"

She ignored me and began to fuck me harder, squeezing her muscles rhythmically. Her face began to flush as a much harder knock interrupted us.

"Alright," a harsh male voice shouted, "you've had your fun. Now get out of there."

She was bucking wildly.

More knocks.

"Don't make me open this door."

This seemed to drive her crazy, and I thought she was going to bounce right off my dick. I was near coming myself. She curled her fingers into my chest hair and let out a long low guttural moan. Her bouncing slowly stopped. I let myself go, coming with a quick spurt. She fell on top of me, kissing me sloppily.

"I'm losing patience," the voice on the other side yelled.

She looked up and yelled, "Can't a girl piss in peace around here?"

"Oh, uhhh," the voice sounded confused. "Sorry, ma'am, I thought a man might be in there."

"Do I sound like a fucking man?"

"No, no you don't. Please excuse me. And take your time."

"Thanks, I will."

"Think he believes it's only you?" I whispered.

"Who cares?" and we kissed some more, until she finally lifted herself up. I watched her gather up her clothes.

"I could fuck you all night."

"That's because you're a loyal little boy, but you better get dressed."

We were ready to leave.

"You first," she said, and unlocked the door and pushed me out, where a small line of women glared.

"Sorry girls," she said, laughing behind me, "but I needed help wiping myself."

We staggered out of the bar as the bartender eyeballed us all the way to the door.

Blondes. Burnt-out blondes.

Like a thirsty man needs water, like the condemned man needs a reprieve, I need dyed blonde pussy.

You see them on the streets, on the train, or in cabs.

And I crave them.

I crave them all.

CROOKED KWAN

Cecilia Tan

ohnny Kwan tried to lie still in the dark, but the bed moved like a ship at rough seas as his partner rocked above him. He felt the droplets of her sweat hit his chest, tap tap, but no coolness, just wet upon wet. Overhead a fan turned, he knew by the creak of it since he could neither see it in the dark nor feel any breeze. All that he could see was the shining outline of her damp cheek, her damp shoulder, her damp breast, in the light from the street that came in the open window. A flash of her blond hair, limp with sweat.

The fan creaked, the bed springs protested, and the sounds of traffic and street Chinese crowded into his ears. His partner braced herself against him with her hands on his shoulders and added her voice to the orchestra, an inarticulate moan as she moved to new heights of pleasure. Johnny Kwan did not move, except to clench his jaw. Even when she sighed she had a foreign sound to her voice, something in the vowels that could be British or American but was certainly not Hongkongese. Two months, Johnny thought, two months until the gates close, and nothing to be done about it. Holding still wasn't working anymore. She began to say things in her low, brassy tone that he didn't understand, and he could not stop what was coming any more than he could stop the British from giving up the place. He bucked once, twice, and came into her, his dark hands sliding across her white breasts in the window light as he sank down deeper and deeper into darkness.

He heard the metallic sound of the pull chain on the fan; she was fumbling in the dark for the light. She snapped on the wall switch and Johnny winced in the yellowy brightness. Her hands searched his jacket pocket for something. She stood up with two cigarettes and a lighter in her hands, put both cigarettes into her mouth and lit them with one puff. He took one.

"You good," he said, not smiling. One only smiles when one wants to placate someone bigger than oneself. "Your name?"

The blond did smile, but she was a girl, a Westerner, and a whore, and they smiled for all sorts of reasons. She spoke some soft syllables and he had to put his hand to his ear for her to repeat them. "Sherrie," she said with exaggerated r's. She sat in a wooden chair by the window and crossed her legs.

Johnny nodded his head. Madame Lun always did good business with girls like these. Back when Iron Circle was in the protection racket, Madame Lun sometimes let men like Johnny sample the goods. But tonight, there was no Iron Circle anymore, and Johnny was a paying customer. He decided he'd hand over the money after he finished the cigarette.

"You like Hong Kong?" he asked, feeling bold with the thought of that money. In all the confusion, Smiling Willy Lim would never know it was gone and Johnny Kwan had no intention of working for him.

"Yeah sure," she said, her eyes out the window on the traffic.

"You good," he repeated. He tried to make his English words come out slow, like the drawl of confidence American movie actors always had. Bravado made him say "Madame Lun, I ask her for you again."

Sherrie snorted half a laugh. "Well, it better be soon honey because in a few weeks I am outta here. When the Brits go, I go. Madame Lun, too. Gone, sayonara, bye bye Chinaman."

Johnny stubbed out his cigarette, not-smiling even harder. The implied insult, that because he couldn't leave he was somehow beneath her, would have earned her a slap from most men. But, one couldn't expect whores to have respect and one didn't pay them to be kind, Johnny told himself. Just pay her and go. He slid his pants on and buckled the belt. He pulled his cotton T-shirt over his head and picked up his western-style button down shirt and jacket. From the inner pocket of the jacket he produced a wad of green, American bills. He tugged a few out of the wad and put them onto the damp bed. But he held out his hand for his lighter before he left the room.

On the street, Johnny Kwan, also known as Crooked Kwan not because of his trade but because of the way his face never seemed to be on quite straight, looked for a taxi. He had more stops to make tonight as he made his best attempt to spend what was formerly Willy Lim's money. Their former boss, J.Y. Fung, head of the Iron Circle, had bought himself a citizenship to Canada and was already on his way to Vancouver where he had legitimate businesses and ties to a powerful ancestral clan association in San Francisco. Smiling Lim, conniver that he was, had tried to take over Iron Circle in J.Y.'s wake but the organization split into factions. Small men with small influence were scrabbling for what little hold they could get in the fading light of Hong Kong's sunset, as the island sank into the great, hulking economic morass that was the People's Republic like the sun into the sea. Already there were mainland tongs taking over the drug trade, and anyone with enough money in the bank had bought their citizenship somewhere else. Madame Lun was probably one of them. Johnny Kwan wandered down the street through the crowd of noodle stands and mah-jongg players and people, the smell of steaming fish and garbage seeping through his still damp skin.

Iron Circle was rust and he knew it, so he was doing what any sensible person would do. He was on a binge.

Working his way up the hill and up in price, he went next to the House of Jade. They put him in another little room with a glass of water on the table and a fan that almost cooled the room. He could feel the breeze it made, anyhow, even if it felt like all it did was re-circulate the heat that had risen back down into the room. There they brought him a bleach-blond who had white skin but didn't look or sound American, but he took her anyway, holding onto her blond hair as he pushed her mouth down on his hard cock. That way he couldn't hear her talk and couldn't see that her pubic hair wasn't bleached. He let her smoke one of his cigarettes and had to buy more before his next stop.

He took a taxi to the House of the Flowering Lotus, where the sheets were red silk like a wedding dress and stained in a puddle as dark as blood when he sweated on them. They had a genuine blond, white woman, who, like Sherrie, tried to get on top to finish him off as quickly as possible. It wasn't necessary. Crooked Kwan wanted quantity now, and although he stayed on top, he was done without much delay. But then he ordered a clean shirt and decided to fuck her again while he waited for it. She lay back on the bed and spread her legs wide, beckoning him by spreading the pink, shaven folds of her cunt wide and fingering herself. So brazen, only a Western woman would act this way, he thought. So this is what a higher price can get you. He approached her but found he was still soft. She took him in her hands and mouth and made him hard again. Another bonus. In a cheap house if a man couldn't get it up he didn't get his money back either. He teased her with the now hard pole, rubbing it against her lips and sliding it around everywhere but into her. She cooed and writhed, and said "Oh come on, sugar, fill me up with that sausage." He made her wait even longer for it. By the time he was fucking her again, his clean shirt arrived without him noticing. This is heaven, he thought, as he buried his face between her white spheres. There was only one place more expensive than House of the Flowering Lotus and he looked forward to trying there next.

"Fay dee ah, quickly!" He banged his gold ring against the dark wood of the table. He had come in to the Palace of Summer Clouds and demanded their best white girl. Some silent, demure women in long silk dresses had seated him here, poured him tea, and withdrew. But surely such a high-class place would not keep him waiting so long. He had drunk two cups of tea already. The air was thick with old incense to mask the odor of sweat and other men.

"Ai," he muttered. The place would be a communist work camp by the time he got any service. An older woman bedecked with too much jade and mascara entered the room. Johnny Kwan tossed some bills onto the table. "Gwai lo," he spat. Someone white. "American, British, Australian, I don't care." She named him a price, an exorbitant, ridiculous price, Johnny knew, but he was in the charade now and threw more bills down.

She plucked the bills from the table with her lacquered claws and held them up to the light. Satisfied they were genuine, she jerked her head to indicate he should follow her. She left him in a room full of ornate woodwork and red paper lanterns, jade statuettes and incense, things probably arranged to meet the expectations of some rich gwai lo who came here to see what an Oriental brothel was "really" like. Johnny stripped out of his shirt and was glad this place was air-conditioned.

The sound of soft footsteps behind him made him turn. In the dim lantern light he could see she wasn't blond, but she was white. She was dolled up in a satin chongsam and had chopsticks in her hair, which just made her look all the more un-Chinese. "Fay dee ah," he said. "Get out your clothes." He slipped off his pants and shoes. She began wriggling out of the dress, fumbling with the cloth buttons.

Too slow, he decided. He pushed her onto the bed and tore the chongsam open. She gasped. Her pubic hair was mousy brown like the hair on her head and he knelt down to put his face in it. That was enough foreplay for him. Holding her at the edge of the bed, he buried himself deep inside her. In the light he could see the darkness of his pubic hair contrasted with hers and he nodded to himself. Her eyes were shut and her head was turned away.

"Open your eyes," he said. He didn't remember what color they were.

She shook her head. Her brown hair came loose from the chopsticks and spilled out over the fine brocade of the bed cover.

"Come on." He thrust harder into her as if he could force her eyes open with his cock. "Open."

She grimaced and shook her head again.

"Aiyah, I thought this was an expensive place with good whores," he said to himself in street Chinese. She made no sign of understanding him.

"You listen," he said as he kept up his rhythm. "You do what I say or your madame will beat you."

But she still did not move or open her eyes.

Johnny Kwan shrugged. Maybe this was a part of the service, he thought. The extra price he paid must have been for this. They think I want to rape this white woman, so she plays uncooperative. Good act. He lifted her up so he could slide further onto the bed without pulling out of her. He slowed down his stroking and began to caress her soft, white breasts. Let's see what kind of whore she really is, he thought. When she starts to go wild with pleasure she will drop this act.

He leaned over to tease her nipples with his tongue and they stood up obediently. He breathed hot in her ear and twirled his fingers around her hard nipples and tugged on them. She still clutched at the bed covers and did not look up. Well, no matter. Johnny Kwan slid his fingers along her stomach until he began to burrow in the crease between their bodies. Every time he pulled back he would slide his finger further down into her cleft, seeking the right spot for her pleasure. She bit her lip as he found it, and he began to stroke it in time with his thrusts.

"Come on, little sister," he said to her, "come to Big Brother Kwan. Open your eyes, little sister, show me eyes." But still she refused. He buried himself deep in her and slapped her across the face and she gasped with shock. "What the matter with you?" She began to cry. Johnny Kwan turned her face toward him but did not pull out of her. He crooned. "Hey, hey, little sister. What wrong?" He'd been a drug runner and a small time hustler but he'd never thought of himself as a bully. He stroked her cheek where he'd hit her.

She opened her eyes. They were a kaleidoscope of colors, brown, with flecks of green, red, eyes like Johnny Kwan had never seen before, not on a woman he was in bed with, anyway. The eyes were also full of tears. He hugged her to him. "Hey, hey, okay, okay," he said as he rocked. He was still fucking her, after all. She wasn't sobbing and the tears stopped.

He held himself above her and made his strokes long and slow. "Okay now?" She nodded and two American-sounding syllables came from her throat. "Uh huh." Johnny Kwan tasted her neck again. "Sweet little sister," he breathed.

Either she was an even better actress than he imagined, or her little act had gotten out of hand there. Well, she was all right now. He decided to slow down even more, to see if he could make it last longer. Maybe she had a few more surprises for him. "Why you cost so much, little sister?"

She blushed. "I . . . I don't know." But that was clearly a lie. "Come on, you got something special? Madame of Summer Clouds wouldn't charge that much for any piece of tail, even gwai lo tail." He quoted the price back to her as if that might remind her which service she was to provide.

Her eyes went wide with recognition and her tears started again. "Well?"

She went limp with resignation. "That old bitch, I can't believe she did that."

That was not what Johnny Kwan expected to hear. "Eh?"

The white girl grimaced. "You and I just paid for her ticket out of Hong Kong, my friend. That was just the amount she needed."

Another bought citizenship, he supposed. If only he'd been stealing this much from Willy Lim all along, he could be in Canada too by now. But he wasn't. But what had the girl said? "You, and I?"

The woman rolled her multi-colored eyes and sighed. "She told me if I didn't . . . service you, that she'd make sure I lost my papers and couldn't stay. With the new government, I don't think the bribe system will work. So I agreed."

He must be hearing her wrong. She seemed to be implying that she wasn't a regular whore, and she wasn't planning on leaving with everyone else.

Crooked Kwan was so puzzled he had to stop fucking for a minute while he thought about it.

"Why you here?" he finally asked.

"I just told you. Because Madame Wing blackmailed me."

"No, no, in Hong Kong."

"Business," she answered. Her mouth was set now, tough, and her voice rasped with sarcasm. "Haven't you heard? The PRC is the world's biggest, fastest growing economy. And Hong Kong is its new doorstep." She lay back with a tired sigh. "Let the old bitch go. I thought she was just trying to humiliate me, but no."

"But, why you? No other white girl?"

She shook her head. "Summer Clouds is where big time white businessmen come to fuck gorgeous Asian women, not the other way around," she said, slowly as if he must be dim not to know it.

Johnny Kwan repeated his earlier question. "Why you here? Summer Clouds, I mean."

"To meet big time white businessmen."

"Ah." Johnny Kwan blinked. Life must look different through multicolor eyes. He still had some money left and could afford to lay low for a while longer. Willy Lim might be dead already in the squabbling, and when the dust cleared, there would be opportunities for Crooked Kwan who had pledged no damaging allegiances. There would be money flowing through Hong Kong and he could drink from that river as well as any man, PRC or no.

She looked down at where he was still sunk into her and then back up at him. "Are you done?"

He did not smile. No, he decided, he was definitely not done.

MEMORIAL DAY

Mike Kimera

"So what was your best?"

"Best what?"

"Best erotic experience."

Mark is a sex bore. He talks about it so much it's a wonder he gets time to do it.

"Mine was with two Swedish twins in a sauna," he says, leaning towards me conspiratorially. "I'd added a day to a Swiss business trip to get some skiing in and these two and I were first back to the hotel from the piste. Well, you know how the Europeans are with saunas, everyone together and no clothes allowed. Just one of these girls would have been amazing—snow white hair, all-over tan and sleek body—but twins! I thought I'd died and gone to pussy heaven."

I hate men who say pussy like that. Like a woman starts and ends at her cunt. But I've known Mark since grade school so I give him some latitude. Turning slightly away from him, I look towards the lake where Helen and Barbara are sunning themselves. They are the best of friends and they tell each other everything. I want to sit quietly beside them and listen to their talk. Instead I am standing next to Mark at the BarBQ pit, burning burgers.

"So anyways, the shock came when the first one took me inside her. In the heat of the sauna her pussy felt cool. No shit. Cool pussy from an ice-maiden in a sauna. How sexy is that! Then, when her sister joined in . . ."

I think Mark is making this up. Maybe the twins were real. Maybe he even saw them in the sauna. But I want to believe that he doesn't cheat on Barbara on his business trips.

I am a little in love with Barbara. Helen pointed it out to me one night as we drove back from dinner at their house. She said that she'd noticed that Barbara is always the last person I look at in a room and that I avoid being alone with her, both sure signs of my attraction. Denial would have been pointless; Helen knows me too well. After a few seconds of guilt-ridden silence, Helen pulled the car over to the side of the road, and right there, in a tree-lined suburban street, where nice neighbors repaint their picket fences every spring, she fucked me. She didn't say a word. Mouth on mine, she freed my cock, pushed aside her panties and rode me. I came like a boy. She grinned at me, held my face in her hands and said, "If you ever call me Barbara while we fuck, I'll cut your dick off." Then she drove us home.

Only when Mark says, "Your turn," do I realise I've missed his sauna-sex story and he is now waiting for mine.

"Come on Pete," he says, "even a terminally married man like you must have had SOME erotic adventures. 'Fess up."

An image of Helen blossoms in my mind. She is 19 and has just let me fuck her for the first time, that's my first time, not hers. She'd insisted that we use her parents' bed. "It will make up for all the times I've had to listen to them screwing," she'd said as she led me into the master bedroom. I am laying on my back, wrists still tied to the headboard, sated and happy, watching her between half closed eyes, pretending to be asleep. She is sitting at her mother's dressing table, brushing her long black hair. The sun streaming through the window behind her seems to me to be a kind of halo. She leans her head to one side so that she can push the comb through the full length of her thick glossy hair. This causes one small upturned breast to push off the silk robe that Helen has "borrowed" from her mother, and to stretch triumphantly up towards the sun. I am hypnotised by the play of light on her hair; the smooth movement of her arm as she wields the brush and the slight but attention-grabbing movement of her silhouetted breast. She puts the brush back on the dressing table, looks at me and smiles. Many times since, I have returned to that moment of still happiness, crowned with the love in her smile.

"Well?" Mark says.

"Sorry Mark," I say, "nobody seems to want erotic adventures with me."

I mean it as a playful way of changing the subject. Mark takes me literally.

"I don't know," he says, "you're not bad looking. I know Barbara thinks you're sexy. You just need to read the signs."

"I think the food is ready now," I say, gathering the half-burnt/half-frozen products of Mark's culinary skill on to plates.

"You must have been tempted. At least once," Mark says.

"I'm happily married Mark. Temptation is easy enough to overcome."

"Ah yes," Mark says, "I'd forgotten about the Peter Brader man of steel act."

I start to walk back towards the lake hoping to bring an end to the conversation before we get in to a fight. Mark has always taken my abstinence from casual sex as a personal affront. Briefly I wonder if he thinks it's all an act and I'm just refusing to share the details with him.

"Barbara really does think you're sexy you know."

I stop and look at him. He laughs.

"No need to look so horrified. She's not going to rape you or anything. But she told me that she admires your serenity. Isn't that a great phrase? Admires your serenity."

I try for a wry smile but Mark is already striding ahead of me so it is lost on him.

"OK girls, the hunters have returned with freshly charred dead animals for their women to feast upon," he shouts.

Sometimes I think Mark is locked in a parallel dimension. The "girls," both in their late twenties, exchange pained glances at Mark's return, but he either doesn't notice or doesn't care.

This meal is a tradition amongst us going back eight years, to when we were both newly married couples. Every Memorial Day we drive out to the lake and have a BarBQ on the public beach. Back then we slept in our trucks and drank beer with our burgers. Now we rent a large cabin and sip Pinot Noir. Sometimes I think the burgers are the last talisman of the days when we had more hope than history.

I have my head in Helen's lap. She smells of sunshine and cotton. I relax, content to listen to her telling Barbara stories about the people in her office. I have never visited Helen's office. I am reluctant to have reality superimposed on the vivid images I have of her colleagues. Barbara and Helen used to work together. Helen introduced Barbara to Mark.

When Barbara laughs at the punch line of Helen's story, it is a raucous laugh that seems to escape from her. I turn my head slightly, knowing that Barbara will have one hand in front of her face. Helen feels me move, recognises the reason and, unseen by the others, pinches my earlobe as she pulls me back to my original position. I look up at her. She mouths the word "later" and I shiver at the thought.

Despite Helen's admonition, I find myself wondering about Barbara's laugh. It reminds me of Miss Honeychurch in "Room with a view," whose passionate nature is discernible only by the way in which she plays piano. With a stab of guilt, accompanied by a sudden erection, I have a flash of Barbara coming as raucously as she laughs.

On our second year out here, we almost got into a group thing. We'd stopped talking and started kissing, still in couples but with each couple acutely aware of the presence of the other. I left the decision to Helen who in turn looked to Barbara. Mark was thinking with his cock and pushed up Barbara's T-shirt to take her nipple into his mouth. The discomfort on Barbara's face was obvious.

Helen grabbed me by the belt and said, more loudly than she needed to, "Come on Peter, I need a bed to tie you to."

I was happy to leave. Barbara smiled her gratitude while trying to keep Mark's fingers out of her shorts. Civilised man that I am, I still could not erase the sight of Barbara's stiff nipple topping a small neat breast that just demanded to be taken into my mouth. Helen knew what I was thinking. When she rode me she held my nipples between her fingernails and used them like a bridle. I was sore for a week but my cock was made of ivory that night.

The scene was never repeated. Barbara confided in Helen her embarrassment at how Mark fucks her. I was puzzled when Helen passed on the remark. She just laughed and said, "Well you've seen him dance haven't you." Mark thinks he dances like John Travolta but he looks more like Fred Flintstone. He dances vigorously, with his eyes closed, paying little attention to either his partner or the rhythm of the music. The magnitude of the criticism made my balls retract.

I am constantly amazed at what women tell each other. Men brag, women tell the truth. It's a frightening thought.

A tinny rendition of the James Bond Theme fractures the silence. Mark has brought his cell phone, even on Memorial Day. Barbara glares at him but he turns his back on her and takes the call. Mark uses an earpiece on his phone. He says he doesn't want to fry the brain cells that survived the drugs. He looks demented as he paces in a circle, apparently talking to himself.

We overhear enough of the conversation to know that he has been summoned back to the city by some European emergency that he must respond to at once. I wonder at that, it's 9 P.M. in Berlin right now. It occurs to me that I have just seen a piece of performance art. Maybe Mark doesn't make his adventures up. Perhaps there is someone waiting for him even now in a city center hotel room.

To my surprise Barbara lets Mark go without complaint, she just sits and watches as he takes the car, leaving her behind like luggage we will forward to him later.

"I'm going to lie down in the cabin for a while," Barbara says once the car is out of sight.

"Are you OK?" I say. Dumb question. Helen digs her fingers into my side to tell me to shut up.

"No Peter, I'm not OK, but I'm trying to get used to it. Not everyone has a marriage like yours. I live with a man who never touches me, but who tries to fuck anything female that can move without a Zimmer frame. He doesn't even have the tact not to embarrass me in front of my friends. So I'm trying to preserve my dignity by not letting myself cry until I get back to my room."

Barbara's eyes are wet but she is standing straight and her voice is strong and clear. She holds my gaze until I look away, then she picks up a bottle of wine and heads back to the cabin. Helen follows her. They talk quietly but passionately. I can't hear what is said. Then they hug in that way women do, halfway between a caress and a handshake.

Helen waits, head on one side, hands on her hips, for my questions. I don't ask any. She looks at me for the longest time. I seldom know what she is thinking. She moves to stand in front of me, tilts my head down towards hers and says, "I love you Peter Brader."

We give Barbara an hour before we return to the cabin. I head into the kitchen to clear away the debris of our meal. Helen goes to check on Barbara. I have just loaded the dishwasher when I hear Helen say, "Come here Peter."

I know from her tone that we have started to play. I am surprised but, out of long habit, I go to her and wait, eyes downcast, for her instructions. I love surrendering to her like this. My cock is already thickening and my heartbeat is elevated. It is so exciting not to know what will happen next. Even so, I am concerned. Surely she's not going to take me here, in the main room. The thought worries and thrills me at the same time.

"Strip Peter."

Helen has never done this before. On our Memorial Weekends she has always used the bedroom for our fucking.

I don't look at her or speak as I strip. I feel exposed standing there, my cock sending semaphore signals of desire to my mistress.

"Put your hands behind your back," Helen says.

The steel cuffs Helen produces from her bag are cold against my wrists. They make me feel pleasantly helpless.

"Peter, I want you to stay hard as long as you can. Let me help you," She ties a soft leather strap around my balls. My cock trembles at her touch. She grins and plants a chaste little kiss just underneath the head.

I wait for her to undress. She doesn't. Instead she reaches into her bag and pulls out a scarf. Standing behind me she blindfolds me with the scarf. I feel her breath on my neck. Her teeth sink into my earlobe as her fist closes around my cock. I groan.

"You wanted Barbara today didn't you," she says.

I nod.

"Say it. Tell me what you were thinking."

"I wanted to know how she sounds when she comes," I say.

She lets go of my cock. A cool finger probes my anus.

"So you prefer her to me?"

"No. I love you. I need you."

"But . . . ?"

"But I like Barbara."

"Would you like her to fuck you?"

"Yes," I say. I think I know where Helen is going with this but I can't believe she really means it.

Helen kisses me. A deep, slow kiss, exploring my mouth with hers. Except it is not Helen. Helen is still behind me.

The kissing stops. Before I can speak Helen presses against my back and whispers, "It will be OK Peter. Trust me." I nod my head slightly and she whispers "Thank you."

I understand the blindfold. It gives us the option to pretend that none of this has happened.

No one is touching me now. I wait. I assume the women are undressing. I wonder if they are touching. Suddenly it occurs to me that, over the years, they may have done more than just touch. My mind doubts that this is true, Helen would have told me, but my cock goes with the image and twitches ludicrously.

A hand, strong and purposeful, pushes on my shoulder, signalling for me to kneel. The floor is hard on my knees. I won't be able to do this for long. I recognise the smell of Helen's sex, seconds before it is pressed against my face. She holds my head and rubs herself against me. My tongue presents itself for use. She presses her labia against my mouth until my head is forced backwards. She rubs me in a figure of eight against her sex, then she is gone.

Seconds later another sex is pressed against my mouth. To my surprise it smells and tastes just like the first. Maybe I can't tell the difference between Helen and Barbara. Maybe Helen is returning to confuse me. The message is clear enough: stop trying to analyse, go with the flow, be the moment, let the sex flow through you. That message is at the heart of my sexuality and I recognise it as their gift to me.

Hands guide me to lie first on my side and then on my back. Cushions are placed under my head and my butt. Care is taken to ensure that I am never touched by both women at the same time. I could let myself imagine that there is only Helen or only Barbara, but now is the time for feeling, not imagining.

A mouth suckles my nipple. The sound of it is loud against the eerie silence that possesses us like a spell. The tongue moves down my belly slowly, skilfully, until it reaches my pubic hair, then it goes away. A hand, warm, strong, grips my cock around the shaft. The palm of a second hand rubs my precum over the head of my cock, making me wriggle and moan. It takes effort not to come, but I control myself.

Attention shifts from my cock to my mouth. Swift butterfly kisses that make me smile. Then tickling. Tickling that goes on until I am giggling helplessly with tears wetting my blindfold.

I am allowed to get my breath back, then I am mounted. My cock slides into ripe wetness that grabs at me eagerly. Hands on my chest. Thighs around my legs. Deep forceful strokes, followed after the shortest of times by a tremor of passion that passes through to my bones. She falls forward on to me, sweat-slick breasts sliding over me, teeth nipping at my neck.

Then she rolls off me, leaving my cock straining for relief, my body demanding stimulus. Both are granted by the mouth that envelops my cock and the swollen labia that descends upon my face. I lick eagerly at first, then become distracted by the play of teeth and tongue and lips upon my cock.

I break the spell of silence, begging to be allowed to come. The mouth releases me as she slides down my body and impales herself on my cock. She does not move, but she squeezes me with her cunt, milking me irresistibly. She is moaning now, but quietly, as if she were gagged. Her hands are on my ankles; her cunt is pressed hard against my pubis. When I start to come, her grip on my ankles tightens and I hear a groan that starts in the back of her throat and becomes an explosive "Fuck!" She stays on me until my cock softens, then she lets it slide out.

I am exhausted. Cool fingers undo the leather around my balls. My cock is patted gently, like a Labrador being rewarded for performing a favorite trick. I find it hard to focus. My awareness always ebbs after I come.

I am being helped up and led somewhere. A bed. Fresh clean linen. The bed feels so comforting after the hardness of the floor. My hands are uncuffed. My arms are massaged vigorously and asexually. Scarves are used to tie my wrists to the headboard.

I am ready to give way to sleep when I hear that unmistakable buzz followed by the smell of latex. My asshole clenches in anticipation.

"Spread Peter," Helen's voice. A calm command she knows will be obeyed.

The vibrator is slim and has a slight curve. It is perfect for stimulating the prostate. I relax and let it slide in, wondering who is holding it. My tired cock starts to rally. I think I hear a giggle from beside the bed, but I am distracted by having my balls sucked one after the other.

My brain is fuzzy. I want to sleep. I want to fuck forever. I turn down the noise in my mind and focus on the cunt that is now raising and lowering itself on my cock. I have no control over the pace. I am a flesh dildo. I am happy.

With the vibrator in place I manage to stay hard until after she comes. I am rewarded with a skilful hand job that drains my balls and takes the last of my energy.

I hear Helen say, "You can sleep now Peter," and I know the game is over. As sleep washes over me, I think I hear a different voice say very quietly "Thank you."

I sleep late. When I awake my hands are free, the blindfold is gone, my ass is sore and my memory is confused. Before I can get out of bed, Helen and Barbara, both fully dressed and looking refreshed and relaxed, bring me breakfast on a tray.

"Good morning sleepyhead," Helen says. "We've brought you something to build up your strength."

"Do I need building up?" I ask.

Helen ignores the question and hands me a glass of cold OJ. Barbara is standing at the foot of the bed. She is smiling, not broadly, but persistently. I doubt she is aware of it.

"Barbara is going to come and stay with us for a while," Helen says.

I look at both of them. Helen posed it as a statement, but we all know it was a question. The silence continues while I think about it.

"It's only until I decide what to do about Mark," Barbara says, "Helen thought I could stay in the guest room for a while."

I think about how long I have known Mark and yet how little I really like him. I consider how comfortable Helen and Barbara are together. I remember the carefully anonymous passion we shared last night. I know that if I say yes it will change things forever in ways that I can't yet predict.

"I'm sorry about you and Mark," I say to Barbara, "but I'm glad you're coming to stay. I'm sure we'll work something out."

The look on Helen's face tells me I'd done the right thing. I don't know if last night will be repeated. I trust Helen to work that out. I do know that I am still naked under the bedclothes and that I desperately need to use the bathroom.

"If you ladies will excuse me," I say, "I have some urgent business to attend to, privately."

Helen grins and leads Barbara by the elbow, saying, "A man's gotta do what a man's gotta do," in a terrible John Wayne accent.

Barbara picks up the theme and says, "Yep, and there are some things a man must do alone." They are both laughing as they leave the room.

I'm still not sure what I've just agreed to, but however it turns out, it won't be dull. I head off to the bathroom, whistling happily.

THE HORSE BUTCHER'S SON

Helena Settimana

This is the way it goes down: you are in the Bureau des Postes in Boulogne-sur-mer trying to mail a postcard to your sister in London while Charles Aznavour is humming "La Vie en Rose" into the back of your head. Of course it is not Charles, who might be dead, but the man is trying hard. The tiny hairs on your neck start to prickle as his breath rolls in a wave over your collar. Eventually he says in English, to no one in particular, "I don't think she is French." This is where you turn with the sweetest smile, and in your plummiest tones, tell him that he is right. This is where your words pile into your throat like dead flies between windowpanes, and know that the singer of the songs is someone you might lie with. You like trying to see the world without leaving your bed. He has black eyes, spiraled, coiled Tunisian hair; biblical teeth.

The crooner suggests a café, and midway through your mocha you are wishing for absinthe and the company of talented dwarves a la Lautrec. You tell him so. He calls for anisette. He is charming, and you are shocked to hear that he is the son of the local horse-butcher. "Horse butcher's sons go to college too" he says and smiles in a distinctly feral, Gallic way. He offers to show you the shop, closed now for the week-end.

The cuts of meat are laid out as in any other butcher shop, and in the back hang the carcasses; the heads, bits of body parts in a bin: tails, bony legs, folds of skin and hide, coils of gut, cocks and balls: refuse. It is here in the cold with dead horses hanging from heavy steel hooks that he kisses you, hot and fevered so that you taste blood, coppery on your lips. His hands are hard and knowing and invasive. They wind like vises around your thighs, creep like small animals into your folds, burrow into the wet, and inhabit you there. You watch the vapor emitting from your mouths, noses puffing, the stacks on steam engines, liquid air rising from manholes in the street.

This is how you come; balanced like a meat puppet around his hand, pulling at his narrow, uncut, olive pisser until your fingers are webbed together by his load.

Later, alone at night, you dream of whores; a clever dwarf with Tunisian hair and of you, you, you, impaled upon a severed horse's cock.

NIGHTHAWKS

M. Christian

1:00 A.M. Phillies coffee house. A cup each: white and sweet for her, black for him. Nick stirred his clockwise, Darlene stirred counter.

"Chasin' the moon tonight?" Nick said, looking over at her. Her hair was the color of fresh copper, and she wore a dress to match. Her face was lean, but not harsh, and her eyes were the green of fresh grass.

"Just watching it travel, I guess. Probably gonna be home before it sets," Darlene said smiling at him. He had a good face, with lots of character: strong chin, good nose, gray eyes hooded beneath luxurious eyebrows. Not a pretty-boy, but handsome on his own.

"Used to be able to make it myself: all the way from the silver coming up to the silver going down. No gray on the roof but I'm not a kid anymore," he said smiling at her. Under the red dress she was slim, but not skinny, breasts full and obvious even through the material.

"You don't look like you're ready to get stuck in a home to me," she said, returning the smile. He wasn't big, but he seemed to be well put together: broad shoulders, and with nothing hanging over his belt. His hands, she noticed, had character. They were like signposts to his soul: strong, elegant, with perfectly clean nails.

"You're just buttering me. Nah, just been burning too much of that midnight oil lately." He wondered about her, instantly picturing her standing in his little place: red dress tossed over a chair, silken slip floating as she walked, showing off her fine lines. He imagined a red-head's soft skin, longs legs stretching beneath the bright white slip, and the twin points of hard nipples on perfect breasts.

"Know it. Just got off a shift myself. Thought a cup might make the trip home a little easier." She wondered about his lips: strong but soft, at first a gentle graze across hers, just a mixing of breaths. Then the initial chaste one, the first touch of his to hers. Heat between them flaring with the first touch of tongues, then the roaring blaze as he tilted her head back for a longer, more penetrating kiss.

"I'm right down on Bleeker. Got a little more to do but ran out of java. Jack's place is always open." He saw himself on his bed, looking down his half-dressed body, T-shirt, shorts, socks, as she climbed up with him. The gleaming white of her slip moving just enough to give him quick snapshots of knotted, deep-brown nipples, a tight tummy, and the distant flash of curled red hairs between her long legs.

"Gotta love Jack. You work graveyard or something?" His hands. Yes, that was next, his hands. Very good hands, and she thought about how he might use them. During the kissing, when it got good, so very good, they would be on her. Not hard grabs, but rather slow grazes across her thighs, up her side, over her shoulder. Then, as the fires grew higher, a gentle rest on her skirt, a cautious knead of the hard muscles. She imagined, and could see herself spread her thighs a little, just enough. But he'd be a good man, and wouldn't dive right in. Instead, she saw him kiss her even harder, swing dancing with her tongue, and his hand rest softly on her breast. At the thought, her nipple crinkled and gently throbbed in the soft support of her bra.

"My own. I'm a hack; got one thing down but have another piece due tomorrow," he was hard and hoped she wouldn't notice—but he was also hard and hoped she *would* notice. She was there, live and real in his mind, smiling up at him as she reached into his boxers and pulled out his very, very hard dick. She kissed it, at first—just a soft little touch to let him know that she wasn't afraid. Then a longer, wetter, harder kiss. In his mind, he was in her mouth, with his sensitive head of his cock grazing the roof of her mouth, as he watched her bright red hair bob up and down with each in, each out.

"Maybe I've read something." She could see his chest, lightly haired with dark nipples and ridges of firm muscles. His shoulders would have a light dusting of freckles, and his arms would be thick but not burly. He would have a good manly chest. Salt, the sensation suddenly on her tongue as she sipped at her coffee. Yes, salt: she wanted—then, there— to kiss that bare chest, taste the bite of his gleaming sweat.

"Not unless you hang out in some very unlady-like places. It pays the bills, though. Where do you sling your hash?" It wasn't that she would do the things he'd seen on playing cards, in stag reels. No, that wasn't what had his dick throbbing on his pants. It was just the thought of her being there, really there, with him in his little place. The way she smiled: he ached to see that same smile as she stroked his dick; as she pulled off her slip to show him her lean body, her firm breasts, her dark nipples, the triangle of red curls down between her legs. He wanted all that, but all that with the smile—more than anything.

"Del Rio's down on 154th. Food's not bad and the joes don't pinch my ass that much." She wanted those strong hands to touch her, to pull her close in a tight clench. She wanted him to hold her, to squeeze her so that her body was pressed against the firmness of his chest, his tight legs, his securing arms. Then—shocking in its quick power—she wanted him in her, to fill her with his kind strength, his barely restrained power.

"Tempting, I have to say; but I'm too much the gentleman." In his mind she was turning, showing him all that she was—all that she had, a proud display of her excitement. Not shy, not hiding under the bed-clothes, but smiling with pleasure. Her breasts, yes; firm, with just a little jiggle as she turned; her thighs, all good lines, a knockout; her bush, looking sweet and inviting, with her legs barely spread so he could see between; her ass, tight, strong, like a perfect pear. And—as she turned for him—always the smile, the brilliant show of red lips and white teeth. She wanted this, wanted him. That was the best part of his fantasy.

"My knight. Just as long as your pen is better than your sword." She was daring in her mind, imagining his strokes into her, his strong pounding between her tight thighs. Thinking, allowing her mind to run hot and humid, she felt herself respond. A quick blush came to her cheeks as the wetness came between her legs. The shame, though, was gone as quick as the hot, wet had come: the dance of their bodies coming together, of his member sliding into that wetness, of his breath on her neck, of his lips grazing his own, was just too damned nice.

"Don't know about that—haven't got any complaints about the sword as of yet." One playing card stuck in his mind, a favorite of his jerk-off fantasies, and her smile would go so well with it: her red, freck-led body straddling him as he lay on his bed, her tits bouncing as she moved her ass up and down on his dick. He could feel her, in his mind: the way her cunt would grip him, the way her so-soft, so-wet lips would push down and pull up with each wild bounce. Smiling, of course, as she fucked herself on his very hard dick.

She felt a new flush, a kind of fear: too much, too much. Good, damned yes, but it was too much: she wanted to touch him, to run a hand across his cheek, to feel the muscles there, the slight sandpaper of his almost-invisible shadow. She wanted to say something, to bring it about. No—no, it was too scary, too present. "This late I don't know if anyone would be able to find anything," she said.

He felt a heaviness. She was still there, fucking herself on his so-hard dick, but part of himself felt the illusion fall. If she came with him she probably wouldn't smile, probably wouldn't show him her body with pride and excitement. Maybe a handjob, maybe just a promise for sometime later that would never come. "I know. Except maybe the moon. Shouldn't stop us from trying though," he said.

"Always willing to try, but you know, I think it's going down," she said, a little bloom springing up. Maybe, maybe, maybe. She touched that hope, and kept smiling at him.

"Happens to all of us. Long nights, too little sleep . . . you know," But, he thought, she just might. The illusion flickered but didn't die— he held it, looking at her pretty face, and smiled back. Maybe . . .

"Too well. Sometimes I think the only thing that keeps me going is the joe," she said. She held it, the dream of him kissing her, of his broad chest, his strong thrusts, the chills and wonderful shivers of him inside her. Not tonight, no, but there's always the next day.

"Good dreams. See you in here tomorrow?" he said, trying to keep the quaver out of his voice, the precious grip on his dream from slipping. It was a good illusion: so real and . . . too complete not to give it a try.

"It's a date. I'll just follow the moon," she said, swallowing back an octave of pleasure. Not today, but maybe later—maybe sometime soon, maybe even tomorrow.

"See ya," he said as she got off the stool and picked up her handbag.

"Bye," she said as she passed him and walked towards the glass doors.

He watched her go, and smiled . . .

At the doors she looked back, and returned it.

THE LADY AND THE CHAUFFEUR

Shivaji Sengupta

As the gigantic 747 screamed upward, carrying us like so many seeds in a massive pea-pod, I looked out the window. The dark sky and the diamond points of lights of New Delhi tilted at an angle. The plane jolted and lunged upward. I could see the Milky Way.

I had just parted from my lover with whom I had the most intense sexual relationship of my life. My heart was heavy, it hurt even to swallow. Yet, I couldn't help smiling, thinking of Raja's thick, manly *lingam* piercing the depth of my darkness, like this night sky, his sperm spilling over and spreading out like the Milky Way on my dark thigh. . . .

On my two sides slept my boys, each leaning against me. Their names are Plavan, flood, and Jeevan, life.

Even though we called him Raja Babu, he wasn't a *babu*, a title usually given to gentlemen in Bengal. I guess, he was called Raja Babu affectionately by the Master of our joint family. The Master is my father-in-law.

Raja was our chauffeur.

When I returned from America with my husband, the future Master of this household, we had become completely unaccustomed to paid help in the house. That is why, when Raja opened the door of the old, aristocratic '64 Ford, I had mistaken him to be a relative.

He was of medium height, very dark skinned, thin, sinewy body, with a shock of jet-black hair falling across his face. The eyes were sharp, incisive. Deep in his dark iris, lurked repressed anger. When he looked at me I was immediately aware of his eyes, they seemed to burn holes through my blouse and sari reaching further inside me than I thought was possible. Instinctively, I resented his gaze. Anger singed my body. But, the next instant, I noticed his hands, sculptured by God. Broad manly palms of glowing warm pink seemed to radiate heat through those long fingers; neatly manicured, pink nails glistening in summer sunlight.

I don't know why, at 36 years of age, after giving birth to two children, just when I thought that sex had no surprises for me, Raja's hands and eyes, pierced through my abdomen like a knife. I remember I was getting in the car, came precariously close to his body, actually brushing past him, distinctly smelling his sweat. My legs buckled. I was certain he sensed my disarray.

He was arrogant, indifferent.

I hated him.

From that first day on, I couldn't settle down in the material comfort of my father-in-law's huge mansion. It irritated me with its splendour. In America, we had a house that was comfortable without being ostentatious. This one, entirely too big for even our household of eight (five family members and three servants), was a sprawling mass of colonial architecture, decorated, or rather flaunted, with antique furniture and paintings. Life size portraits of generational patriarchs hung sedately on the walls with no apparent organizational design. Despite their stationery silence, I felt they would jump at me, like prowling tigers, when I turned the corners of long, eerie hallways lined with dusty oil paintings of demure princely ladies, dim as dreams.

Aristotrash.

In this labyrinth of hallways and balconies, Raja, the driver, seemed to be everywhere, silent like shadow. When I asked him irritably what he was doing near me, he would simply reply with two words: "Master said."

I felt like screaming. "The Master is not my master! Not even my husband is! Get out!" But not a word escaped my lips. I seemed to be both revolted and hypnotized by the family's aristocratic arrogance and Raja's eyes. He was always there, in the next room, out on the balcony, standing in waiting beside the glittering Ford. He never spoke unless spoken to, never smiled.

Except when he was with my kids. In their company his whole face went through a transformation. He would laugh and play. Glee replaced gloom. I loved to see Raja and my boys whoop it up, kicking a ball around in the back yard.

My two sons, Plavan and Jeevan, were everything to me. I gave them those names, conscious of the flood of emotional intensity within me that I have always suppressed, of the life they would bring me as my sons. My husband, a real estate developer, had always preferred money to me or my boys. In America, life in the suburbs, would have been unbearable but for the kids. My life was full with them.

But here in Delhi, the boys were swooped up by their grandmother, uncles and aunts, their numerous cousins. I hardly saw them. Even at night, the grandmother would insist that they slept with her, leaving me alone and bored. But Raja played with my sons near me. He never took them *away*. And that was the only time when I saw him as a normal young man, happy.

Even after months of his unfailing proximity, I couldn't get used to the new sensations he created in my body. Raja was always inside me, his fingertips on my veins, X-ray eyes tingling the very core of my being. Between my legs was a perpetual cry of spring.

"What every man needs is to be cuckolded, at least once!" The Master said to his son, puffing on his pipe, drinking gin and lime, his corpulent body comfortably ensconced on a divan fitted with enormous pillows, embroidered with lace and tiny mirrors.

Father-in-law and husband were chatting in the luxurious living room decorated with oriental bric-a-brac, the Master expounding on the sexual liberation of women. I was there in the background, directing servants silently, to serve the men, ignored completely by them.

"Look at American men! They behave themselves because their wives are free to fuck others!" said the patriarch, laughing boisterously at his own provocation.

My husband drank his gin silently. He has never stood up to his father, shown him fossilized respect. In his father's presence, he was like an old St. Bernard: quiet, faithful, serious without purpose.

"In our country," the Master went on pontificating, "men are too preoccupied with the image of Sita and Sati—did you notice the words are anagramatical in English? Heh heh-heh!" Impressed with his own discovery, he went on, "We, so called educated Indians, want our wives to be spotlessly innocent, like Sita! And then want them burnt—metaphorically—with us on the funeral pyre, Sati! Our women are not free sexually. And, if you are not free sexually, you are not free!" The father completed his diatribe on Indian customs with tremendous self-importance.

I thought of Mataji, my mother-in-law. Years of sexual neglect from her husband, his endless philandering, ruthlessly claiming the bodies of the physically endowed female servants. Sleeping with him was a condition for employment, like paying tax. Mataji never complained. Her once beautiful body simply shrivelled up due to lack of attention. Her face was like that of a tired nurse, waiting on her husband's body, tired from fucking other women. It was inconceivable that she had the kind of freedom her master was theorizing about. Sati refers to an ancient Indian custom of wives dying with their husbands by jumping into the funeral pyre. Mataji, as far as I could see, was being burned, skewered slowly to death. But, of course, the Master was completely oblivious to that. Whenever the Master pronounced generalizations about every Indian, he excepted himself.

Looking around the room, he suddenly noticed me, and loudly asked for my approval of his views. He was distinctly drunk. "Hello, there, daughter-in-law!" He guffawed, "Wouldn't you like the freedom to fuck whomever you please? It's healthy, you know, good for the libido!"

I felt like smacking him.

The next few days I resolutely ignored Raja.

My husband was busy getting the family business together and hardly had time for his children, or me, except for a midnight fuck, between wake and sleep. He noticed that I was bored, listless.

"What happened?" he asked one day, "Aren't you happy here?"

"No."

Uneasy silence.

The heat in Delhi was tremendous, the balcony outside, sizzled. The lush green banana trees created a shadow in one corner. We noticed Raja sitting there, crouching like a granite sculpture, sweat glistening like silver.

"I know!" Hubby shouted out his eureka. "Why don't you learn to drive? There is very little motor traffic here, you will only have to learn to dodge the cows." He laughed.

Before I could agree, he settled the issue. "Raja!" he commanded authoritatively, "From tomorrow, early dawn, take my wife out and teach her to drive!"

Raja, who had entered silently, nodded and left the room.

The driving lessons drove me wild. In the front bench seat of the Ford, Raja insisted on sitting right next to me, hips touching. He had to be near the controls—and controlled my body! His hands touched me on every pretext. The dry, excessively warm palms covering over mine on the steering wheel, gripping my fist as it held the gear knob, leg brushing against mine, slowly, I am sure, deliberately as he pressed in the clutch.

One time, his upper arm rubbed against my breast for what seemed like a long second.

By then I had stopped caring. Opening up my body in secret, I began to enjoy Raja's hot, throbbing presence. He never said anything, except issuing cryptic driving instructions.

This went on for several weeks. I was calmer now about him. Raja, too, had shed his apparent indifference. A man of few words, his face definitely lit up when I came out ready for my lesson dressed in *kameez*, a long, loose shirt reaching to my knees, buttoning at the back, and *shalwar* baggy pants, gathered and tied around the waist with string. Indian women, perhaps because of the intense heat, do not wear panties underneath the *shalwar*. However, bras were necessary with the *kameez* because of the thinness of the fabric.

Even when I would ride with the rest of the family, Raja, at the driver's seat, stared at me through the rear view mirror, his eyes touching my nipples, caressing. It was during one of those moments, I suddenly became his lover, without giving my body to him, without ever exchanging any words.

I made love to my husband, and waited the whole night patiently for dawn, to be with Raja.

But the nights were unbearably long. Those were the hot months in India. Air-conditioners broke down periodically, abandoning us to the elements. For relief, my husband and I slept on the flat rooftop, safely enclosed for privacy. He had his routine fuck. I stared at the indigo sky.

One night I went to look for Raja, tip-toeing in the darkness to where he had often slept when it was too late for him to go home. I saw his sleeping body, naked except for the briefs, mouth open, dead to the world. How innocently, self-contentedly he slept, while I burned! Hating him, I came back to my sleeping husband.

"What happened? Where did you go?" He asked sleepily.

"To check on the boys."

One day, Raja told me that there was an exhibition of local arts and crafts in a village near where we practiced driving. I asked my husband if I could go to the fair after the driving lesson. He readily agreed.

That day Raja was more reckless about touching me. Outwardly, he was the same quiet driving instructor, but our bodies touched longer. He curled his fingers over my fist, his palm damp with sweat, his thigh brushed my leg while steering the car when it veered, but when brought under control, he was in no hurry to move away.

Then, just as the lesson ended, when I had shifted to the passenger's seat, something got into my eye. Painful and uncomfortable, I tried in vain to remove the grit. Instantly, it became red and teared profusely. Raja moved in to help.

Gently, looming very, very close to me, he removed the offending particle. I sensed instant relief, and a rush of involuntary tears.

Then, in a moment of blinding heat, I felt Raja's parched lips brushing my cheeks, kissing my nose, his hot touch scalding me.

I couldn't react at all, just sat there, utterly passive, as by now Raja took my body into his arms and was crushing me, kissing me blindly, groaning, sighing, babbling in Hindi, *"Aur mai sahan nahi kar sakta, bhabiji, mai mar jaunga!"* He was telling me he couldn't bear it any longer, calling me his lady, he was saying he would die if he could not have me. He wasn't being macho, the great seducer, just a miserable man, seeking sanctuary.

Raja kissed me again and again, every part of my face, finally sucking in my lips, his hot tongue thrusting in my mouth, staying inside. He sucked in my tongue so hard that it hurt. His tongue leapt in and caressed every part of my mouth.

I had my eyes tightly shut, feeling him, smelling his mildly spiced hair oil, cheap shaving lotion. Raja's hand went to my breasts over the *kameez* and squeezed them in desperation. His fingers on my nipples sent a searing sensation, deep inside me, and clutched between my legs. I opened my eyes and saw the sky, diffused with hot, hazy blue, the smooth steady glide of an eagle, trees adorned with thorns, devoid of leaves.

Raja pressed his face on my chest, licking the fabric over my nipple, biting it through the shirt and bra. My breath caught in my throat. I felt a sharp, overwhelming sensation, and had a long, slow orgasm, surprising myself. Pantiless, I was drenched, the liquid pouring down my thighs like sweat. I hid my face in his thick hair as his head still lay cradled in my breasts. I was hoping that he would not notice that I came, because, despite weeks of anticipation, I still had not expected to go this far. I felt shame, not guilt.

My body shook and shook.

Giving me time to recover, Raja's hand crept under my *kameez* to my stomach, my body stiffening as I felt his warm fingers tracing a line along my belly and waist, finding the string of the *shalwar*, and with a single, determined pull, untying them.

Instantly, I straightened up. "Not here!"

Raja let go of me at once, emptiness rushing into me at the sudden loss of contact.

"I am sorry, Madam, I got carried away. Please forgive. We will go to the fair." He said, looking very straight through the windshield, body erect, starting the car.

"No, not to the fair," I said, my throat very dry. "To your house."

*   *   *

Raja lived in a garage with two tiny windows. When we entered I couldn't help being vaguely conscious of a tidy room, with a single bed under one of the windows. There was a standing fan.

Having entered, there was no escape, I was thinking, still feeling the wetness between my legs, sticky, the matted texture of my pubic hair. I smelled my own sweat, the spice in his bedroom, and sperm on Raja.

Anxious to make me comfortable, he moved around busily, doing nothing. He did not know that at that moment no place held more excitement for me than that unpretentious little garage.

Raja offered me water. I took it. He offered to play music on a little tape recorder. I said no.

He embraced me.

Hungrily, he pulled my body to him, and kissed me full in the mouth, our bodies joining. I could feel him so close, the terrible monster at the base of his belly, hard, rubbing against my thigh. The fan was full on my face, my breath almost stopped.

Raja's tongue was deep inside me now, my mouth having opened instinctively. His eyes were closed as he felt me, oh God, how he felt me all over! His hand was at the back of my neck, massaged roughly below my shoulder, then my back, feeling, for a fleeting second, the elastic bands of my bra, his hand travelled down to the small of my back, while all the time he savagely kissed me, licking my neck, throat, a long sleek tongue.

His hands grabbed roughly the cheeks of my bottom.

A long moan escaped from him, as the rough clutching of his hands slowed down to a caress, long fingers probing the cleft . . .

Everything he did I watched him doing it with every pore of my body. It was a strange and perverse curiosity. I am a grown woman, mother of kids, and yet, what Raja was doing to me, was new, spontaneous. All along, since I had made up my mind to give myself to him, I told myself this was pure lust. But now, plunged into the eye of his storm, I began to feel a strange love for him that I didn't think I was capable of any more.

He caressed me for a long time. Squeezed and massaged my breasts, kissing them, while I still had my clothes on. Finally, after eons of seconds when everything was in slow motion, he slipped his hand under my *shalwar*, and creeping up my back, with one deft movement unclasped the hook of the bra.

My breasts sprang loose, falling out of the case, the nipples meeting urgent fingers, coming up in hard little knobs. Raja caressed my stomach, one of them finding my navel, invaded it, creating a sharp, almost unbearable tingling that instantly shot through my groin and stung my clitoris. No one had played with my belly button before.

Soon, Raja found the string of my *shalwar* again, but this time there was no going back. He lingered on for a slow second, fondling it, then pulled, undoing it authoritatively.

Without warning, in a split second, my *shalwar* left my waist and rushed to the floor. I was naked underneath the *kameez*, its knee length hiding me from him for the moment.

Raja straightened up and pulled me closer to him, his penis prodding my lower belly like a hard arrow root.

Sleek warm hands stroked my naked buttocks, so smooth and sensual were his hands, so utterly mesmerizing that, of their own accord my legs parted and Raja's hands slipped moistly into my sopping wet vagina, instantly, driving up within me, thousands of fingers, hard and yet so soft, chaotic yet so deliberate. My body wracked with spasms.

I gripped Raja's pants and unbuckled his belt, and, sliding down his trousers and underwear, freed his large, thick manhood. Like his fingers, it was dark brown, the tip, pink.

With one swift movement he carried me to the bed, my head on his chest, his one arm under my neck, the other against the back of my thighs. I was conscious of the hem of my *kameez* hitched up. With dark, passionate, wild eyes, he looked at my bushy abdomen, his *bhabiji's yoni*, his Mistress' cunt.

He sat me down with surprising tenderness and holding the hem, he raised the *kameez* over my shoulders and took it off completely.

I was naked.

Gently, very gently, he lay me down. Gently, very gently, he put his own body on top of mine, his *lingam* ensconced between my thighs, just below my hairy mound. Gently, he dipped his head and took my nipple in his mouth. The distended, dark nipple felt like it would never stop growing.

Raja played with my nipples, nuzzling and nibbling them, making me moan. After months of sleepy lovemaking with my husband, I wanted to be ravished. Raja, too, moaned softly with every long suck.

He gently spread his legs on either side of me, his phallus springing up like a bucked horse, as he lowered his haunches to sit on my upper thigh. I saw his face was like someone possessed. I took him in my hand, and he let out a loud groan. Eyes so dark, so wild! The tip of his penis, dewed by a drop of cum. His face was contorted just slightly, curling, succulent lips parted, a neatly groomed mustache partially framed a sexy red mouth.

Raja saw me watching him. He grew some more. I held his lean, tight buttocks in the palm of my hands and squeezed them, one finger rubbed the crack in between, revelling in it slightly corrugated sensation, the dampness, its faint tell-tale smell.

Raja held me tightly at the hip and with my tongue I burned his neck and chest. His hand caressed the inside of my thighs.

Then, after a long, high time, shaking beneath every accelerating tremor of my body, Raja entered me.

I felt him slide wetly inside, then an enormous thrust that completely took my breath away. I opened my mouth wide to cry out his name. Momentarily, Raja's face showed fear, perhaps he thought I was going to scream, I felt so utterly, overwhelmingly penetrated by his long, thick cock. My breath caught so sharply, and my body stiffened so much that, for a few seconds, Raja stopped, his face a mixture of surprise and concern.

But I soon grew used to him inside, my vaginal muscles adjusting. I heard a long moan come out of me as my eyes closed with the tight fit of Raja's love, now all the way inside me. His face was so near me, I could feel his jagged breath. My eyes closed, I suddenly remembered his face so close to mine in the car, not a few hours ago, when he took the grit out of my eye. That memory served to make the present experience all the more exquisite, with him now deep inside the folds of my liquidly wet being, feeling Raja throb so deep inside me that he was touching my cervix, I heard him moan as I started to move beneath him. Then, from the center of his rising storm, Raja began his slow, deliberate ride home.

I felt him go, slippery, in and out, in and out. Every time he withdrew, taking the length of his hard muscle almost to the rim of my soft, wetly open vagina, I feared losing him and held him tight, drawing him to me, holding his sweat-sleek torso between my thighs, I rocked him as a sea rocks a boat, the mother her child. Deep in the throes of ravaging sex, I held Raja between my legs and I don't know how, I don't know why, Jeevan and Plavan, my two sons, appeared in a vision. No, even then I didn't feel guilty. I thought of Raja playing with my boys, and I embraced him with even more vigour. Raja's movement increased with every thrust. With every thrust, he tore through my insides, hot, burning hot, I couldn't distinguish pleasure from pain, and I cried out as he roughly pushed my legs back, crushing my breasts.

Raja's eyes were now wild, his tongue hanging out, as he thrust even harder and harder. I forgot where I was, so incredible was the pleasure-pain. I held him and screamed out my agony and ecstasy, expecting him to pour himself into me any minute.

But he did not. He just kept going, screaming, jabbering something with incredible speed in a local Hindi dialect that I vaguely understood. He was slamming into me, panting out,*"Sali, teri chut ko mai phata doonga! Teri ghulam hu mai ya tera Raja!"* Bitch! I will bust your cunt with my cock. Am I your servant or your lord! With each word he thrust, slamming into me making me groan, making him moan out the words. I still had enough brain left to understand that he was cursing my whole family, cursing our wealth, our position, cursing the great divide. Yet here he was, deep inside me, joined so absolutely, obliterating all differences between us with this intense and powerful lovemaking. Strangely, his words, hostile and violent, didn't upset me one bit, only made me want to fuck him harder, forever. My juices came oozing out, Raja aware of every bit of physical change in me, began to part the cheeks of my *nitam* with his hand and feel the moisture with his finger, feeling the ooze run down the furrow. His fingers reached the tight puckered hole and massaged it with passion. I felt the hot, hard, burning sensation. I don't know where he found the super human strength. A fire burned deep inside me, sharp and strong, spreading like hot lava through my entire body with his each feverish thrust. A dam broke within me. Wetness spread all over the bed sheet.

Suddenly as Raja stopped for a second to recuperate, wiping the sweat that was blinding his eye, his torso shook, he erupted violently inside me, the like I'd never experienced before. It was like a hot, blunt electric rod vibrating. Raja's eyes opened wide, he pulled back his head, opened his mouth to show a pink tongue that reminded me of hot flickering fire, he drew in his breath with a deep, blood curdling groan, pulled himself back all the way out, and slammed it in with the force of his entire body, but at the same time, with super human force, arching up my shoulder and neck, he held my head with one hand, he let me look: the dark *lingam,* its thick stem slick with the passion of my *yoni.*

It felt like thousands of volts of electric shock, from head to toe. He roared his orgasm out of his body. I actually saw his come. I shouted out his name, and he called out to me, for the first time uttering my name, *Sooooneeeetaaa!!!* Its sound entering into every tremor of my body. Tears streamed down my face, my throat was parched. I bit into his shoulders to stop myself from trembling. Raja's head dipped down and his mouth sucked in my nipple, increasing my tremors, I sucked in the skin of his shoulder to battle the trembling.

There we were, two lost souls, servant and lady, lover and beloved, our bodies entwined, drenched with sweat. I was crying softly. I kissed him all over his face, mouth, eyes, eye-brows, lips, licked at his ear and whispered amidst tears, "*Tu mere ghulam nahi, mere suhag, mere raja, raja!*" Raja sobbed.

Later as my lover slept in post-orgasmic peace, I looked down at our drenched bodies. His sperm was all over my thighs, still a little white against the expanse of my dark thighs. I thought of the Milky Way in a night sky.

Adultery.

I thought about that word practically all the time. *Post sexualis gravitas.* Seriousness sets in after the love-making, said the Roman poet, Catallus.

What does one do after one fucks a servant of the house? How could I have behaved with him in front of all those relatives, my husband and the Master of the house, the father-in-law? It was impossible to make love to Raja again, there just wasn't the opportunity. There was also guilt, and rationalizations.

Absorbed by every inch of his fondling, every time we had the chance, I nevertheless tried to make peace with myself for what I was doing with him, seducing this servant who was also at least ten years younger. Pure lust, I kept telling myself, just as men indulge in pure lust. I had the same right.

No more driving lessons. Raja and I went several times in his garage early in the morning and made long, passionate love.

Raja made love with such furious intensity, such passion. I could never tell whether he loved me or was satisfying his enormous lust. But after, Raja Babu would be so tender. We would just lie there for as long as stolen time would permit, Raja stroking my naked body, covered with sweat, saying nothing. His face, though, was a picture of serenity and tranquil emotion. A tender finger would play with a curl on my forehead. He would sigh. When I questioned him, he would smile and say, "*Kuch bhi nahi.*" Nothing, at all. There, in his little room, with the fan circulating warm air, staring into the slice of summer haze, I would be filled with peace.

When I left the bed to dress—the bathroom was like an outhouse so that I couldn't use it for fear of being seen—he would lie in bed watching me with his large lustful eyes, intense, quiet.

One day as he was watching me put back my bra, I suddenly remembered again his face, reflected in the rear view mirror. The thought brought on another surge of desire in me. Raja must have been thinking of the same thing, because I saw his flaccid penis slowly began to stir. The head like an angry pink mushroom, announced its presence. With nothing on but bra, I quickly went toward him and kissed it. "*Aaja! Mai teri chut ko chatu!*" The direct, coarse imperative made my heart beat faster! No body had ever gone down on me before! No body had ever spoken dirty. This had been one of my deepest fantasies. But we were so late! I saw Raja's face, eyes dreamy, wild, desire diffusing his face like the white on a Japanese Kabuki. Mouth open. Pure lust.

Throwing caution to the wind, I climbed on the bed, Raja taking hold of my hips and turning me around so that my mouth was on his mushroom head again, and he was slowly stroking the globes of my *nitam* lovingly, breathing into me his passion.

He opened me up with his large warm hands. I felt vulnerable, like I was some gigantic fruit. Raja sighed as the smell of my sex, saturated with his sperm, permeated the room. I felt his breath on my open vagina, tingling, then a hot wet tongue, surprisingly hard, plunged into me, fast and flickering like a serpent's tongue, darting out, laving the entire opening, stabbing my clitoris. Before I had time to react, I felt my vitals being sucked in, a huge, tight, moist suck, Raja's upper lip, mustache pricking me, pressuring it, and then the sucking began again!

Groaning, I sunk my mouth on his member, opening wide to accommodate it, my tongue moving on it as fast as his, keeping rhythm, I kept the stem in my grip and flicked my tongue at the underside of the thick bulbous head.

Raja's body jolted upwards as he almost bit into me, and, in the next instant, my mouth flooded with the acrid, sharp taste of his come, pungent salty. But even in the throes of his erupting orgasm, Raja never stopped sucking me and my body vibrated with yet another coming.

As Raja drove me home, I sat primly on the back seat, and slept. We knew that if we kept going to his place, sooner or later, people would know. We would get caught.

But for now we really couldn't control our lust. At every opportunity, *half* an opportunity, Raja and I made love, or, if intercourse was impossible, he caught me on the stairwell to shove his hand down my *kameez* to feel my breasts. Once he accosted me as I was coming down stairs. Appearing almost literally from nowhere, he made me stand a few steps above him on a landing and, undoing the string of my *shalwar*, he sucked at my labia, his tongue stabbing at that spot where passion bursts into millions of stars.

There, standing in broad daylight, within a few feet from whoever who was near, I had a massive orgasm. By the time he disappeared, swift as a cat, I was breathless, tears in my eyes.

A few days later our family, Master and all, were invited to a relative's house for the whole day. Just before dinner it was discovered that our hosts were a few utensils short and needed to borrow from us. We didn't live far away so *Mataji*, my mother-in-law, asked me to go with the car to get the utensils. All the servants were busy helping with the meal.

Raja drove me home. He was quiet and officious during the short ride. When we arrived at our house, we found that there was no electricity. Another evening of power economizing by the government.

It was quite dark now, so Raja lit a candle as I entered the small pantry, Raja following. The pantry had shelves in it where the utensils were kept neatly in rows. Raja held the candle aloft as I reached for the shelf. He stuck the candle on a table near him, and, just as I had bent over to grab a utensil Raja grabbed me by my waist. He pushed me over some more and quickly lifted up my sari and petticoat, and bunching them around my waist, exposed my whole, naked backside to him.

"*Are Ram! Mum batti men kitni sunder lagti hai tere chuter!*" Raja exclaimed in a mad babble, saying in his dialect how sexy the cheeks of my open derriere looked in candlelight."

His frank but coarse praise of body never failed to excite me. With my husband, I was used to silent sex, no words of affection, never mind sexy words. He even came so silently that I would not even know that he did. The contrast between him and Raja was overwhelming. Raja used obscene words while making love, the kind that shocked and excited me at the same time.

The single candlelight cast huge shadows on sidewall, and I saw the gigantic reflection of my lover leaning over on my back. My pussy was soaking wet in anticipation, the strong smell of my sex filled up the tiny windowless room and mixed with the smell of curry and pepper.

I felt him penetrate me like I have never felt before, his fat, thick cock filling me, stretching me, until his flat stomach pressed against me. Raja began making love to me, moving in and out, in and out, the bulbous head brushing my aching clitoris. There, in utter darkness of the little room, lit by a single candle, Raja and I made love in tremendous frenzy, like it would be our last. He gurgled and groaned out his orgasm, biting my ear, pressing a finger deep inside my other opening, his balls rubbing heavily against the lips of my open sex. Like always, he came so much that his come oozed out of me and rolled down my thighs. Raja crouched in front of me and with a wet handkerchief, gently and carefully wiped his sperm from my cunt and thighs, the feel of his fingers wrapped up in the damp cloth produced the most tingling sensation on my clitoris and in the entire region of my abdomen.

Satiated, we went back into the car to return to our relatives. Darkness and intimacy was replaced by a gaggle of relatives and loud music.

Then the inevitable happened. We got caught.

The first one to find out was the Master. I had just woken up from an afternoon siesta when my favourite maidservant, Srila, came crying in and said the Master wanted to see me, that he was very, very angry.

That was when I knew.

As I made my way to the regal living room, the maidservant was chanting the name of Hari, the Hindu God. My inside froze. I felt nothing.

The Master was kind. He told me he had fired Raja on the spot, and had ordered his eviction because the garage in which Raja lived was owned by the Master himself. He would drive him out of, not only the city but the state.

He commanded me to face my husband but first he would learn of his wife's adultery from his own father.

That evening my husband came into our bedroom where I sat on a chair, unable to move or feel. His face was a contorted mass of pain and shame. For a long time he didn't say a word, just looked at me pathetically, pursed his lips and sat spellbound, looking down at the floor. After a long time, he spoke.

"A thousand mercies of the Lord Hari that papa found out before the neighborhood did!"

I looked at his face, absolutely stunned. So that was what he was thinking about! He did not feel jealous or upset, simply an instinct to safe guard the family's name. I was unable to reply.

"Listen!" He suddenly almost shouted. "Masterji won't forgive you, so you cannot bloody well stay here, this is his house. He has asked me to send you away, alone, back to America. If you go quietly, without talking about this—this—disgusting affair, we will give you enough money to settle you for life. A million dollars. But if you don't, we will haul you out of here and Masterji's disciplinary staff will put you through unimaginable torture."

"I will go quietly," I said feeling nothing but determination. "But I want the boys."

"No!" he said, "Masterji's orders!"

I said nothing. I knew enough of Indian law to realize that when it came to issues of who would keep the children if the parents divorced, Indian civil law invariably sided with the husband and his family, never with the mother regardless of how young the children were. Now, with proven adultery, the mother would have no chance. But Jeevan and

Plavan were only eight, going on nine. They needed their mother. My life in America would be utterly empty without my children. I was determined to have them but said nothing at the moment. I had other cards to play.

The next day, I told my maid, Srila, about Raja and me. I was sure that by now the servants have heard rumors. But Srila and I were very friendly. I had given her cosmetics from America, and she was completely loyal to me. I told her what I did. Waiting for the shock in her to subside, I ordered her to spread the news, tell the neighborhood that Masterji's daughter-in-law fucked his driver. She had to wait for me to give her the order, I said, shoving into her hands two thousand rupees.

Srila, whose loyalty was one hundred per cent to me also found out where Raja Babu had gone and carried from me a verbal message in which I asked him to wait for further instructions from me.

Having done these things, I sought a meeting with Masterji.

It was late at night when the Grand Master granted me the visit, upstairs in a large bedroom that could have easily competed with royalty.

The floor was of pure Medici marble from Italy, cool to my bare feet. Though the walls were a garish green, they were decorated with crossed swords, their handles bejewelled with ruby and mother of pearl. The chandelier was lavish as was the heavily decked mahogany bed on an elevated marble base. There, against massive pillows of maroon velvet, reclined the Maharaja—Masterji—dressed for the occasion with a huge turban studded with diamonds and rubies that complimented his enormous white mustache. He was puffing at a hookah, a long, standing pipe that one smokes via a long, thin nozzle. I could tell from the smell that what he was smoking was not tobacco but hashish.

He saw me and beckoned me to come in. Then, silently, he indicated that I sit on the bed. I did, almost on its edge, as far away as I could be from him.

"This matter of the boys," he said dreamily. "Why don't you let us keep them? They'll be fine here!"

"They are too young to be without their mother," I said without fanfare.

Masterji chuckled and deliberately moved his elephant body, parting his legs so that his long loose robe parted to show me *his* enormous manhood, the balls heavy, pendulous. Ensuring that I saw his assets, he laughed lasciviously,

"What *sort* of mother, eh?"

I didn't reply. I didn't want to cross him because here, in this house,

I was outnumbered. They could cut my throat and no one outside would know. I sat motionless. Masterji watched me, quietly.

"If you tell the world about your screwing our driver I will have you and the driver killed, you know that, don't you?"

Again, I didn't say anything. "Let's see you deal with American law," I said in silence.

"We are giving you a million dollars. A *million*! It's not enough?"

"Master," I said straightening up, deciding to play political. "You are kind and generous with your money. But I am a mother, however my morals may seem to you. Jeevan and Plavan need me. Please let me go away with them. I will do nothing to harm your family. Ever."

Again the Master moved to one side, his huge corpulent body like a huge billowy wave. Again, he parted his robe to show me his penis, that in the dim green light seemed more like the bullet of a Royal Enfield.

Puffing at the hashish filled hookah, his eyes turned lustful. I turned my head toward the door and saw them closed. Someone had locked them silently. We were alone, bathed in the greenish light of the bed-room, sweetened by the smell of the intoxicating weed.

"You can take the boys," the Master said smiling underneath the white mustache. "But, first, I will ask you to do something for me that shouldn't be too difficult for you!"

He wants to fuck me, I thought. If that's what will get me the boys, I will, I decided. I looked at him straight in the eye. Let *him* utter the words.

"I want you to undo your *shalwar* and show me your *chut*, cunt, just like you showed him. Then I want you to do certain other things."

"What?" My voice was calm.

"You will see, nothing so difficult, or bad—for a person of your character."

I took a deep breath, moved more into his bed and leaned against the mahogany bedpost. Closed my eyes.

"You have to keep your eyes open," he said in a quiet tone. The bed moved heavily.

I saw the Master had completely removed his robe, and placed his huge buttocks on a large pillow. He opened the massive thighs. His short, stocky member was now erect, looking like a miniature cannon shaft on his huge round sac.

I proceeded to undo the string of my *shalwar*, looking at him straight in the eye. My eyes must have been daring because I felt dared. "What if he does not keep his promise?" I thought. Well, we'll see. I felt a strange kind of excitement at the pit of my belly.

I moved up my *kameez* slowly to my waist, and starting to push the loose pants from around my waist.

A huge ornate mirror was directly opposite me, beyond the bedpost. In it, dimly, I saw a woman reclining on the bed, slowly taking off her *shalwar*, her dark midriff appearing slowly on the mirror, darkly.

I became incredibly aroused.

I pushed down the *shalwar* below my waist, watching the old man's eyes riveted on my abdomen. I watched the woman in the large mirror, watched with fascination, as the dark, hairy triangle of my pussy revealed itself to him.

The room was absolutely silent, except for the sound of his hookah, purring sensually with each puff.

I bent my legs up just a little while I completely took off the *shalwar*, then leaned back and languidly parted my knees to give Masterji a full view of myself, the cunt of red oleander, the cunt that his son and driver have used.

Masterji's cock was now fully erect, twitching.

I knew that in a few moments he would ask me to sit on him and I was ready. But he surprised me.

"Masturbate with me," he commanded me dreamily as he started to stroke himself, and catching its stem in a fist, began a slow but deliberate up and down movement.

I became incredibly horny. Opened the cuntlips with my hands and began to rub my clitoris. I shivered.

We both masturbated in unison, he jerking off, taking a long time, which was OK with me because it took me a long time to come. The room filled with the smell of my sex and mixed with the smell of the hashish. I almost lay myself down and lifting up my buttocks and hips began to massage the entire slit of my cunt, the jewel inside, and plunged two fingers deep inside myself. My eyes closed of their own accord but opening them just a little bit, I saw the old man now about to come. His cock had grown to be quite thick and so large that I thought would be impossible at his age. He stared at my cunt, his eyes glistening, as I masturbated. Suddenly, thick, white come began to shoot upward from his twitching cock, a spurt landing on my thigh, as I myself came with a deep, drawn out sigh.

But even after the mutual orgasm, he wasn't done. Lying back on one of the huge pillows, he ordered me to straddle his chest so that he could suck me. I obliged.

Masterji held my waist firmly as I brought my nether lips up to his face. Lowering his head, he first just nibbled at my pubic hair, pulling lightly on them, and then licked the labia, long and slow, breathing in its strong smell. He looked up at me and smiled in a childlike manner and said, "Ah! The scent of a woman after she comes!"

He squeezed my buttocks and sucked my entire cunt, the swollen lips and eventually the clitoris. He was an expert at oral sex and soon brought my body completely under his control. I rode his chest, shivered and moaned as he sucked and sucked, teasing my clitoris with the tip of his tongue. With his middle finger he penetrated my vagina and rubbed my G-Spot. I pressed my cunt to his face and felt him part my behind and massage my anus. He stabbed my clitoris with his tongue, he sucked it in until I came like a storm, screaming and shivering, skewered by his thick index finger deep into my rectum.

He let me go.

"I have given instructions. Tomorrow you and your boys will leave this house," he said in a tired voice, turning to his side to sleep. The million dollar bank draft is on the table there," he pointed to his desk. "Make your travel arrangements fast. You don't have time." He turned around, showed me his mountainous naked buttocks and went to sleep.

I tidied myself, unlocked the door and went to my bedroom. My husband wasn't there. But, for the first time, since I had come to India, I saw Jeevan and Plavan sleeping like two little angels on my bed.

Something welled up in me. I ran toward them, held both sleeping boys and cried like a baby.

The next day, I sent money to Raja Babu to get his passport and visa. He would follow us within a month of our departure.

That night, when my boys and I stepped out of the taxi at the Indira Gandhi International Air Port, we saw Raja waiting for us. Jeevan and Plavan rushed to greet him. He hugged them both. Where was he, the boys complained. He explained gently, he had to go away for a while. Would he go to America with them? No, he said, laughing pleasantly, but he would follow. Promise? asked the boys. He promised.

He then looked at me, serene, quiet, confident.

"I knew we were not momentary," he said in Hindi after a few seconds of silence.

I smiled. I felt like I was his wife. The intercom was announcing our flight.

"That's for us," I said.

"Yes, I know a little English," he laughed.

"You will learn more in America," I said.

"Yes, in your arms!"

THREE PENNIES

Jason Rubis

Will's room was dark. I reached for the light-switch, but Will put his hand on mine and said, "Don't. It's more romantic this way." His smile was barely visible.

"Are you sure you're not just worried about the others?" I asked, moving past him and sitting gingerly down on the mattress rammed up against the far wall. His bed, apparently. The sounds of the party continued to filter through the door even after Will shut it.

"Are *you*?" he asked, folding his arms at me.

I shrugged.

"I mean, you're the big, strong heterosexual. *I'm* the fluffy little Asian queerboy. And I live here. I'm a known quantity. I'm known in these parts, pardner."

"Yeah? What are you known *for*?" I asked, instantly sort of regretting it. I hadn't made up my mind about anything, I reminded myself. I wasn't supposed to be encouraging him. But when he walked across the room to me, it wasn't with the ass-swinging Bitch-Princess walk he'd affected downstairs. His shoulders were a little slumped and it struck me that he looked kind of tired.

"Various shit. Cattle-rustling. A little petty larceny here and there. Rob banks." He stopped in front of me and pressed one bare foot against my sneaker. "And now you have a choice: I can either finish up by saying 'I also suck dick like a goddamn vacuum-cleaner,' or 'I sometimes kidnap cute white boys.' What'll it be?"

"Have a seat," I said, patting the mattress.

Will shrugged and sank down beside me, stretching out his legs. He pushed his fingers through his hair once, then again, tilting his head back like it really felt good to do that.

"Don't be pissed at me for saying this, but you really look like a girl now. Especially in this light. Anybody'd look at you . . ."

"Sissy-boy," he lisped, rotating his shoulders. "Long haa-irr. Big red lips. Don't play *sports*. Play with *dolls*. Little chinky *fag* boy." He half-turned and leaned into my lap, staring up at me with his long brown eyes. "Is that why you tried so hard to get me to talk to you, down in the kitchen? You like boys like me? And don't pretend you don't like me doing this; I can feel your dick under my head, and it's *hard*."

I laughed. He smiled and bounced his head up and down on my groin. "Think I can make you come if I do this long enough? Bouncy-bouncy . . ."

I touched his neck. Gently. "Quit," I told him. When I tried to take my hand away he caught my wrist and pressed my fingers to his throat. I could feel his pulse.

I looked around his room, trying to will my erection away. "You really play with dolls?" I asked him.

"I still got my Barbies. See 'em up there, on the bookshelf? They belonged to my sister, but guess who played with 'em most? Take a wild guess."

I peered up at the row of dolls on the shelf, five of them held erect by plastic stands, backed by rows of cassettes and paperbacks. As far as I could tell, they were all blonde.

"Did they ever make an Asian Barbie?" I asked.

"Sure, they made *me*. Then they broke the mold. Can you see me batting my eyes?"

"Yeah, I can see you."

"Will-iko and Her Dream House. Barbie *hates* Will-iko, because all the boys like *me* best. I can see you too. Peek-a-boo."

"Were you hot for Ken when you were a kid?"

"A little. I like you better."

"I'm not as good-looking as Ken. I have glasses."

"Glasses can come off." His hands rose, and, gentle as wasps, lifted my glasses away. "Peek-a-boo," he said again, whispering this time.

"I can't see you as good now."

"Can you see me doing obscene things at you with my tongue? Nyah. Nyaaaaah."

"Brat," I whispered, and dug my fingers into his belly. He kicked and muffled a scream with his fingers.

"I'll scream rape," he told me softly. "I'll tell everybody you're up here trying to stick your cock in my ass. Trying to fuck me . . . shit!" he said suddenly, giggling and bouncing his head on me again. "*Somebody's* hard-on came back awful fast."

I laughed with him. "Why are you doing this?"

"Doing what?"

"Trying to seduce me."

"Because you want me to seduce you. And I'm horny. You know, *horny*? I want to have someone touch me and give me big gooshy kisses and do things that make me come."

"And I'm the lucky guy, huh?"

"Looks that way, doesn't it? Nobody else wanted to come up here and visit with me."

"And you think I'm some kind of stud-muffin?"

"*Oh* no," he says, wagging a finger in my face. "I know how this works. You won't believe me if I say yes, and you'll get all pouty if I say no. You're all alike."

"Who's all alike?"

"Boys like you. Straight boys, isn't that what you like to be called? Do you want to take my clothes off?"

". . ."

"You know we're going to end up naked sooner or later. You know you're going to kiss me. You know you're going to play with my dick, just to see what it feels like. Because it'll be hard, and that'll be proof that you got me hot. Proof you can't get from a girl."

I pursed my lips. Will sighed and crossed his ankles.

"Do you want me to put a dress on?" he asked dryly. "I have— well, it's not a dress. It's a little frilly lingerie-thingy. I got it from my sister. I put it on sometimes, just 'cause I like it. It feels good. And I *really* look like a girl in it. Would that make you feel better?"

"I . . . no, that's okay."

"Wanna tickle me some more? Dominate me, kind of? I'll let you, but you have to do it to my feet, not my belly. They're not as ticklish, 'cause I go barefoot so much." He half got up, swiveled around on his ass and pushed his feet into my hands. They were long and delicate. I fingered his toes; the bones felt as light as a bird's. He wiggled them invitingly.

"Go ahead," he said, folding his hands behind his head. "They don't smell."

I patted his ankles. "I think I should go," I said. "This is . . . I don't know, this doesn't feel right."

"Too late," he smiled, nudging one foot against my belly. "Every-body knows you're up here by now. All your little friends will think we had hot and heavy sex whatever you do, whatever you say."

I knew he was right. I closed my eyes and kept them closed a while. I heard Will taking a deep breath. "Listen. You're nice, okay? You have nice eyes. And a sexy mouth. Broad shoulders. And I like your voice, your sense of humor. I'd like to hear you talking to me while I fall asleep, after we both come. I'm going to undress now," he said, taking his feet away and pulling his T-shirt up over his head. When the shirt came off, his hair was tousled, hanging in his eyes. He smoothed it away and said "Hey . . . how about I pay you?"

"What?"

"Pay you. To sleep with me here tonight. Then you can tell everyone you're a hustler, that I came to you crazed with lust for your hot white body and tempted you with ungodly sums of money . . . with . . ." he dug in the pockets of his jeans. Eventually he pulled his fist out and held it out to me. Three pennies gleamed in his palm. "Three cents," he said, smiling goofily.

The laughter came out of me in a flood. I couldn't stop. Will laughed too, pulling my pocket open with one finger and pushing the coins into it.

"Congratulations my son, you are now a fag *and* a whore," he said, unbuttoning my shirt with quick, slender fingers. "Now gimme." He spread my shirt open and pressed his lips to my chest. I could feel my back slowly arching. I couldn't stop it. I shrugged my shirt all the way off and Will bit my shoulder.

I could hear music booming suddenly up from downstairs; one of Will's housemates had put on something obnoxious and metallic. Somewhere in the house a girl was laughing, screeching like a parrot. My arms went around Will and hugged him to me. He smelled like spice and sweat. His cock pressed through his jeans against my leg. Then his mouth found mine and rubbed briefly against it before he kissed me.

"Come on," he told me, hooking a hand onto my shoulder and pulling me down like gravity. His voice was tender and breathy with excitement.

I pulled back from him one last time, just a little. "Will, I don't . . . I . . ."

His tongue found my ear. "Too late. I already paid for you. Plus, I got your shirt off. Know what that means? That means I can do *this* to you." He reached up and I felt his fingertips skating over my spine. My back arched again and I groaned. His fingers slid down to my ribs. *Oh God.* I bit back a harsh giggle. Will giggled for me.

"See? I can tickle too. I know how to make you purr. I am in total control. Submit to Will-iko. Will-iko says to get naked now." He was already unzipping his jeans, jerking his hips from side to side as he worked them down his legs.

By the time I got my own pants off, he was naked, stretched out on the mattress. His body surprised me a little; I guess I was still unconsciously expecting him to be a girl under his clothes. But his narrow shoulders and hips were as angular as mine, his chest as flat, with little brown nipples that reminded me of the pennies he had thrust into my pocket. There was a small puff of black hair between his legs, and under that his cock, long and hard and curved a little to one side. He reached down and made a fist around it. I found myself echoing the motion, my hand creeping down to touch myself. My initial surprise was fading; it was like he was coming into focus for me. My eyes were translating him.

I got down beside him and touched his knee. "You're beautiful," I told him. He smiled and lifted his leg, pointing his toes.

"Of course I am. I am the beautiful and sensuous Will-iko. All boys must in time come to Will-iko. Or come in time *on* Will-iko. You know. Either way is good."

I was clumsy at first. "Like this," he said gently, guiding my arms around his waist. "Yeah. Good boy. Now kiss my neck."

"Am I that stupid?" I asked, mumbling at his throat.

"No, but you like me telling you like this, don't you? That's okay, you can bump your hips like that. Hold me tight, yeah. Where's your ass?"

Nails dug into my cheeks. I'd never had anyone grab me like that before. It felt good. "Mmm. Now kiss my mouth. Tongue, yeah . . . mmm."

We lay like that for a long time. His skin was hot; it shifted over his bones as I hugged him over and over. His mouth worked against mine, thrusting his tongue in and making me taste wine. Finally he pulled back a little and took me in his hands; they felt larger than I expected they would, soft but a little rough. I shut my eyes and let my lips part while he played with me.

"Suck or fuck?" his voice asked me after a while. "Or do you want us to just rub off on each other?"

"I don't know," I said truthfully. "I've never . . ."

"Here, get on top of me. Now we just do this—mm-hmm—until we find a nice angle. Until it feels good, and you just want to rub and rub . . . okay? I don't have lube, but I don't think it'll take long . . . you find your place?"

My cock was resting in the little groove between his balls and his thigh. His was pushing up through my pubic hair, the head not quite poking my navel. "Yeah . . . it's good."

"Okay . . . then fuck me. Fuck me, okay? Yeah, like that. That's nice."

I moved with the friction we made, my ass going back and forth like a piston. Will threw his head back, biting one finger tightly between his teeth. His eyes weren't closed. He was squinting at me, watching me, and after a minute he started making gasping, whimpering noises around his finger. When he stopped biting and slipped the finger into his mouth to suck it, still looking right at me, I came. I rolled off him, gasping. My cock felt brush-burned. I could feel it dribbling onto the mattress.

Will's belly was gleaming wet, but what was on him was all mine. His knees were poked up and his fist was around his cock again, jerking it rapidly back and forth. I realized he hadn't come yet. I got up and, without thinking about it, pushed his hands away and started pulling gently at his dick. I did it hand over hand, the way I do myself under the covers at night, until his finger went back in his mouth. A moment later he made a ragged, crying sound and something hot spouted out of him, onto my hands.

"Aww. Aww, a mess. Here, wait." He took my wrists and grabbed a box of tissue from beside the mattress. I was shaking. When my hands were clean he kissed my fingers one by one.

"You too," I told him, taking my hand away and gesturing at his stomach.

"It's okay," he said, grabbing a fresh handful of tissue and dabbing daintily at his belly. "I'm practiced. I jerk off every day of my life, all over myself. I should just bathe in the stuff and be done with it. I bet it's good for your skin. What's wrong?"

I was still shaking. I coughed and then again, made a hitching noise deep in my chest.

"Aw no, come on," he said. He knelt beside me and pulled me to him. "Don't. Is it because I said you were a fag and a whore? I take it back, okay? You can just be a whore, alright? Come on . . ."

I wasn't crying, but the hitching noise wouldn't stop. I felt like a freak. "So what now?" I wriggled. "Let me go, okay?"

Will didn't move. "No, I don't think so. I think you need this." Part of me wanted to shove him roughly away, but I ended up leaning into his arms with my eyes shut tight.

He kissed my hair. "What do you mean?" he asked. "What do you mean, what now?"

"I mean, *what now*? Are we like boyfriends now, or what?"

He didn't say anything for a moment. Then, "Are you familiar with the term 'fuck-buddies'?"

I coughed explosively and started laughing. It was grating and ugly sounding, but it felt pretty damned good. Will laughed with me, shrilly, and we started rocking back and forth together in each other's arms. For some reason that made us laugh even harder.

"Trust me," he said, bumping his forehead against mine. "You're the same as you were this morning. You just did some stuff, that's all. Some new stuff. You wanted to, and you did it. What's the problem? You never had Thai food, so you go out and eat Thai food one night . . . you don't spazz out about that, do you? Thai food's good. Maybe you'll feel like some tomorrow night. Maybe you'll eat a *lot* of Thai food from now on. Who cares? You won't wake up tomorrow morning with slanted eyes . . . trust me on that one. You'll do exactly what you want to do."

"Yeah?"

"Hell yes, boy. How do you think I live *my* fabulous life? All I ask is that you don't turn over-night into a gung-ho queer. That shit is *so* dreary. I swear to God, the first time I see you in pride-rings and engineer boots—*pfft*! it's over!"

I stopped laughing finally and pulled a sigh. I was enormously tired all of a sudden, emptied out and exhausted. "You still haven't told me what's gonna happen next," I told him softly, squeezing his shoulder like I'd keep bugging him until he told me. The truth was, I just wanted him to go on talking, so I could keep listening to him.

"Oh, you want a little story, huh? Well . . ." he pulled me down beside him and pulled a blanket over us. I pushed up next to him and he nuzzled my chest. "We're going to go to sleep here tonight. It'll take a while, because we'll talk some, you know, whispering like kids do, keep trying to make each other laugh. Every time you think you're falling asleep I'll tickle your feet with my toes, just because I'm a brat. But tomorrow morning we're going to get up real early, before everyone else does, when they're all in bed with hang-overs. It'll still be dark out. We're gonna go out for breakfast. I'll keep snitching bacon off your plate because, as previously noted, I am a brat. Then we'll order some more coffee and I'll point out the window. Know what I'll be pointing at? The sun, coming up one more time, the way it always does. It'll be fucking gorgeous."

AWAKENING MOMENT

D. E. Rider

"Well, I think we've got what we need," said Sol. He smiled, and I'm sure I smiled too. The bed—that is what he was eyeing.

The room was lovely: a nice view, a decadent bath, complete with mirrors and Jacuzzi. The kids at Mom's, the afternoon off. An evening away from it all. Our fifteenth anniversary.

And I knew what Sol was thinking: trying out that bed. "Restrain yourself, loverboy," I said, keeping my tone light. I didn't want to discourage him, but it had been a lot of years since we were indulging in the daytime: we had the entire evening and night to ourselves. But I found myself thinking about those first few crazy months when the afternoon was far from out of the question . . . well, back then we'd already have had our clothes off by this point, both of us. But that was then.

I thought about the pool: the day was just a little bit cool though I was sure the pool was heated. Sol took my hand while I was thinking and I found myself kissing him, then laying my head against his chest as he held me. Fifteen years.

"So, what are you up for?" he said. We didn't really have any afternoon plans other than being lazy around the pool.

"Oh, I don't know." I briefly wondered if Sol's first idea might be the right one.

"Let's go out."

"Out?"

"Somewhere where we can walk."

That seemed appealing and soon we found ourselves driving off. I'm sure there were lots of places around to walk, but somehow you don't pick out walks in your own hometown. We were headed out of town and I began to wonder what Sol had in mind. "You know where we're going?" I asked.

"I've got some idea," he said.

It was a state park, a few miles out of town. It had a few paths: one especially easy one around part of a lake, and I found myself warming to the idea. The place was deserted.

It was a little cool, but the walk was very pleasant: the lake was pretty. And we had the walk all to ourselves. We didn't say anything, but just walked, arms around each other. Soon I found myself in his arms again, we'd paused and kissed again. "Best fifteen years of *my* life," he said when we broke it.

All I managed to reply was a "mmm."

"Come," he said and I found myself being led. Off the path.

"Sol," I said letting him know I wasn't sure what was going on and he'd better not get too crazy.

"Come on!" was all he replied. Soon the path was out of sight and suddenly I was in his arms again.

"What have you got in mind?" I asked after we'd kissed.

He laughed. "Don't worry," he said, his voice giving the impression that he was going to behave himself, but I wondered whether that was really his intent. Next I found he'd put his jacket on the ground and was wanting me to sit on it with him.

"You can just get those ideas out of your mind," I said after we'd kissed again.

"Well who's bringing up ideas?" he answered and kissed me again.

He'd certainly put ideas in *my* head. Did he think we'd do much out here? That's something we'd certainly never done, even in our crazy days. "Just relax," he said, but I knew the idea was in his mind. "All I want is a kiss," he said, continuing. "A *real* kiss."

Well, that was something: a declaration of his intentions. And a kiss was certainly all right, so I relaxed and we did our best.

When we broke that one, I found his hand on the front of my shirt. "No," I said, but smiled, trying to make sure he didn't go into a huff or something.

He didn't stop. His hand wandered slowly over my breasts. "You know you like it," he said.

And I knew what he was thinking. There was one time, back during our crazy days when we were outside: in a different park. He'd made me come: I come pretty easily when he touches my breasts. He'd pulled up my top right out there in the park—well, no one was around—and it had happened. Now I felt him fingering the buttons of my shirt. I reached up and held his fingers still.

I realized it could happen. I was ready for something. If we were instantly transported back to the hotel room at that moment, we'd definitely have our afternoon delight. His fingers struggled out of my grip and I felt a button being opened.

"Oh, no," I said, still trying to keep my voice light about it. I grabbed his head and pulled him into a kiss. In a moment I wondered whether it was distracting me more than him: he had a couple of buttons open and his hand was inside. Through my bra, I felt him cup my breast.

"Please, no!" I said. I'm sure he could hear I was serious.

His hand withdrew and he buttoned the buttons. But while he did it, he smiled and said: "OK, but you *owe* me."

I thought about it as we walked out. I suppose of all the problems that I might be confronted with in life, a randy husband who loved me surely had to be pretty low on the list. He had been a good sport: we walked out arms around each other.

The park was still basically deserted. We reached the car to find just one other car coming in, and as we drove out a couple from the car walked out the way we had just returned from.

"Young love," said Sol as we drove by them on the way out. I found myself figuring they would be more daring than we had been: perhaps they were still in their crazy stage. Why else would they be walking out there like that? Why had we walked out like that?

We drove back quietly and I thought about the pool—even though it was cool out it wasn't too bad and if the pool were heated, it should be pleasant enough. "Think it's not too cold for the pool?" I said. Sol didn't answer right away and I looked at him.

Suddenly he grinned and looked back at me. "Are you a hard one to convince?" he said. Oh that. The moment for that had passed. But I briefly wondered whether I was going to have to let him have his way. I felt a little trapped, but was desperate that it not show. Not on our anniversary.

"We'll have to see," I said, trying to give him an enigmatic smile. The rest of the way, my mind was busy: how would I get him off this kick? But what was really wrong with his idea? Was I resisting for any good reason? Had I gotten too set in our ways? A part of me felt it was so immature to fool around during the day: what with the kids, we never did anything like that.

But I remembered that pool. We didn't get many chances for a nice heated pool. Once we were in the room, I said, "Are you going in?" I dug for my suit.

Sol didn't answer and I tossed him his suit. Thinking of Sol's mood,

I briefly considered changing in the bathroom, but rejected the idea as absurd.

Yes, his hands went around me as soon as I was undressed. "Sol," I said, just a little disapproving.

"Can't I kiss my wife?"

I would have said *we know what's really on your mind* but he was kissing me before I managed it. There I stood, naked, kissing him.

When we finally broke it, I said: "Sol, tonight." With as much finality as I could manage.

"There's nothing wrong with the daytime. What do you think that couple in the state park were up to?"

"So you noticed." The girl had been quite something. Sol missed little.

"I'm not blind. I guess you did too," he answered. "Maybe we should have followed them back in."

"Wanted to see them in action?" I asked. I realized we were beginning to get a little daring in our conversation and my nakedness suddenly seemed too suggestive. I grabbed the bottom of my suit and started to put it on.

"Or we could have shown them how it's done," said Sol. I realized he had his shirt off: his chest was bare.

"And joined them?" I asked. Now I felt the devil had hold of me. "You looking for a taste of her?" I had the bottom on and started with the top.

"How about you?" he answered. I looked at him: a little smirk.

I wondered if he meant me and the woman. He could have meant me and the man, but I knew Sol: he knew about me and Sherry and he wouldn't forget. I decided he was being ambiguous on purpose.

Somehow I flashed on that woman in the park. Young. Pretty. I seemed to remember her rather well. Not skinny, but with a figure: but a chest that would have men looking. Tall. If we were to kiss, my head would be tilted up as if I were kissing a man. But my body would be pressed against her soft body, her soft breasts. When we'd pause, she'd smile down at me, her arms wrapped around me.

Sol had come over and I felt I'd been woolgathering. He was smiling and now I wondered if I'd let things get out of hand. He gently placed me down on the bed and removed my bottom. Then he was naked.

I did like it: I was ready and he felt wonderful inside me. He managed a little kiss while we were in the midst of it, though that tends to be a little awkward. He was gentle and slow. And I was happy, pool or no pool.

He'd definitely thought about me and that woman in the park: he wouldn't forget my telling him about Sherry. Not that there was much to tell, just the one kiss. It had been back before I knew Sol. Sherry had shown up one Saturday afternoon to tell me her news: that she was getting married. She'd been my best friend for a long time and I knew very well what she thought of John and I couldn't have been happier for her.

We'd hugged, as soon as she'd told me. No, it's not what you think: we were cheek-to-cheek, arms around each other, revelling in her news. But it was a long hug and I loved the warmth of her body.

Then we'd finished and were both talking again, almost too giddy for real conversation. And I'd suddenly insisted on being the first to kiss the bride. No, I hadn't been looking for anything like that. But then the kiss *was* just a little too long. Well, more than a little. I opened my eyes to discover I had her head in my hands, and found myself watching the way she kissed me, her eyes closed.

Then it was over. But it had been too long: we both knew that, though now we were both silent. Tongue-tied. I forced myself to drag her into the kitchen to sit down for tea, and soon we were talking wedding plans and arrangements. We talked another half-hour, never mentioning the kiss. But I'd liked it. And Sherry: I could have sworn the moment after that kiss, as she stood there, she'd have done anything. Anything at all.

And then she'd had to run. And I'd told her again how happy I was for her. And somehow we'd ended up in another kiss, our arms around each other. It was over in a couple of seconds, but afterwards there'd been her hand on my back.

I still remember that hand. Little more than a friendly pat. But definitely more: the way it had finally lingered for a moment, briefly moving, softly. I'd thought back to that very moment many times since: the moment had passed and she'd left. But there had been an invitation in it: many times since then I've been absolutely certain of it. Her lingering hand: one little sign of response from me and she wouldn't have withdrawn it.

I knew that. I knew it while we parted and after I shut the door. And as I discreetly watched her through the window as she drove off. And as I found myself in bed moments later, touching myself. I imagined the two of us together: together in bed. Kissing. Dressed, but lying down in that very bed, kissing each other.

But that had been enough: that fantasy and my fingers were enough to take me to it. I'd lain there exhausted for half an hour afterwards.

And now it was enough again: the memory of that day many years before. Sol inside me—did he know what I was thinking? I knew he'd thought of my kiss with Sherry, but I hadn't told him about my being in bed afterward. Now here we were: joined. And my memories bringing me right to the moment. Yes, for *that* moment, I didn't mind skipping the pool.

He held me that night as we fell asleep. Dinner had been just what we'd been looking for. The bottle of wine was gone. Sol had been game as we'd retired, but I'd declined.

It had been for his sake, actually. Sort of. I knew we weren't as young as we had been and after that afternoon, it wouldn't be the same for Sol. I figured he must know that though he gave no sign: he just seemed to buy my line about being blissfully tired and looking forward to the morning.

Well, he'd *almost* gone along with it. "OK, but in the middle of the night, I'm going to wake you—like this." His hand slipped up my thigh, slipping toward the inside, caressing. I'd caught it before it reached me and I think I giggled. "I'm not asking: I'm telling you," he added as he withdrew his hand.

He was true to *that* word: I awoke to his hand on my vagina. I was wet. He must have sensed I was now awake: he gave me a little "shh."

In a second we were spooning. Silent sex in the middle of the night: not a word to be spoken. He was gentle, but he knows my body. He took his time but it didn't take long before I didn't just want it: I needed it.

He obliged. I loved the feeling of him inside me. He stopped his movement so that we just lay there for a while, joined. We did nothing except that his fingers continued to idly play with my nipple. For me that can do a lot and in a minute I grabbed his fingers to make him stop. He took that as a signal to start his hips again, but he started very slowly.

It was so deliciously slow. Him inside me. I recalled our day: our afternoon indulgence. His comment about that girl and how that had triggered my memories. The picture of her in the park came back in my mind. Her light-brown, shoulder-length hair. Her dark eyes and dark skin: I must have noticed more than I'd thought. Her face was so pretty and smooth: I could picture her naked brown body. Pressed against mine in bed as she kissed me, our arms locked around each other. The feel of her soft breasts, so womanly. I *know* Sol noticed them: while I know he likes mine, he's only human and wouldn't fail to appreciate the more generous breasts of other women.

The feeling of her soft body pressed against mine. Her lips, kissing. She'd roll on top of me, looking down at me, smiling. I'd run my hands up and down her back, feeling her skin. Down past her rear to the backs of her thighs and up again. She'd kiss me again and roll us sideways and do the same to my back. And then slip her hand between our bodies, while we still kissed. And her fingers would be on me and I would be hers.

And I would come . . . I came: it felt so good the way he'd increased our rhythm, all while he still touched my nipple. I felt my body stiffen as if I were stretching on just waking up some morning. But I made no sound, or I don't think I did: it's hard to remember.

We lay there, him still inside me, but I knew he'd soften and our joining would be over. But it was so nice there in his arms. Not a single word between us: all of it through the silent understanding of lovers. I felt him finally out of me and he rolled on his back. I pressed my back against him: he doesn't mind that. Soon I heard the slow breaths of his sleep.

She wouldn't be asleep so quickly. She'd hold me and kiss me again. And what would she think of Sol lying there, sleeping?

She'd know what to do: after all she was my fantasy. She'd be on top of him, straddling him and kiss him awake again. I shifted to lying on my back as I thought of her. She'd smile at me. And wink. As she lifted herself to lower herself on him. Yes, he'd be ready again: finding another woman taking charge like that, so young.

I lay there with my eyes shut, my fingers on myself, feeling it coming yet again. The image of that woman in my head, taking Sol despite himself. Riding him. Using him for her own pleasure as he lay there, his eyes taking in the image of her naked body rising and falling. He'd have no chance, no chance at all. I came again.

Sol snored. I lay there, too exhausted to sleep for the moment, but I knew I'd be sleeping soon. I rolled on my side again and scooted to where my back was against Sol's side. What would Sol think of these images dancing in my head? I thought about telling him in the morning. But . . .

But I knew somehow it would be *too* important to him. Not just a casual little thing: not just a shared little fantasy. He'd be interested. I'd be embarrassed. If he quizzed me about it, it would be horrible. If he didn't, I'd still know he was thinking about it and it would be just as bad. No. This was something that he was never going to know about.

Un Petit Greniet Ensoleille
A Wee Sunny Garret

Elana White

It had been a bad year. Chantal's marriage lay in tatters at her feet. Every step she took unsettled the smouldering ashes, choking her with guilt and rage. Everything reminded her of the failure. The love had gone and they had denied it far too long. They had begun to hate one another. She had lost herself.

How could he have changed so much, she wondered. Why couldn't I fix it? I should have tried harder. Did I stop loving him because he was so bitter, or did he become bitter after I stopped loving him?

The worst thing was remembering the time before. When the love had still been there. The loss of that good man stung her more deeply than anything else. Her throat closed down painfully every time those thoughts began to whisper. Those happy memories were worse than all the memories of the screaming fights and sleeplessness and savage thrumming resentment.

Flight had seemed the only response to the pain. An attempt to leave behind the hateful fires that burned in her soul. Surely they could not continue to smoulder here. Surely his sickness could not follow this far.

The pain had driven her out of her own country, away from her home, to this small village in France, where the sun shone and the air felt like a caress. It was where her Grandmamma Chantal had been born. She took a tiny room above a cafe. She owned nothing. At night she worked in the cafe, serving stew and tea to the few tired old fishermen who stopped there before going to their empty houses to sleep alone. They did not trouble her. Her beauty was not sufficient for them. Her halting French too much trouble to bother overcoming.

Every night when the cafe closed she climbed the narrow ancient stairs to her room, pulled the blind over the window and undressed. The shade on the single lamp was yellowed with age and cast a gentle light into the small room. She would sit on the edge of her little bed and stare at her face in the cracked mirror on the bureau as she brushed her long brown hair. Three months she had been there and the haunted look still lay like a caul over her features. She wondered if she would always look this way. She remembered how her eyes used to shine. She missed herself.

After turning off the light, she would raise the shade again so the sweet night air could come in the window. Her bed lay along the wall under the window and before sleeping she would sit up and look out for a time, over the tiled rooftops. When the moon was full she would sit up far into the night, transfixed by it.

She liked to be woken by the warm French sunshine as it crept, dappled, through the lace curtain and across her body. She would rise and take her bath in the huge iron tub in the shared bathroom across the hall, peeking out the door before hurrying from one room to the other in her robe. She used an old tin cup to pour water over her head to wet her hair for the shampoo. She liked the way the air cooled her shoulders and breasts as she scrubbed her hair, and the contrasting heat of the water when she rinsed.

One morning, her robe clinging to her damp skin, her hair in a tangle from the towel drying, she was half-way across the hall when someone emerged from the room next to the bath. She gasped and sprang for her room, turning to look out briefly as she shut the door. The tall young man saw her and smiled broadly just before her door clicked shut. She stood stock still at the door, holding her breath, as his footsteps passed her room and clumped down the stairs.

No one had told her there was a new roomer. The next day, as she bathed, she knew he was in his room. She heard a muffled thump and the floor creaked now and then as he moved. She felt exposed somehow, knowing he was there. Knowing she would have to cross the hall again, that he might see her. She tried not to splash too loudly and she winced when she pulled the plug and the water slurped noisily down the drain, betraying the fact that she was about to cross the hall. There was a listening silence from the next room.

After that first glimpse, she didn't see him again for weeks, though she was intensely aware of his presence. Small sounds came through the floorboards. His footsteps thumped in the hall. She giggled at his unabashed splashing and singing in the bathtub. He bathed at night.

She became familiar with his rhythms and timed her own so that she would not encounter him. She never saw him in the cafe at night. He arrived home before she went down to work, had his bath and then stayed in his room all evening. She began to wonder what he did in there all alone every night. She never heard other voices. Never smelled perfume in the hallway. She knew from the brief glimpse she had had of him that he was a striking man and wondered why he never brought women to his room. It wasn't until she saw him again that she realized how much he had consumed her thoughts.

He came home late one evening and encountered her on the stairs as she went down to begin her shift. He had stopped on the landing where the stairs turned and was silently reading some mail when she came down the stairs and almost walked into him.

"Oh!"

He looked up, eyes unfocused, but smiled widely when he saw her. "*Bonjour!*" he said.

She smiled faintly and said "Hello."

"Ahh, you are Chantal, the Canadian woman who works in the cafe. It is so nice to meet you finally." He held out his hand and she took it hesitantly, worried that he might do something European, like kiss it. But he just shook it briefly, politely, and said "I am Armande." He loomed over her on the cramped landing, not moving. The bare bulb over their heads cast his eyes deep into shadow, but she saw them glitter. She saw the smile on his lush mouth.

"Umm . . . nice to meet you. C-could I get by please, I have to get to work."

"Of course." He pressed his back to the wall, holding his letter to his chest, but still she couldn't avoid brushing against him slightly as she passed. She hoped the harsh shadows from the overhead light would not reveal her blush. Head lowered, eyes darting nervously, she hurried down the stairs.

Near midnight, coming out of the kitchen with a pot of tea, she saw Armande sitting at a table in the back. He was lighting the candle in front of him and the sudden flare of the match caught her eye or she might not have noticed him there. With a graceful gesture he let her know that he wanted her to come over.

"I thought I would enjoy some wine this evening." He grinned at her. The candlelight softened the shadows on his face and she noticed how long and thick his lashes were. It was too dark to see the colour of his eyes.

"Chantal?"

Chantal blinked and seemed to wake up with a start. "What? Sorry. Red or white?"

"Red, I think. You choose the bottle."

She hurried away, feeling foolish and embarrassed. Her cheeks burned again. God, what is it about him that does that to me, she asked herself sharply, determined not to let it happen again. But she couldn't ignore the slight quivering in her stomach as she hurried down to the wine cellar. Standing before the huge dusty wine rack she desperately tried to remember what Andre, the cafe owner, had taught her about wine. Cabernet Sauvignon for sure, she thought. Can't go wrong with a good Cab. What year, what year? Her fingers trailed through the air over the stacked, dusty bottles. She wasn't sure how much he wanted to spend. 1994—Andre had said there were some very good wines that year, and they would be reasonably priced because they weren't too old. She selected one from the rack and examined the label, still uncertain about all the unfamiliar terms. She hoped it was a good one. She rushed back upstairs with the bottle and tried to calm her breath as she reached for a glass over the bar.

When she showed him the bottle, he beamed at her, delighted. "A very good choice, Chantal. Are you a connoisseur?"

"Me?" she laughed nervously. "No, not at all. I hardly know a thing about wine."

"Except that you like it, yes?"

She felt a grin spread across her face and she laughed softly. "Yes." He laughed with her and held out his glass, holding it delicately by the stem. His hands were large, the fingers long and graceful-looking.

She opened the bottle for him, her hands trembling slightly, and poured a small amount. He took a sip and swirled it around in his mouth, his eyes a little distant. Then he sucked some air in through his teeth to help his tongue and nose better distinguish the unique flavours in the wine. Chantal was familiar with the technique. Andre had taught her. But seeing Armande do it made her suck the air into her own lungs. He looked a little primal, baring his white teeth like that. Unexpected images came into her mind, startling her, making the wine gurgle as she shakily filled his glass.

She took his money, left him to his wine and went about cleaning up the tables. It was almost time to close. She was intensely conscious of his gaze following her. It made her nervous and she almost dropped some dishes as she went through the door into the kitchen. She resolved to tell him to stop staring when she came out, but when she emerged from the kitchen he was gone. His table was bare—he'd taken the wine and his glass with him. She shrugged, relieved to be free of his staring eyes, but also irritated with herself when she realized how disappointed she was that he had left. She finished closing up and climbed the stairs to her room.

Later, as she brushed her hair, she thought about him. She had hardly stopped thinking of him since she had almost walked into him on the stairs. Armande. She repeated his name to herself, savouring the exotic sound of it. Absently, as the brush stroked her hair, as the rhythm of her arm lulled her, she fell into a fantasy that clouded her vision and stole the minutes from her. He was kissing her with his beautiful full lips, he was holding her tightly to his body, burying his face in her neck, nuzzling her. He was . . .

There was a tapping at her door. She blinked. Her eyes cleared and discovered her reflection, startling her with the sudden beauty she found there. Her cheeks glowed with colour, her eyes were clear and luminous. Her lips were parted, rosy and moist, as if she had just been kissed. The tapping came at the door again, and she caught her breath. It's him! came her first frantic thought. But then she realized it could not be him. Why would he come to her door so late at night? Why would he come to her door at all? It must be Andre, come to complain about something. She took the four steps to the door and opened it impatiently, scowling.

It was Armande. Her eyes widened at the sight of him standing there with the almost-full bottle of wine and two glasses. He was smiling. She wondered if he ever stopped smiling.

"Bon soir!" he said brightly, as if it weren't two o'clock in the morning and he'd just met her a few hours before. "Look at all this wine I have." He raised the bottle. "I could never drink it all by myself. What a shame to waste it . . . would you help me drink it up?"

Chantal pulled her robe more tightly around her and looked down the hall to the open door of his room. The light was off. "It's two in the morning!"

"Yes! It is! May I come in?" Chantal was as afraid to let him in as she was to turn him away. Armande must have sensed the internal struggle she was waging and pulled his face into such a pitiable expression that Chantal burst into helpless laughter and opened the door. He breezed past her and looked around. "Small room!" he commented. There was an old wooden chair next to the bureau, but he ignored it and sat down happily on the end of the bed, holding the glasses out to her.

They finished the wine and when it was gone, Chantal tip-toed down to the kitchen and made them a pot of tea. They sat up until the sky began to grow pink and the fishermen could be heard outside her window, trudging down to the docks. They talked of everything, followed the conversation wherever it took them, thrilled at how much they had in common, in spite of being raised in different cultures. Their voices sometimes rose too much when they discovered another common point and they rocked with suppressed giggles and shushed each other, expecting at any moment to hear Andre's angry wife banging her cane on the ceiling of her room below them.

Chantal delighted in Armande's beautiful voice, his perfect accented English. She was astonished at how at ease she felt with him. He made her laugh. He seemed so cheerful and bright. He was a writer, he told her, come to this small town from Arles to find some peace while he finished his book. He worked as a labourer during the day, to pay the rent, and wrote at night.

As he told her about his large family, Chantal watched him, his expressive gestures, his animated face. His appearance, at rest, seemed so at odds with his cheerful demeanor. She was sure he would look dangerous to her if she met him on a dark street. He was very tall, long limbed, broad shouldered. He was dark. He seemed to fill her tiny attic room. She felt safe with him. His high cheekbones and shapely eyebrows framed two deep blue eyes that sparkled merrily when he laughed. He had a beautiful smile.

Armande became pensive just before he left that morning, looking at her strangely, bringing her nervousness back for a moment. He rose quickly, bid her adieu and left. She heard his door close softly.

She didn't see him again that day. Or the next. Every time the door opened in the cafe she would look around, hoping to see him smiling there. She found herself taking more care with her makeup, brushing her hair a little differently so that it framed her face more flatteringly. She bought a pretty dress to wear. The fishermen started to smile at her when she brought them their food. She smiled back.

On the third night he appeared in the cafe again, as suddenly as the first time, and again he ordered wine and again he brought most of it with him to her room after she finished working, sitting up with her late into the night. He began to meet her every two or three nights this way, sitting on the end of her bed, telling her his stories, listening to hers. He shared some of his writing with her, reading quietly while she stared at his pliant lips as they formed each word, thrilling at the sound of each syllable from his French tongue, even though she understood little of what he said. She began to fall in love with him.

One night, about a month after their first meeting, Chantal prepared to go down to work with a feeling of dread in her stomach. She had not seen Armande for five nights. He had not told her he was going to be away. She scolded herself for feeling so bereft. He had never indicated any special feeling for her, other than a pleasure at her company over the wine they both loved. She knew she had no right to expect him to be there.

As she opened her door to go down to the cafe, she heard footsteps on the stairs. Armande looked up at her as he reached the top. He looked haggard and worn.

"Armande! What's wrong?" She rushed to meet him, stopping short. She had almost flown into his arms without even thinking. She stepped back. "Where have you been? You look terrible."

"Why thank you," he said quietly with a sad smile, trying to make a joke. He gave her a look that was so complex it frightened her, filled with sadness and longing both. And before she could ask again, he stepped toward her and enfolded her in his arms, swaying, burying his face in her hair.

"*Cherie*, I had to go home. My uncle . . . *mon oncle* Gustav . . . he died in a crash. My mama is overcome with grief. He was her little brother. He was my friend." His breath touched her ear and Chantal put her arms around his neck to comfort him. She felt his body tremble. He held her tightly to him and she felt the tension in the muscles of his back. She closed her eyes, feeling guilty at the pleasure she took from his grieving embrace, her heart soaring at his unexpected endearment.

It was too much. He held her too tightly, too long. She feared he could feel her heart pounding in her breast. She released her hold on him and tried to move away, but he caught her around the waist with one arm and pulled her to him again, pressing his whole body to her. "Please don't go," he whispered. His other hand laced into her hair and he held her there, her breasts crushed against his chest, the long firm length of his thighs pressing along hers. He was going to kiss her. He looked at her desperately, taking in her flushed cheeks, her wide, almost frightened eyes, her startled, parted lips. But when he bent to her, his lips went not to her mouth, but her ear, and he said, in a trembling voice, "I will come down for wine tonight." And then he released her softly, trailing his fingertips along her arms, and went quickly to his room without looking back.

Chantal had to hold tightly to the bannister as she went down the stairs to the cafe. Her legs felt weak and she couldn't focus her eyes— they were too intently focused inward on the physical memory of his body against hers, his thighs . . . his hips brushing hers as he bent into their embrace.

He came down much later than usual that night. She had already begun to close the cafe. He noticed his bottle of wine already waiting for him behind the bar. Instead of sitting down at his table he picked up the wine and two glasses and gestured with them up the stairs. Chantal nodded from across the room, understanding his silent message. He would wait upstairs. But this was not the usual routine, said the question in her eyes. He did not answer it.

A little while later, as she neared the top of the stairs, she noticed the scent of lavender. The door to the bath was open and she looked in to see Armande, fully dressed, straightening up with a bottle of scented oil in his hand. There were candles melted to the rim of the tub and a glass of wine on a low stool where it could be reached while reclining in the water. He must have found her robe—the emerald green silk one that she never wore—hanging on the back of her door, for it now hung neatly on the hook beside the enormous bathtub.

Armande crossed the room in three silent graceful steps and stood before her, smiling down into her questioning face. He touched her cheek with the back of his fingers.

"You looked so distressed when I left you earlier, *cherie.* I'm so sorry."

"Armande," Chantal said, surprised, "you don't need to apologize. I was just worried about you. You've been through such a bad time. You looked so . . ."

Armande hushed her with a gentle caress of his fingertip on her lips. It smelled of lavender. "Shhh . . . *mon petit* . . . I've drawn you a nice warm bath, you see? I think you need to relax. I want you to get in and soak and drink your wine and then I want you to join me and we will have a nice chat. OK?" He smiled at her and his eyes seemed so startlingly blue that she could only nod and watch as he turned off the overhead light, locked the door from the inside and then pulled it shut behind him as he left.

At first she sat up rigidly in the water, ignoring the wine, just looking at the door as if she could see through it. He was in her room, sitting on her bed, waiting for her. She could feel him in there. She fidgeted with the soap dish. She stretched out her legs and then crossed them under her again.

A knock came at the door.

"You are not relaxing," his sing-song voice teased. "I can hear you splashing in there." She started slightly and giggled. She could hear the smile in his voice when he spoke again. "Have some wine, *cherie.* Lie back and close your eyes. I'll knock in fifteen minutes."

So, she did as she was told. She took a sip of wine and lay back. The water was just the right temperature and the scent of lavender soothed her, even through the riot of thoughts that tumbled through her mind. Poor man, she thought. He was the one who should be getting pampered and taken care of. So sad to lose his uncle like that. What was he up to? She shivered as she remembered their embrace in the hallway earlier. There was more there than just one friend taking comfort from another. She had felt it, and she knew he had also. She had seen it in his eyes. Her heart beat faster as she remembered that look. The desperate passion that had been there.

When Armande knocked again, Chantal awoke from a wide-eyed trance of his hands on her and found that her own hands had strayed to stroke her thighs and her breasts. She was terrified to get out of the tub now. What was waiting for her out there? Did she want it? Her body and her heart told her that she did. She stepped out of the tub, dried herself off carefully and put on her robe.

As she crossed the hallway she was painfully conscious of how the silk robe clung to her warm, moist skin. Her breasts bobbed with every step, brushing her nipples against the fabric. She felt it hugging her buttocks as she walked. Feeling exposed, she had tied the sash so tightly that all she had accomplished was to pull the robe more snugly against her curves. She clung to her bundle of clothes and entered her room.

Armande was there, sitting cross-legged on the end of her bed as he always did. But usually he leaned back against the wall, nothing but his face turned toward her. Tonight his whole body faced the head of the bed, where she would sit in a moment. She saw the usual bottle of wine and glasses on the deep windowsill. But there was a candle there tonight as well, flickering gently in the light breeze. Her lamp was safely on, though it seemed dimmer for some reason. The light in the room was mellow and soft. Soothing. Save for a few small, insignificant details, all was as it usually was, and she relaxed a little, feeling silly for being so nervous. Just another all-night chat, like so many others.

She dropped her clothes on the chair by her dresser and quickly took her place on the head of the bed. Armande was watching her quietly, a small smile on his face. She tucked the robe up under her knees and brought them to her chest. A protective posture that she couldn't help taking. She was so aware of the way her naked breasts made the glossy silk quiver as she moved and breathed. She wrapped an arm around her knees and reached for the fresh glass of wine he had poured for her. She needed something to do with her hands.

Armande began to talk. She watched him as he spoke, as she always did. He was dressed all in black. He rested his elbows on his knees as he spoke and fiddled with a loose thread on the blanket. His sleeves were pushed up to just below his elbows. Chantal watched the long muscles in his forearms work as his graceful fingers worried the thread. The high neck of his sweater accentuated the paleness of his face. There were ragged spots of colour high on his cheeks and his full lips seemed very red. There was a tenderness around his eyes, a slight pinkishness around the rims that made the irises so brilliantly blue she had to hold her breath.

He told her about his Uncle Gustav. His voice was soft and low and trembled a little now and then. He looked around the room as he spoke, as if he was afraid to meet her eyes. He did not gesture as much as usual.

At first, Chantal assumed his strange quietude was caused by his uncle's death. But even though it was Gustav that he spoke of, Chantal began to realize it was not his uncle that occupied his mind. Not entirely. There was something else distracting him when he paused for a breath or a sip of wine.

Once or twice, when he told her something that brought the laughter back into his face, he leaned forward and put his hand on her foot. His warm palm so briefly touched her and trailed away as he sat back again, leaving her reeling. He coaxed her into telling him of her favourite uncle. Uncle Ted, who had always made her laugh with funny faces and tickles. Armande listened, grinning at the bedspread as she spoke.

Golden dawn was beginning to overpower the little candle in her window. She had long before turned the lamp off, unable to bear the sight of him so utterly beautiful in the light. When she fell silent he did not respond. She saw the smile slowly leave his face. His lips parted. There was a long moment filled with silence and anticipation. And then he reached out and drew the tip of his middle finger slowly, delicately, down the silken skin on the top of her naked foot, from the bend at her ankle to the hollow place at the base of her toes. He caressed that spot with the lightest touch she had ever felt. It was barely there, yet it shot through her entire body, frightening her and exhilarating her completely.

But when he withdrew, he looked at the clock beside her bed. He looked out the window. His face glowed in the warm light of the sun. He looked almost childlike, confused.

He was about to go. She knew it as surely as she knew that she did not want him to go. He was about to force a smile and look at her shoulder or her chin and get up from her bed and leave her alone. And if he did she would never forgive herself for allowing it. For she knew, somehow without knowing it, she knew that if he left her now he would go back to Arles and she would never see him again.

She let go of her knees and rolled them to the side, rising up before him at the very moment that he drew in the breath with which he would say goodbye to her. She knelt before him and challenged him with her eyes. Challenged him to move, to leave. When he hesitated, she bent to him, steadying herself with her hands on his strong shoulders, and kissed him on the mouth. She kissed him without hesitation, without doubt, because she knew more than anything else in this moment that she loved him and could not let him go.

His hands came up to hold her face. He pulled away from her kiss and looked into her eyes with an expression so incomprehensible she felt sure she had made a huge mistake and her eyes filled with tears. She looked down. Her body sagged and she bit back a sob.

"Ohh, *mon cher Chantal, mon petit oiseau.*" His words pulled her eyes back to his and she saw the tears swimming in them. *"Je t'aime,"* he whispered. *"Je t'aime, ma belle!"* He said it with all the passion she felt and as he pushed her back and lay beside her she trembled at the feel of his long body stretched out beside hers.

He leaned on one elbow above her, stroking her cheek with his fingertips, running them down her neck to her throat. He brushed them over her lashes, lightly, ran them along her brows, traced the outline of one small ear. She drowned in his eyes and when she could not live one moment more without kissing him, she put her hand on the back of his neck and pulled him to her.

He kissed her as if he had never kissed a woman before. With such reverence, such care, as if it would be the only kiss he would ever know. She felt his lips brush hers so lightly. He kissed the corner of her mouth. She sighed and took his bottom lip between hers, sucking gently. The tip of his tongue touched hers, making her moan. He continued to caress her face, her hair. Her hands roamed up and down his sides and back.

They explored one another's faces with their mouths, tasting earlobes, touching tongues to eyebrows, nibbling the corner of a jaw, breathing on the fullness of a cheek. They kissed as if they would kiss forever, never needing more than the kiss, all their hungers satisfied in this one blessed act.

But together, in one unspoken moment, his hand brushed her breast, she tugged on the waistband of his pants and then he was off the bed, undressing before her. She watched, rapt, how the skin of his sides slid over his ribs as he pulled his sweater over his head, his flat belly heaving with his quickened breath. He undid his pants with swift, practiced movements, his eyes never leaving her face as he slid them down his legs and stepped out of them. She caught her breath.

"You're so beautiful," she sighed, and held her arms out for his return to her. As he lowered himself to her again, he slowly tugged on the sash of her robe, releasing its tight cling on her waist. He pushed the robe open slowly, as if revealing a great solemn treasure, whispering exotic endearments, sighing. He caressed her breasts so gently. Her nipples rose to hard little peaks and he bent and tasted them with his lips and his tongue. Chantal's head pressed back into the pillow as she arched herself up into him.

With his mouth on her nipple, he trailed his hand over her ribs and her belly, plucked at the edge of her navel, grazed lightly over the tight curls at the top of her legs and then dipped reverently into her moist passion with a movement so deft and gentle that she cried out and clutched him to her, spreading her legs and thrusting her hips into his hand.

She had never known such a perfect touch. He continued to suckle her breast as he moved his fingers between her legs. She closed her eyes and clung to him and opened herself to him more fully than she had ever done with any man before. He moaned and dipped into her slickness. She felt his fingers inside her and tightened her muscles as if she would keep him there always. But he withdrew them and slowly slid them up, their slippery tips finding her heat, caressing it the way he had her foot, so lightly it was almost not a touch at all. But it was enough. It was too much. It was all she ever wanted for the rest of her life.

When she felt that her soul would leave her body, when the hot flush of blood stained her face and her chest and her lungs had filled with the constant staccato intake of breath, half a heartbeat from her outburst, Armande took his fingers away and moved over her, leaning on one arm and cradling her face in his hand.

"Open your eyes, *cher*, look at me," Armande whispered, "Look at me, my love." Chantal's eyes fluttered open, her hands came up to hold his face. They stared, utterly focused, into one anothers' eyes as Armande slowly moved himself into her. She saw in his eyes the moment when he felt her intimate embrace. She saw the quivering, at the corners of his mouth, his exquisite tension. He groaned and closed his eyes for a single agonizing moment and then opened them as he gasped, still slipping deeper. Chantal whimpered with the thrill his surrender gave her. The look in his eyes was overwhelming her.

Slowly, slowly, his length slid along Chantal's throbbing centre and she gasped, wide-eyed, reaching for her release in his eyes, her hips making small motions to tempt him further into her, but he stopped, stilled, holding his breath when he saw she was about to peak. He waited for her to subside a little before continuing.

When he could go no farther, he began to withdraw just as slowly. He moved luxuriously into her and out again, each time just a tiny bit faster. Chantal moaned helplessly and closed her eyes. "Open your eyes, *cher*, watch me. I want to see your eyes when you come for me."

His words pushed her over the edge finally. They sent a deep primitive thrill through her entire body. She felt it in her stomach and her womb and finally, explosively, crashingly, as Armande's perfect hardness caressed her core one last time, she shuddered, crying out his name, her hips bucking into his. He felt her clench around him, pulling the seed up through him, milking him. They fell into one another's eyes, weeping, trembling, staring wide-eyed and exultant into the only place they ever wanted to be again. Together.

Outside, in the cobblestoned street, an old fisherman looked up, startled at the sudden cries he heard above him, from the attic room of Andre's cafe. He smiled, doffed his hat to the window and continued down to the dock with a new spring in his step.

HOUSE OF SEDALIA

Clayton Holiday

It was about five o'clock on a Saturday afternoon in April, when a gentleman arrived at the House of Sedalia, a dignified establishment on 1410 Lexington Boulevard. Located a few blocks west of Grand Avenue, the house was a detached, two-story structure in the company of other freestanding houses on the west side of the street.

Sedalia Dodier's father originally purchased the property in the Grande-Prairie neighborhood of North-Central St. Louis. The house, built in 1887, was acquired by wealthy attorney Marcel Dodier in 1904. The Dodier family had direct links to the old St. Louis French aristocracy, and made their initial fortune from the fur trade of the early 19th century. Marcel Dodier had turned a $100,000 inheritance into a $750,000 estate at the end of a lifetime of wise investments.

When Marcel Dodier bought the house at 1410 Lexington Boulevard, it was a typical St. Louis street, and the red bricks helped absorb the sun. Across the street from the house was St. Michael's Church.

By the outbreak of World War Two, Lexington Boulevard was still regarded as a very respectable neighborhood, solidly upper-middle class.

The House of Sedalia was Late-Victorian (1880–1900), which used the formal design of *Italiante* architecture for the detail of the cornice, the segmental arched windows, and the brackets below the windows. Some Richardsonian Romanesque Revival influence showed in the large arched window on the first floor. Other architectural elements of the house on Lexington Boulevard included windows double hung with transoms above. The center of each of the triple windows and the upper floor window centered above the door were "front windows," since the lower sashes were larger than the upper sashes.

The House of Sedalia did not depend for its effect on fancy landscaping and a large lot, but rather tended toward a public presence by favoring a two-story shape on a small lot set back from the street; it has a token front yard, and a modest back yard. The house had a predominance of red brick for the body of the building, with an entablature resting above the white cornice, supported by stone brackets. The single-family dwelling featured a flat roof, with stone exterior windowsills of limestone, some contemporary plumbing, and two back porches. The foundation was native stone from Carthage, Missouri.

From the sidewalk, two limestone steps led directly across a small walkway to four more limestone steps to the protruding front entrance. Once inside the main door, there was a small vestibule, with another door into the house, common in cold weather towns like St. Louis. A staircase, just beyond the front door, ran along the north wall for access to the bedrooms on the second floor. At the top of the stairs there was a window for cross ventilation, from east-to-west. The layout of the house, on both floors, followed a "side-hall plan." The floor plan had double-parlors with the support spaces behind this.

The "guest" emerged from his 1944 two-tone Mercury, quite sure of what was to follow. He looked at the nameplate on the wrought-iron fence and glanced at the identification: *Sedalia*. He already felt himself draining of obligation and stress, as if he was about to escape a malignant world. He proceeded along the walkway, ascended the four limestone steps and pressed the doorbell.

The "guest" was soon received at the door by Octavio Flores, a young dwarf who worked as a maid for Sedalia. Originally from Tamazunchale, a small, sleepy town in the Sierra Occidental of Mexico, some Azteca ancestry perhaps accounted for her bantam physical size.

Octavio smiled and curtseyed before the "guest." She wore a black serving dress, with a lace apron, and a cap for her hair. She kept a little strand of hair waxed into a rococo curlicue on her forehead. In this upholstery, Octavio was the perfect maid.

The young dwarf conducted the "guest" to the high-ceiling salon where he was cordially greeted by the hostess. There was a clean white cloth on a large table, and the surrounding chairs were wide and leather soft. Red and white wines were at either end of the table, in carafes. The room was hung with impressive paintings in modest antique frames.

Like much of the interior, the decor embodied some Country-French character, charm and understated luxury. Inspired by the sun-drenched colors of Southern France, the harmonious mingling of fabrics, soothing textures, pleasing patterns and leather furnishings mirrored life within the salon. The "guest" loved the splendor and elegance of the whole dwelling. The house was a perfect refuge.

Wasting little time, Sedalia deliberately pulled the "guest" close for a kiss with her crimson, heart-shaped lips. Her hair, which was curly and worn cut to the neck, fell very beautifully about her face. A little surprised, he returned Sedalia's deliberate affection. The 5'4" brunette wore a studded black basque corset, cut high along the top edge and high over the hips, and black leather high heel stiletto pumps. Her cleavage was tantalizing. Since Sedalia wore no panties or stockings, her exquisite cunt and lavish dark pubic hair created the most gratifying exhibit.

"Welcome," she said.

The 30 year-old Sedalia Dodier was intelligent, socially substantial and classy. It was not so much her looks, although she made the most of her physical assets, but her manner that was striking: circumspect and ladylike, yet always strongly sexual in its overtones. There was a dangerous sense of irony which she usually kept sheathed, but which the "guest" found especially appealing. He knew she had more life in her eyelashes than he did in his whole snobbish body.

By the time Sedalia was born in 1914, the Dodier family had been shaped and influenced by the endless drama of the squandering and consolidation of wealth. Imprisoned in picture frames on the walls leading to the second-floor were photographs of earlier Dodier family members. From this Sedalia had a keen perception about human nature: you are what you make people think you are.

Yet as the world order was changing, Sedalia enjoyed the promiscuity of an exclusive set. She was bored with the political twaddle served up in the newspapers every day. For her, St. Louis was like Rome at the end of the Republic, when patrician women loitered on dark streets, giving themselves to strangers.

The "guest" was a good ten years older than Sedalia. He had a sharp, but wayward intelligence. He strongly resembled "Black Jack" Bouvier. With hair parted as if by calipers, dark face ripely handsome, the "guest" had made a reputation as a sexual corsair sailing through society parties of St. Louis. Because of his matinee-idol looks, people of both sexes found him physically attractive. Occasionally at a party, he would take his cock out and insist that someone examine it to reassure him that he was not syphilitic. Many times other males obliged him.

The "guest" often displayed a moral numbness. He simply wanted a hostess already famed for her depravity, who would supply dubious pleasures for a consideration. The "guest" was just like a degenerate aristocrat in the grand style of 19th century Europe. He existed upon alcohol: mint juleps, brandy-smashes, whiskey-skies, gin-sling, cocktail sherry, rum-salads, streaks of lightning, and morning glory. Yet the magnificence of his love for Lebanese hashish was well known in defined St. Louis circles.

In fact, the "guest" prided himself as an aficionado of hashish and vastly preferred the Lebanese influence over samples from Tehran or Kabul. He wished he had been a member of the Hashish Club, the unofficial name given to a group of writers and artists in the years just before the Second French Republic who experimented with the drug. Some of those people included William Blake, Samuel Coleridge, Thomas De Quincey, Edgar Allan Poe, and Charles Pierre Baudelaire.

In general, the "guest" delighted in knowing most people thought the word assassin is adapted from the Arabic word *haschishin* for hashish user. He knew the word is derived from al-Hassan ibn-al-Sabbah, the head of an 11th century Persian religious sect, who used hashish to enlist the aid of young men into his private army, known as assassins (*aschishin*—or follower of Hassan). It was from his mountain home that Hassan ibn-al-Sabbah obtained evil celebrity among the Crusaders, and spread terror through the Mohammedan world.

Before sitting in a low leather armchair, the "guest" removed his dark blue suit jacket and began to release his tie. He carefully handed these items to Octavio. The maid expressed herself, in broken English, with a mind perhaps ten or eleven years old. She enjoyed talk about the private lives of ghosts and archbishops. She also told jokes at which her own laughter sounded in the air before anyone else. Octavio became easily excited by the war, or the clientele of the house, and often talked in a frantic stream of Spanish that verged on hysteria and kept the "guest" pleasurably buoyant. Nothing perturbed Octavio, and she flitted through the rooms of the house like a gentle grinning little monkey, with the same bright inhuman gaze.

As the "guest" continued disrobing, Sedalia drew the curtains closed, and the atmosphere in the salon, heated by hashish smoldering in an incense burner, became erotically sultry.

Sedalia also alerted the "guest" to his favorite music on the gramophone: Claude Debussy's "Prelude to the Afternoon of a Faun." Debussy was his favorite composer. The Symbolists believed art should appeal to the senses before the intellect. That's what the "guest" found most appealing about Debussy.

"Are you ready for our game?" Sedalia asked.

"Yes, let's begin," he answered.

The rules of the game were straightforward. The "guest" remained blindfolded at all times. A young male took a woman to the love seat in the living room and inserted his stiff cock into her well-moistened cunt. He fucked the woman for two minutes. Afterward he approached the "guest," who sucked his cock to determine which woman had just been serviced. The "guest" had to correctly identify the woman by the taste of the young male's cock. If the "guest" failed this test, he submitted to anal sodomy from Sedalia, using a strap-on dildo. His compliance lasted a full five minutes for each incorrect answer.

Octavio used a warm washcloth to cleanse the young male before each entry into a new woman.

However, if the "guest" responded correctly, he had the pleasure of sexual relations with Sedalia on his terms. The "guest" acquiesced to this prescribed ritual because he so enjoyed violating conventions. He had no use for moral pretense, and loved being a voyeur to these amatory games. Besides, he was mesmerized by his own depravity. The true appeal for the "guest" was always the splendid and excruciating passion of masochism.

The mistress quickly summoned four women. The ladies, dressed in arousing clothing, entered the room immediately. The "guest" was thoroughly familiar with this quartet:

Adelaide: early 30s, well-kept figure, medium height, green eyes and long red hair. She wore a red babydoll, no panties, stay-up stockings with white lace tops, and black leather open toe pumps. She had a thick crop of triangular shaped pubic hair. Consequently, her cunt resembled an inverted pyramid. She was very restful to a tired eye.

Heloise: late 20s, full-figured, 5'3", with short brunette hair. Her eyes were beautiful, clearly brown, the long lashes curving upwards. She wore a black leather cut-away basque corset, which left her breasts fully exposed. Non-piercing silver jewelry was affixed to her nipples. She had pink-tinted, smooth skin with a scant patch of dark pubic hair in splendid contrast. She wore black hold-up stockings with lace tops and a pair of black leather sling-back heels.

Justine: mid-30s, plump, average height, large breasts, blue eyes, and long brunette hair. Her flesh was beautifully white. She wore a black garter belt with suspenders and black high heel stiletto pumps. She also wore two silver-black nipple flowers made of leather with small chains on her breasts. She had a pretty cunt, a very fully developed clitoris, and curly, luxuriant pubic hair.

Margot: mid-20s, slender, 5'8", blue eyes, with soft, blond hair swept away from her face and ears. She was very charming. She wore a fully boned black leather corset with front lace, long black gloves and leopard-stockings. For foot apparel, she wore some attractive open-side black leather pumps. She had soft, downy pubic hair.

The foursome always reminded the "guest" of whores photographed in the Paris brothels by Brassai, the Hungarian-born French photographer. Yet the truth was that this quartet of women held scarcely any attraction for him. The "guest" found each voluptuary to be so tedious and unoriginal, so willfully jaded and dull.

Gunter Steinberg also accompanied the women. He was a Jewish refugee from Germany, who fled with his family when he was still a young boy. Now Gunter was in his mid-20s, he had blue eyes and blond hair. He was 5'11" and his body was muscular, like a broad sweep of hard flesh, accented by a firm ass. He wore only a long black leather cape. He had a noble, well-proportioned shaft standing out 7" from his belly, and looked an inch and a half in diameter. The "guest" was visibly impressed; he achieved an erection instantly.

Once the blindfold was secured on the "guest," Gunter beckoned silently for one of the women to join him. Justine moved across the room like an angel-guided courtesan. The "guest" heard the sound of spiked heels cross the wooden floor, and stop in the vicinity of the loveseat, directly across from him. Justine laid down across the soft cushions. Gunter removed his cape, leaned over and fondled her large breasts. He slipped his index finger across the lips of her cunt; it oozed slow, like honey.

Then without any resistance Gunter lay on Justine. Her thighs opened easily. He quickly placed a hand over her mouth to help suppress her moans of pleasure. No one wished to tip the advantage of the game toward the "guest." Gunter adjusted his cock, grasped her ass firmly, and thrusted energetically. He deluged her cunt for several minutes.

All the while, the "guest" sat gracefully in his chair, listening to the audible sounds of two bodies slapping against each other during heated coitus.

After the requisite two minutes, Sedalia asked Gunter to cease his activity and approach the "guest." As Gunter drew near, Sedalia helped guide his glistening cock into the impatient mouth of the "guest." His lips parted effortlessly and he proceeded to fillet the blond German stud.

Always the consummate professional, Gunter merely stood with his hands on his hips and offered his cock to the "guest." Otherwise, he remained indifferent.

The "guest" worked his tongue expertly around the uncircumcised head of Gunter's cock. The taste was sweet and pleasing. However, the smell of Gunter's leather cape distracted him mildly. Yet the "guest" concentrated on identifying the mystery cunt.

After two full minutes, Sedalia stepped forward and gently retrieved the thick cock from his supple mouth.

"Time is up," she announced. "How do you answer?"

The "guest" licked his lips once more. "The taste on Gunter's cock is decidedly agreeable," the "guest" said, "and the fragrance pleasing to smell. I'm certain the cunt belongs to Adelaide."

Sedalia removed his blindfold. The smiles on the surrounding faces told the "guest" his answer was erroneous.

Octavio emerged from the hallway, carrying the accouterments for Sedalia's next role: a harness and strap-on dildo. The "guest," disappointed only momentarily, was a genuine sportsman. He fully accepted the rules of the game. Besides, he had consorted for so long with dilettantes of exchangeable gender, that he forgot how many women had strapped on dildos and entered him as men. After rising he bent over the arm of the chair and offered himself to Sedalia. The "guest" felt exposed and vulnerable.

Octavio helped secure the black leather harness firmly around the waist of her mistress. The dildo, made of dark Brazilian rubber, was meant to suggest the cock of a well-endowed Negro. The item was particularly expensive and had to be obtained from a special habitué in Mexico City. The dildo stuck out lewdly from between Sedalia's thighs, just above her cunt, and bobbed gently up and down.

Gunter and the quartet of women gathered on every side to watch Sedalia. Octavio helped prepare the "guest" by applying some clear, glistening KY jelly to his sphincter. The cold, greasy lubricant caused him to shudder a little. She also smeared the lubricant over the length of the dildo. The "guest" thought it looked like Octavio was masturbating Sedalia. In fact, the slimy gel reminded him of semen.

Sedalia's hands sensuously attended his entire body, stopping finally at his cheeks. Her hand continued to play with his ass, spreading his cheeks further apart. The "guest" felt her start to finger fuck him and he softly murmured approval.

Sedalia began her invasion cautiously, parting his ass with delicacy. Slowly and deliberately, she began pumping the "guest." His knees buckled slightly, and in spite of himself, the "guest" moaned out loud each time the thick dildo went a little deeper. Finally, with a quick arch of her legs, Sedalia forced the dildo completely into his ass. She leaned over and spoke in his ear confidentially.

"I love fucking you in front of Gunter and my girls," Sedalia said. "How does it feel to be treated like the whore you are?" she asked.

As the in-and-out continued, perspiration rolled down the back of the "guest," and the room seemed hot and the air smelled of sex. He was impaled on her deep, slowly articulated strokes, which burned like a hot poker inside him. Each stroke of her dildo made him bite his lower lip, yet he felt himself becoming strongly aroused and continued thrusting back at Sedalia, as she made the fake object twist and plunge. The sensation of Sedalia's breasts rubbing against his back, combined with the steady rhythm of the dildo, made him wild. The "guest" felt the pleasure growing inside him, building like a potent storm. His body shuddered and swayed as if he was in a somnambulistic trance, seeking enslavement.

As the "guest" was fucked by Sedalia, he seemed to pass in and out of consciousness. His knowledge of reality became vague and imprecise: Hail many, fell of greats, the Lord is with thee, Blessed art thou among women, and blessed is the fruit of thy womb, Jesus. Holy Mary, Mother of God, pray for us sinn finners, now, and in the hour of our death. Blessed Mary Margaret Anycock, we pray to St. Vincent de Paul, St. Martin of Tours, St. Anonymous, St. Eponymous, St. Pseudonymous, St. Homonymous, St. Synonymous, St. James of Compostella. Amen.

Languidly, he felt his attention drawn to a Requiem Mass across the street at St. Michael's Church. A devout Catholic, the "guest" cherished the Church's pagan dedication to cruelty. The torture of martyrs filled his imagination with perverse reverie. From the Messiah lashed and nailed to a coarse wooden cross, the most barbaric form of punishment in the Roman world, to the waxed saints' corpses under glass, tattered armbones in gold vaults, half-nude St. Sebastian pierced by arrows, and St. Lucy holding her eyeballs out on a platter.

Through the open window of the church the fragrant incense wafted and with it the fragrant names of she who was conceived without sin, Holy Mary, Pray for us; Holy Mother of God, Holy Virgin of virgins, Mother of Christ, Mother of divine grace, Mother most pure, Mother most chaste, Mother inviolate, Mother undefiled, Mother most amiable, Mother most admirable, Mother of good counsel, Mother of our Creator, Mother of our Savior, Virgin most prudent, Virgin most venerable, Virgin most renowned, Virgin most powerful, Virgin most merciful, Virgin most faithful, Mirror of justice, Seat of wisdom, Cause of our joy, spiritual vessel, Vessel of honor, Singular vessel of devotion, Mystical rose, Tower of David, Tower of ivory, House of gold, Ark of the covenant, Gate of heaven, Morning star, Health of the sick, Refuge of sinners, Comforter of the afflicted, Help of Christians, Queen of angels, Queen of patriarchs, Queen of prophets, Queen of apostles, Queen of martyrs, Queen of confessors, Queen of virgins, Queen of all saints, Queen conceived without original sin, Queen assumed into heaven, Queen of the most holy Rosary, Queen of peace. Lamb of God, Who takest away the sins of the world, Spare us O Lord. Lamb of God, Who takest away the sins of the world, Graciously hear us O Lord. Lamb of God, Who takest away the sins of the world, Have mercy on us. Pray for us O holy Mother of God, That we may be made worthy of the promises of Christ. Pour forth, we beseech Thee, O Lord, Thy grace into our hearts; that we to whom the Incarnation of Christ Thy Son was made known by the message of an angel, may by His passion and cross be brought to the glory of His Resurrection; through the same Christ Our Lord. Amen. May the divine assistance remain always with us. Amen. And may the souls of the faithful departed, through the mercy of God, rest in peace. Amen.

Suddenly a climax was on him, like a cloud burst, and the "guest" could contain himself no longer. He released a long trembling moan and, weak kneed, fell to the floor exhausted.

Then Father Collins, so kind and holy, offered the Introit for the Requiem Mass.

—*Propitaire quaesumus, Domine,*
[Have pity, we pray you, Lord,]
animae famulitu, pro qua hostian
[on the soul of your servant, for whom we offer]
laudia tibi immolamus, majestatem,
[the sacrifice of praise, humbly,]
tuam suppliciter deprecantes:
[entreating your majesty that through]
ut, per haec piae placationis officia,
[our holy offering of expiation]
pervenire mereatur ad requiem sempiternam.
[he may attain to eternal rest.]
Omnis caro ad te veniet.
[All flesh will come to thee.]
Per Dominum nostrum.
[Through our Lord.]
Amen.

After Octavio helped revive the "guest" with smelling salts, he resumed his status in the leather chair, watching the Spring wind blow the curtains outward. They were like the sails of a ship, he thought. Yet before sporting his blindfold, the "guest" briefly indulged his appetite for more hashish. The remedy always made him feel miraculously reassured, happy and secure. His concerns were distant as the sound of rain.

Gunter quietly motioned for Heloise, the 5'3", full-figured brunette. He pulled her close to him on the loveseat. Gunter was wonderfully cool and collected. He put up her legs so that her heels were near his chest, her plump thighs against his stomach. Gunter mounted her supple belly and lodged his cock well up her hot, soft cunt and pushed hard. One hand caressed her belly, the other rubbed her clitoris. When Heloise shut her eyes, she appeared otherworldly, and she tried to muffle the invariant murmurs of rapture which escaped from her mouth.

After the requisite time limit, Gunter's moist cock flopped out of her used cunt. Again, the young German man stood and offered himself to the "guest," who worked his tongue deftly around the head of Gunter's cock. The taste of cunt was luscious and satisfying. The "guest" sighed approvingly.

Two minutes later, Sedalia stepped forward and calmly retrieved the thick cock from his obliging mouth.

"Time is up," she declared. "What's your answer?"

The "guest" licked his lips one last time.

"The taste on Gunter's cock is positively arousing," the "guest" said, "and the scent delightful to smell. I'm convinced the cunt belongs to Heloise."

Sedalia removed his blindfold. This time the smiles on the surrounding faces told the "guest" his answer was exact.

Now the "guest" summoned Sedalia to his side. He arose and, after Octavio handed him a small knife, swiftly ripped her studded black basque corset, letting the shreds of leather clothing flutter to the floor like exotic butterflies. The "guest" gratified his eyes, now that Sedalia stood naked in front of everyone, except for her black leather high heel stiletto pumps.

He stood next to Sedalia and inhaled.

"I adore Chanel perfume," he remarked. "Now put your hands up over your head."

Sedalia did, and he lightly ran his hands over her arms, her armpits and her breasts. She was immensely aroused by his touch. His hands wandered over her until they came to her cunt.

"Spread your legs," he said.

Sedalia spread her legs as ordered, and the "guest" skillfully examined the outside of her cunt. His middle finger easily slipped inside her, and she couldn't help but moan. Her cunt was extremely moist. His finger still inside her, he looked her in the face.

"What a lovely smell your cunt has," he said, putting his fingers just withdrawn from her thighs up to his nose.

The "guest" kissed her enchanting breasts, stroked her dark-haired motte, and peeped at the jagged opening to her cunt.

"Feel my cock," he commanded.

Sedalia reached for his swollen member and fondled it.

"Now, suck it," he said.

Sedalia was one of the most unreservedly sensual people he knew. She gracefully went to her knees and absorbed his cock with devotion.

Meanwhile, Octavio prepared another pipe of hashish. The "guest" inhaled while Sedalia ministered to him.

The "guest" signaled for Sedalia to stop, and he disengaged from her mouth. She remained on her knees.

"Kiss my balls," he said.

Sedalia, by nature, was luxurious and her sexual appetite was so great that one man could not satisfy her. In the past, the "guest" had witnessed Sedalia indulge her craving for carnal ecstasy. It added greatly to her pleasure to know he was a spectator.

Before he fucked Sedalia, the "guest" invited Gunter to stand before her and provide his cock for oral sex. As the young German libertine advanced toward Sedalia, there was admiration and lust in her eyes.

"I won't do this," she taunted. "I'm a well behaved woman."

Then Sedalia leaned forward and Gunter deliberately thrusted himself into her painted lips. His swollen penis still tasted of used cunt.

The "guest" knelt down reverently and positioned himself in between her legs, spreading them apart. His hands opened Sedalia's lips for inspection and he used his tongue to lap up the abundant wetness. His tongue darted around her swollen clit, while her tongue swirled around Gunter's bulging cock.

Sedalia's oral actions gradually decreased and her sucking became less furious, as Gunter unleashed his considerable orgasm in her mouth.

Afterward the "guest" fucked Sedalia unceremoniously on the large table in the salon. Everyone watched and there was no conversation, except for Sedalia's frantic whimpering. Her body writhed under him, her hips met his every thrust. Each time, the "guest" plunged deeper into her, extending her legs over his shoulders for deeper penetration. His fingers in her ass stretched Sedalia and impaled her.

"Fuck me harder," she said. "Please, I beg you."

Soon Sedalia was thoroughly sensitive to his movements, her cunt constricted, a visible pleasure overtook her, and her frame quivered dramatically. His eyes rolled in the convulsions of orgasm; a beatitude of abandonment and holy grace possessed the "guest." If there was anything that filled him with faith, it was this blissful gleam of heaven. He always felt cleansed and innocent after he worshipped in the House of Sedalia. She was the cherished paramour, the desired mistress, the exalted, perfumed whore.

The "guest" watched his sex stream out of her cunt and over the white tablecloth. He genuflected and made the sign of the cross. The "guest" stood up and turned on one of the lights, but the room was full of shadows. A profound conviction of the illusion of everything seized him.

SHAPING LUST

Natasha Rostova

She had missed so much. She wanted to relive her past, not for the sake of righting wrongs or correcting mistakes, but because what had slid through her fingers seemed so painfully, utterly important that it was as if she hadn't even become fully shaped. As if part of her lay bent and cracked behind a wall of bricks, tangled in mortar she had applied with her own hand. The dry plane of her soul had become a battlefield, for in her heart she knew the truth, but her mind and conduct tended to lie.

She detested it, this lack, this void that reminded her every day of how she had somehow slipped, as if she had skidded to a halt while everyone else brushed past her. Ignored, no, they hadn't ignored her, not at all.

They looked her way, spoke to her, asked her questions, but they moved on while she remained still, like the fluid swirls of a marble relief sculpture she had once seen. The battling figures were caught, frozen, and yet saturated with the violent compulsion to move, to dislocate the rigid confines of the carefully constructed work.

She clutched her hands together, feeling her fingers tremble, feeling like a child at a carnival booth, treasures that dangled so temptingly beyond her grasp, aching for the sensation of the soft, plush animals, the plastic trinkets, between her palms. Her thoughts splashed around like so many waves, suffused with hope and lust and want.

And when he came to her one night, she knew she had found a way to unsettle the boundaries, resolving that she would deny herself nothing, brimming with the need to be wholly consumed.

She sat in a coffeehouse amidst the temperate rumble of voices, drinking in the luscious, thick scents of coffee and chocolate. It had been snowing all day, puffs of white vacillating with the force of a light wind, coating the sidewalks like flour. She sat near the window, safe and quiet with book in hand, indulging in the familiar melancholy that settled underneath her skin occasionally. She was good at pretending not to know.

She noticed him enter the coffeehouse, bringing with him a rush of frozen air, noticed his legs encased in worn jeans, the parka that looked as if it had been through more than one winter with him. She noticed his dark hair dusted lightly with melting snow, the way his hand slid into his back pocket as he reached for his wallet, the way he handed the money directly to the cashier instead of placing it on the counter.

When he turned around, she lowered her gaze to her book, pretending, always pretending—remember, she was good at that—pretending that he hadn't glanced in her direction, that he hadn't noticed her as she had noticed him. A chair scraped against the floor, a heavy, ceramic coffee mug made a dull click on the polished table.

Her eyes scanned the same sentence over and over, wrapping around the words as if willing them to make sense, her skin alert to his proximity. She would do nothing, she knew she wouldn't, but her movements were slightly more self-conscious as she sipped her coffee and patted her lips with a napkin.

The melancholy grew thicker, for this was like reading a book and already knowing the ending. No surprises here, nothing altered, the raging figures embedded in stone would not shift one centimeter, the dusty archives of history would not change to suit her whims.

She broke off a portion of muffin with her fingertips, no longer surprised by the fact that she so easily felt another person's gaze on her, for any invasion into her space, into the circle she had constructed around herself, brought all of her senses to full perception.

In one twist, that awareness could slip into apprehension, but not here, not with the ropes of chocolate, voices, and classical music in the air, not with the man whose jeans were worn at the knee. And as much as she desired change, her isolation protected her the way nothing else ever could.

When her coffee had chilled and the muffin had been reduced to crumbs, she closed her book and got ready to leave. She was still aware of his intermittent gaze as she stood and slipped on her coat, but was unprepared for his words.

"Excuse me?"

She looked up, off-kilter suddenly, for this wasn't the way the script was written. "Yes?"

"I couldn't help . . . I mean, I wanted to ask you if I could buy you another cup of coffee." He had a nice voice, reminding her of dusky, chestnut-colored coffee beans. The hesitancy of his words eased away a little of her unsteadiness.

She opened her mouth to refuse, but a split-second alteration nudged at her, and she found herself agreeing. "Yes, thanks. I'd like that."

He looked at her for a moment, almost as if he didn't think he had heard her right. "You know, you have very pretty eyes."

She couldn't help smiling; it was such a cliché line, but she did know certain truths about herself. "Thank you."

He told her his name as she slipped her fingers into his, breaking through her isolation and taking pleasure from the warm, dry sensation of his hand. He went to the counter and she sat down, rather pleased, but also apprehensive. Pretense was no longer an option, not now that she had openly acknowledged him.

When he returned, he sat across from her and asked about her. His brown-eyed gaze was intent and fixed as she told him about what she did. She was not used to being the focus of such direct attention, but she appreciated it, appreciated him for liking how she looked, for liking what she said and how she said it.

She had put her book on the table, and he picked up the worn, dog-eared paperback. "A Tree Grows in Brooklyn."

"It was one of my favorites," she explained, reaching for a plastic cup of cream. "When I was a teenager. I read it again every five years or so."

"Why?"

She looked up, startled. "Why? Because it's a good book. And it reminds me of me."

He smiled kindly, his brown eyes warm. She sensed then, with an intuition that had no sense of reason, time, or space, that she had nothing to fear from him, that he would not hurt her. A thought both comforting and unsettling, for had she not insulated herself because of the very fear that people demanded in return what they gave?

"You seem like you would have a good enough memory," he said. "That you wouldn't need reminding."

Yes, she thought, too good sometimes. Sometimes she wished she could forget, forget who she was, what she was, what she expected of herself. The demands she placed on herself were greater than anyone else could ask. If she didn't think or recollect so much, perhaps those demands would lessen.

She took the book back, brushing his fingers with hers, no rippling shivers, but a pleasant warmth. She looked at him for a moment, suddenly wanting to touch the slight stubble on his cheeks, to brush the pad of her thumb over his lower lip, over the bridge of his imperfect nose. No, nothing, nothing to fear.

"Can I walk you home, then?" His words were polite, traditional, and yet sounded like a response to her thoughts.

She nodded, slipping the book about youth and lost innocence back into her bag. They walked back out into the snowy night, boots crunching through the snow. Streetlamps cast burnt, golden circles on the white drifts. They walked up a hill to her apartment, bent forward slightly, breath in puffs of smoke, each silent in thought. She could taste the crisp air upon her tongue, like sharp crystal and light.

She was glad he didn't speak, not wanting to have to try and construct her own emotions into words, since she knew that was what he would expect from her. Instead, she slipped her gloved hand down his arm, pausing at the edge of his parka sleeve.

She tucked her fingers underneath the material, brushing them against the bare skin of his wrist. His response was minimal, a quick sideways glance that made the light flash and flare briefly in his eyes.

He followed her into the elevator, their faces reddened from the cold, and she stripped off her gloves after pressing the button. She thought she would be uncertain about this, that her self-protective instincts would conquer the need that had begun to simmer inside her, but then she looked at his ruddy cheeks, his dark eyelashes embellished with tiny flakes of snow. A kind of complacency settled in her, a ripe warmth evoked by her pure admission of what she wanted, what he wanted.

When they got to her apartment, they left their boots by the door. She hung his parka next to hers in the closet. He paused by the long window in the living room, looking out at the panorama of snow-covered buildings and trees, the sky colored saffron from the lights.

"Great view," he said.

"Yes. And it changes every day."

"How so?"

She approached the window and stood beside him. "Sometimes everything is glazed in fog, as if someone took a paintbrush and swept it over the scene. Sometimes the outlines of buildings are so sharp and clear that it hurts your eyes. And when the setting or rising sun hits the right way, everything is saturated in a feathery, cherry-colored light."

He turned to look at her, reaching out to trace his finger over one of her dark eyebrows. His gaze scrutinized her face for a moment before slipping down to her bow-shaped lips. "May I kiss you?"

"I'd like it if you would." As she said the words, she knew she was allowing him into her secluded circle, which would then no longer be completely hers.

He bent forward, brushing his mouth lightly over hers. His lips were dry, cold, but warmed quickly as she slipped her hand around to the back of his neck, tucking her fingers underneath the soft, flannel collar of his shirt.

She drew herself to him, gathering in the sensation of his mouth on hers, this primal mating dance that made her heart thrum like a taut, musical instrument. God, it was remarkable, even this modest contact, for it was as if she had finally given herself permission to touch, to be touched, to want, to be wanted.

She parted her lips under his, allowing him to invade her, his tongue sweeping the wet cavern of her mouth with a sudden swiftness. Her acceptance of him made him pull her closer, his hands sliding down to clutch at her hips, forcing their lower bodies into intimate contact. She was wearing black, cotton stretch pants that proved to be a thin barrier between them.

The roughness of his jeans pressed against her, and she felt his growing erection. A quiver of excitement glided through her, thrilling her, prickling her skin. His mouth slid hotly against hers, his teeth nipping at the plump fullness of her lower lip, his tongue licking at the corners of her mouth. His breathing began to increase, and she sensed his growing urgency, her own body echoing its own response of basic need.

He put one hand on the back of her neck, cupping her head in his palm as he angled his mouth more securely over hers. The dark, curly strands of her hair spilled over his hand, and she let her body fall against his, a soft moan escaping her lips as her breasts crushed against his chest. He was solid and good.

A sumptuous heat began to rise inside her, assuaging any lingering inhibitions. She slid her tongue into his mouth, tasting the hot muskiness of him, yielding to him as she simultaneously demanded his surrender.

She wanted him naked, wanted to shape her hands over his flesh, to feel the structure of his body with all its flaws and perfections. Her fingers tugged at the buttons of his shirt, baring his chest to her touch. Her palms smoothed over gentle swells of muscle, a light mat of crisp hairs.

He was not the brawny, bronzed ideal of fiction, but she didn't want that, didn't want fiction or fantasy or illusions. She wanted him, exclusively, this kind man with her now. She stroked her hands over his chest, their mouths still hungry, still devouring, his tongue skimming the glossy surface of her teeth, their breath merging in intermittent gasps.

He bent his head, pressing his mouth against her neck. She closed her eyes, her chest heaving against him, her senses swimming with the luscious sensations of heat and desire. Her blood grew thick with it, burning, painting her pale skin with the coral evidence of need.

She pulled away from him, her fingers trembling as she unfastened the buttons on her shirt—such a faded, old shirt, really, how many years had she had it now? Discarded, the shirt fell to the floor with a whispered softness. She stood before him, her small breasts cupped by a rather worn, lace bra, but she knew it didn't matter to him, that he wouldn't care that she wasn't wearing something more provocative.

She looked at him, their eyes clashing with a sexual force that fairly charged the air. His hands shook as he reached for the front clasp of the bra, fumbling slightly before finally releasing it and baring her breasts to his gaze and touch.

Her heart hammered ceaselessly inside her head, filling her mind and body with the voluptuous pleasure of sensuality. His heated breath brushed against her forehead, stirring tendrils of dark hair as he took her breasts in his hands, rubbing his fingers over the large, brown nipples that were already peaked.

"So pretty," he whispered, his lips moving against the damp skin of her temple. "Everything about you is so pretty."

Sensations radiated down her spine, settling in the juncture between her legs. She leaned her head against his chest, letting out her breath in a slow exhale, closing her eyes. The lush richness of this indulgence seemed to burst through her, raining delicate showers of sparks through her entire body. She took his hands in hers, tracing her fingers over the lines in his palms as she guided him towards the bedroom.

She lowered herself onto the bed, stretching her body out in a luxurious cat-like movement, letting him grasp the waistband of her pants and pull them over the curves of her hips and legs. He gazed with unhidden rapture at the sight of her bare thighs, the secret folds of her vulva concealed by a triangle of dark hair. She would have been anxious about being so revealed, so unfolded, in front of him, but he gazed at her naked body with an expression of such rapacious hunger that any embarrassment quickly waned.

And then he came over her, his brown eyes smoky as he captured her nipple between his lips, swirling his tongue around the areola. At the feeling of her sensitive flesh being so deliciously tormented, she drew in a sharp breath and delved one hand into his thick hair, silently urging him to continue. He turned his attention to her left breast, running his tongue along the juicy crevice underneath it, his fingers plucking and pulling at her right nipple until she began to writhe and pant under his sensual ministrations.

Her sex surged with heat and dampness, and she opened her trembling legs in both a plea and an invitation. His fingers delved into the lush, humid heat of her labia, his thumb swirling around her swollen clitoris until the ache became so painfully sweet that she wanted to touch him in return. He pulled away only briefly to divest himself of his jeans, muttering a groan of relief as his hard, slender penis sprang free from painful confinement.

She lifted herself up on her elbows, her hair falling in disheveled curls around her bare shoulders, her eyes covetous as she now drank in the sight of his nakedness. His erection was lovely, a compact stalk of hardness made all the more engaging by a slight leftward tilt. She was seized by a sudden desire to taste him. Grasping his wrist, she tugged him onto the bed and told him to lie back.

And then she plied his body with her hands and lips, sucking lightly on his nipples, skimming her palms over the planes of his chest, discovering the mole on his right hip, the configuration of his ribcage as his back arched slightly, the way his muscles tensed whenever her tongue darted out to taste him.

She moved lower, sinking her teeth into a thin ridge of muscle, scraping her fingernails lightly over his abdomen, reveling in the sound of his strained breathing and moans. Oh, how delicious, how thoroughly resplendent to touch and explore him like this, to allow her own body to revel in such carnality. She touched his penis with her fingertips.

"You don't have to . . . ," he began.

Eyeing the rampant member, she murmured, "I know I don't have to."

But she did. She bent and slid her lips over the hard knob of his phallus, darting her tongue into the little indentation as she eased her hand lower to caress the twin sacs tucked tightly below. He let out a low groan at the first touch of her hot mouth, his body stiffening slightly in an effort to retain control. She wrapped her hand around the base of his penis, sliding her enclosed fist up to the tip and back down again, loving the sensation of his smooth skin, his pulsing blood and heat.

She eased her mouth down onto his member, taking him in slowly, relishing the salty tang of him against the surface of her tongue, glad that he wasn't so large it would cause her discomfort. He tasted delicious, all warm male and desire, fairly throbbing against the cavern of her mouth.

Her tongue laved the surface of his penis as her fingers continued to stroke and touch the tight, wrinkled skin of his sacs. Her own body grew even hotter as a result of this pleasure-giving, her clitoris beginning to ache with the painful need for release.

"Wait," he gasped, reaching down to thread his fingers through her hair. "Please. . . . wait."

She pulled back, still enclosing his rigid phallus with her hand. His eyes were glazed, his chest heaving with a mixture of pain and pleasure. She released him from her grip, moving up to stroke her tongue swiftly across his lower lip. The knowledge that she had incited him to the brink of discipline thrilled her to no end.

She rubbed her hands over his chest, her fingers toying with his flat, male nipples as she straddled his leg and pressed her open vulva against his thigh. Ah, God, that was so good, that stimulation of rigid muscles and coarse hair against the sensitive folds of her labia, teasing the knot of her clitoris until she succumbed and shifted her body against his thigh. A ribbon of luscious tension constricted in her loins.

"Yesss. . . ." The drawn-out word emerged from him on a choked hiss as she pressed her taut clitoris against him. "Do it. Ride me."

She placed her hands on either side of his head, clutching the bed-covers in her fists, her body slick with perspiration as she strained voluptuously. Her back arched in a white curve as she rode his thigh to urge herself towards utter stimulation, impelled by the voracious flames thrashing her body, by his throaty murmurs of encouragement.

The exposed folds of her vulva rubbed furiously against his leg, her clitoris hard and aching. His hands dug into her hips, moving with the increasing frenzy of her body, pushing her onto him. She let out a low groan. Her head fell forward, her face curtained by a swath of hair as her rapture peaked and her body vibrated with a series of violently pleasurable shudders. Her sex swelled with moisture, bathing his hair-roughened skin with the viscous evidence of her ecstasy.

"Oh, fuck. . . ." She collapsed forward onto him, burying her face against his shoulder as her legs spread and splayed fully across his thighs. The throbbing length of his erection pulsed insistently against her. She drew in a heaving breath, her blood still simmering with arousal, her senses filled with the scent of his clean maleness and her own excitement.

His hands skimmed down her back, his fingers tracing the gentle bumps and curve of her spine even as his own body remained tense and rigid underneath her. His hot breath brushed against her hair and cheek, and she turned her head slightly to press her full lips onto the pulse that beat so passionately in the hollow of his throat.

Her breasts moved against his slick chest, creating a savory friction that sparked a renewed burst of longing through her nerves. His palms moved to cup her bottom, kneading and massaging the resilient flesh. His fingertips darted curiously into the shadowy cleft between the globes, and the sensation of his touch on her tender skin made her squirm on top of him. One finger slipped down to the aperture of her anus, almost hesitantly tracing the puckered ring before probing inside.

She tensed at first, but she was so unfettered, so gloriously open, that the forbidden orifice yielded easily. His other fingers dipped into the scorching fissure between her legs, two digits sliding into the slick, oiled passage that ached to be filled.

Her inner walls pulsed against his fingers, clenching around him as if desperate to keep him inside her. She stared down at him, her dark eyes smoldering with lust and the need to be consumed, the need that had plagued her. She suddenly wanted to shatter the boundaries, not simply unsettle them, not shift or move them, but destroy them, obliterate them.

"Do you want me to fuck you?" she whispered huskily.

His eyes darkened, and he nodded. She reached back and put her hand over his, their fingers colliding against the wet folds of her sex as he slipped his hand away from her. She grasped his rampant erection, guiding it into her slowly, letting their bodies merge with a deep, lush ease that made them both emit pained moans. His stalk filled her, fit her, vibrating against her, expanding the humid warmth of her passage with a wash of heat.

"Oh, yes . . ." She drew in a breath, resting her hands on his chest, her fingernails digging into his skin. Her body burned. "Oh, yeah . . ."

She lifted her body and brought it down again onto him, letting the sleek, heavy friction guide her movements. He reached up to capture her swaying breasts in his hands, her nipples like hard pebbles pressing against him. She shifted her torso forward so that her breasts would fill his palms completely, reveling in the feeling of his hands on her, his hard penis inside her.

She moved her body up and down with increasing frenzy, letting him slide halfway out of her before forcing herself down again, her bottom slamming against his thighs. Broken groans spilled from her throat each time she compelled their bodies into total unity. His hardness jarred through her, making her blood flame, firing the passion in her sex and in her mind. Her moisture bathed his phallus, flowing down to dampen the very juncture of their union.

His hands slid from her breasts to her waist, clutching at her tightly as he lifted himself and rolled them both over so that he now hovered over her. Her eyes drifted closed as her legs spread fully open for him, wrapping around his thighs and allowing him total penetration.

He thrust into her with a movement of his hips, wincing with the pleasure of utter submersion into her tense, humid passage. Bending his head, he licked a bead of sweat that trickled between her breasts, pushing into her with a frenzied rhythm that scorched them both.

Her entire body shook under the force of his thrusts, her sex swelling with blood and arousal. The intensity of sexual pleasure wrapped her in a hazy mist, stunning her into the surrender of her mind, of every ounce of her being. A tear suddenly slipped out of the corner of her eye, melting down into the glossy strands of her hair.

She turned her face away from him, hoping he wouldn't notice, and then unbearably relieved when he did. He cupped her face in his hands, pressing a kiss of such sweetness against her lips that the gesture stood in complete contrast to the rough carnality of their bodies. She accepted both from him, took both from him, parting her lips to let him into her mouth the way she had let his hardness into her body.

Hooking his hands underneath her thighs, he spread her even further apart for his thrusts, constantly filling her with this licentious, repetitive pounding. She buried her hands in his hair, drank from his mouth as pressure began to build in her body again.

Her hips writhed with hot fervor underneath him, pushing upwards as if she were trying to impale herself even more violently on his pulsing member. He reached down between their bodies, his fingers splaying over the burning, sensitive nub of her clitoris, stroking her, driving her pleasure.

"Come," he whispered, his voice deepening with the command. "Come on me, on my hand, all over my cock."

The husky order sent her over the edge. Embers sparked and burst within her, skittering quivers of rapture over her nerves again, causing her to cry out. She clutched his buttocks in her hands, forcing him into her until he could go no further.

"Stop," she hissed.

"I can't . . ."

She gripped his hard penis with her inner muscles, tightening them around him until their combined heat and her constriction made his muscles tense. And then a final squeeze from her, enclosing and immersing his penis, incited a series of hot, wet splashes.

A hoarse groan escaped him, a violent shudder of his body. His expression contorted almost as if he were in pain, and she knew he was, that razor-sharp boundary between pleasure and pain where the two merge together and distinction is impossible.

He fell on top of her, his breath rasping against her breasts, their chests heaving. She closed her eyes, drawing in the clean scent of his hair, knowing that the sensation of his body on hers would be etched in her memory forever. They eased apart slowly, limbs tangling together as their bodies separated. Heat and lust continued to linger in the air, and they both fell asleep under the carnal canopy.

She woke a few hours later, her body both sated and still humming with arousal. She slipped out of bed and reached for a cotton robe that she had once purchased on a trip to Indonesia. The vivid colors bled together at the edges, reminding her of what a melted stained glass window might look like. Wrapping the robe around her naked body, she went to the bedroom window and stared out at the saffron sky.

It was still snowing, but the city lights bleached out the whiteness, and she could only see a few swaying flakes. She pushed her hair away from her forehead, fully aware that the cracked space of her isolation was now evidence. Evidence of her ability, her strength, to displace whatever limits, or even whatever demands, she might set upon herself.

Pretend, yes, she would always pretend—remember, she was good at that. But it wasn't for negative reasons, not to hurt anyone. Only because her self-protection would not allow otherwise. Only because it would keep her safe.

The bedcovers rustled. She turned, glancing at him as he propped himself up on an elbow.

"Can't you sleep?" he mumbled sleepily.

"Not always. Sometimes I have insomnia, or I have too many dreams."

He looked at her for a moment through the dim light. "You're okay, though?"

She turned back to the window, hugging her arms around herself, drawing the vivid, cotton colors closer to her body.

She nodded. "Yes. Yes, I'm fine."

AQUA MARINA

Portia Da Costa

I only went there by chance. I was jilted and lonely, and I happened to be passing. My heart was sore, and my body a mass of cravings.

It was a bizarre phenomenon, silly really. I was unhappy, but I was desperate for sex. Two mutually exclusive states had arrived simultaneously. God knows how, because I certainly didn't.

I'd been lured into the gallery by an image in the window—a solitary siren of a nude, lit dramatically and mounted on a bolt of blue velvet. It wasn't a voluptuous body, the curves were minimal; but something about the figure intrigued me. She was a thin girl, pale and sylphine, with hair as black as sea-coal and long narrow eyes to match.

I hadn't expected it, but inside the spartan, white-walled gallery, the exhibition was *all* of her. My skinny naked girl. Inside she sometimes wore clothes, but it was her in every frame, every medium, every pose. And I understood what it was about her that had connected with my strange, erotic mood.

My girl was as sorrowful as I was. She too was lost, pining for something or someone. I got an impression of a sea nymph, of an eternal state of waiting; someone who'd been left by a lover, for all time.

The softer pictures were especially potent. In watercolours she glowed: ethereal, washed-out and yearning. She was a Lorelei mermaid but she had legs and a living woman's vulva. Her sex was abandoned like mine—and like mine it was crying for attention. I followed her trail through a series of silent showrooms, and she looked down at me coolly, a poem in alabaster and black. And shades of blue. One of the nameplates revealed her identity, Aqua Marina, and I smiled a little wanly at its aptness. Beneath it I read the artist's name too, Ruth Hamer, and felt better for her being a woman. A woman who worshipped this Marina. A woman who'd been obsessed, just like me.

The gallery was half-empty as I wandered around, but the exhibition itself had clearly been successful. "SOLD" stickers were everywhere and I felt childishly jealous? Other people would be taking my Marina away with them. Hanging her in their homes and their bedrooms. Other women would possess her, have a piece of her, and I couldn't afford even the smallest canvas. I could only look and dream. And want and want.

Was she real? I posed myself the question while I rambled from room to room. She *seemed* to have life. Her foam-white body almost throbbed with it.

In the last deserted room, a single large nude knocked me sideways. My body pounding with desire, yet strangely weakened, I sat down on a velvet-covered bench to gather my wits.

Aqua Marina was reclining on a rumpled blanket; her pale legs parted, her dark hair tumbling backwards. The tilt of her head made her neck a long white line: she looked vulnerable, wanton, inviting. I wanted to kiss her, bite her almost; adore her skin with my tongue and with my teeth. In the hollow of her throat there was a blue vein's shadow, and I imagined I could feel its frantic beating.

This particular "Aqua Marina" was more robust than all the others; she looked denser somehow, her colours more vivid and more singing. Frozen before her, I implored her to make a move.

Then gasped with shock when a soft voice said, "Are you impressed?"

A thin pale girl was sitting on the bench beside me. A girl with long black hair wound in two plaited coils. A dark-eyed sprite in an ocean blue dress.

Aqua Marina.

My surprise soon faded. It so was natural that she should be there. And alive. Not even the most talented of artists could only have *imagined* her!

"It's you!" It sounded stupid and I cringed. I wasn't usually this gauche when I wanted someone.

And I did want her.

Fully clothed, she was still sublimely exotic. The blue dress seemed almost an integral part of her, and her sharp perfume made my quim run hot and wet. The smell was fresh and ozonic, but another scent hovered beneath it. Something discrete yet oh-so familiar; she wanted me, and what I smelt was lust.

"Yes," she said evenly, "and I've been watching you. Following you around the gallery. I can see it in your face that you desire me, and I wanted to tell you just how good that makes me feel."

Her eyes were very bright but very dark—twin wells of bottomless near-black cobalt. Her hair too was the same odd shade—but more black and less blue—and her flawless skin was a perfect, stunning white. The colour of bleached shingle yet smooth and soft and moist. Her lips were matte, thinnish, but tempting as red wine, and her lush gown was as oceanic as her name. A complex construction of many floating panels it rippled and fluttered like wild water as she moved. At her waist, it had a loose, rosette-like feature, which I imagined covered a single ingenious fastening.

The dress made me smile, for the first time in her presence. It was a cliché. So obvious. So her.

"Do you like me?" she enquired, her smile twinkling. Her high spirits seemed weird after the *tristesse* of the pictures.

I felt confused. Was she asking if I liked *her*? Herself . . . Or her image as the exquisitely painted nude?

The painting itself now puzzled me too. It looked different somehow. The legs were more opened, the vulva more gaping, wetter. Its seeping arousal was much, much more than likeable. I nodded but I couldn't seem to speak.

"Good!" she exclaimed, showing her small white teeth and clapping her small white hands. "Then you shall see the original!"

Her fingers flew to her waist, and my suspicions about the dress were confirmed. With one flick, the drifting panels were divided, and beneath it Aqua Marina was as naked as her beautifully crafted image, her body so delicate that my own felt gross and lumpen. My idea of touching her seemed suddenly quite obscene. My fingers were too big, too square-tipped. I'd hurt her. I even flinched when she reached down to touch herself.

With no thought that we might be discovered, she started to stroke her breasts; pulling on her dark, pointed nipples, cupping her girlish curves, kneading and pounding with a roughness that was alarming. Her bared pubis, however, she totally ignored.

But *I* couldn't ignore it. It was there on the wall, and there just inches in front of me; veiled by a wisp of black hair that hid nothing and revealed much. The whole of her shining vulva was laid open before my eyes, but even so she made the lewd view even lewder.

Still massaging her breasts, she bent one knee and put her foot up on the bench. The other leg she straightened and stretched, pushing her foot sideways so her thighs were starkly wide.

Her head was thrown back in ecstasy, her quim wet, dark and pouting. With a grunt she shook out the weight of her hair, and just like magic the twin black coils unwound. A fall of crimped waves cascaded across her shoulders and down her back, and some slid forward to rest on her busy fingers. Her hips pumped slowly, the rhythm steady, a living tide.

The paintings and drawings, no matter how explicit, were nothing beside the fabulous reality—this manic wraith rubbing hungrily at her nipples. I forgot the images, forgot the gallery, forgot the other art-lovers who might find us any second. Fumbling, my fingers sweaty, I wrenched open my jacket, popping its buttons in my haste.

"Ah yes!" cooed Aqua Marina, her eyes opening, then focusing on my struggles. Abandoning her own teats, she darted forward, fingers flexed.

There was a moment of awkwardness. My camisole was tight and my breasts were large and heavy; the thin, stretched satin wouldn't yield. Marina cried out, her soft voice strangely fierce; then she yanked violently on the stubborn, twisted camisole, pulled it downwards and eased out my bulging breasts. They looked like two fruits laid on a platform of rucked-up silk.

My skin flushed and my body glowed with heat. My bosom looked bovine beside her pallid daintiness, and my nipples were twin studs of bloated lust. I was a monster beside my fey, mysterious lover.

Yet even so, she fell on me as if I were everything desirable! Her eyes passionate, she lunged her face towards my chest. She was ravenous, rapacious, overwhelming; snagging one nipple in her mouth while her fingers grabbed the other. Her shining hair dropped heavily across my blushing, burning skin, and covered her eyes, her lips and my deep shame.

Beneath that curtain of blue-black silk she nipped and sucked me. All I could see was her hair, and the sharp white line of her parting; but dear God, the marvellous things she made me feel! Relentless suction, acute pincer-like pressure, both syncopated, and both continuously varying. Her tongue flicked and licked; her fingers closed tight, made pain, then relaxed. I heard a shouting voice, but in my frenzy I didn't recognise it. Then, to my amazement, I realised it was me. Me, groaning and laughing. Me, crying out like a wild and savage beast.

The sensations in my breasts were like nothing I'd ever felt. Women had caressed me before often enough, but Marina was playing me like a virtuosa, rousing my flesh as if it were far finer and more deserving. I suddenly felt infinitely precious and bathed in her grace, and between my scissoring legs the delicious resonances throbbed and sang. I had my hands buried helplessly in the fall of her silken hair, but what she was doing made me itch to put them elsewhere. With a broken groan, I reached down towards my jeans.

"My darling, let me!" cried Marina, divine as Venus, rising from my bosom and dashing away my hands. With a deftness that defied the eye, she unfastened my buttoned flies, then pushed her hand in beneficently between them. Between the denim and me. One long, burrowing digit nudged aside my soaking panties, then dove blindly but with confidence inside them. With a little sigh, she took possession of my nest.

"Lift your hips, sweetheart. Let me in."

Tears dripped from my eyes and I obeyed her, shuffling my bulky body so she could better caress my core.

Her hand was so small, and the fingers cool and narrow, but when she touched my clit I exploded in a mighty surge. The pleasure was so enormous I bit my tongue. I tasted blood, rich and coppery, then forgot it. Black heat engulfed my loins like a great dark wave.

I cried and whined, but she stopped me with a kiss; plugging the sound while her finger continued its plunder.

On and on, she rubbed me. I was drowning in her power, just a mote in her vortex; spinning and bobbing between her mouth and her slim, white hand. I could do nothing except come and come and come.

When at last I surfaced, I seemed to rise up into her vulva. The very gaping maw of her sex. It was just a design in pigment, floating on the wall before me, but it shone and glistened like a thing of living flesh. I could smell the juices. Salt and pungent, they made my dry mouth run with spittle. I groaned again—tormented by a killing need to taste her—and my fingertips churned furiously in her fluids.

Her fluids? Aqua Marina's? No, I realised sadly, they weren't hers . . .

Feeling empty I dragged my hand out from my jeans. The gamey seabed odour was from *me*. My own juices on my aching cramping fingers. I'd masturbated, cried out and come to orgasm; and all because of a lifeless, painted image.

"She used to get me that way too."

Embarrassment was a crimson shock rushing through me. But with it came a strange new surge of hope.

It wasn't Aqua Marina who'd spoken, but a rather ordinary looking red-haired woman who was standing beside me. Like me, she was staring hard at Marina's portrait that hung above us, her stance relaxed and her hands stuffed in her pockets. Her tact, in not looking at me while I straightened my clothes, made me warm to her, and my first urge—to up and run—was swiftly past.

When she turned towards me and smiled it disappeared completely. And deep inside, my feelings were suddenly warmer.

She was no great beauty, no goddess like Aqua Marina, but her eyes were sparkling, and her deep pink mouth was generous. Her softly peppered freckles were both abundant and strangely alluring.

"It used to happen all the time," she went on, her tone more wistful as she sat down on the bench beside me. "One minute I was painting or drawing. And the next I was frigging myself senseless!" She shrugged and her unexpected grin was disarming. "Sorry. I should introduce myself. I'm Ruth Hamer."

The artist held out her hand. I lifted my own hand, caught my scent on it, then snatched it back again.

Ruth chuckled. "Not to worry." She glanced up at the naked woman above us. "I'll take it as a compliment. I like it that a figment of *my* imagination can inspire such lust in others."

"You mean she's not real?" I whispered. But the pictures were so vibrant, so alive . . .

"I was obsessed with her for a year," Ruth said quietly. "I nearly had a nervous breakdown. Stupid, isn't it? Falling in love with few daubs of paint and pencil."

"No, it isn't! *I* could love her . . ."

But love who? Marina? Or the visionary who'd given her life? This warm, real woman who looked better and better to me with every second that passed.

"Listen . . ." Ruth paused, seemed to make a decision, then stood up. "Let's go for a drink or something. I'm looking for a new model, and I want someone sexy. With curves. Not a scrawny little sea-creature like her!" She nodded in the direction of her former love.

"Thanks. I'd love to." And it was true.

I wasn't quite sure what I was agreeing to, but suddenly—revived by the heat in Ruth's eyes—I wanted it badly. I felt the familiar tingling trickle between my thighs.

"Goodbye, Aqua Marina," I murmured towards the wall as we left. "I owe you."

I could almost imagine she winked at me, and smiled.

THE CIVIL SERVANT

James Martin

Women are not like men. I'm not speaking of just the plumbing. I mean, my wife's got a decent job training some semi-executive types. Every once in a while they send her a woman from one of the field offices that needs some sort of adjusting. Usually those women bunk down at our place.

See what I mean? Someone comes to visit me on business and they've got a choice of Motel 6 or the Hyatt, depending on how much loose change they want to wring from their per diem. Nope, for these women it's the spare bedroom, the one that houses a menagerie of stuffed animals just for special occasions such as this. And at night I gotta get dressed just to pee.

So I'm driving through three and a half inches of slush to pick up someone named Linda at the airport. That's another thing, my wife won't drive when there's the slightest dampness on the road. So I'm whipping in and out of traffic because it gets her goat and finally the traffic gets so clogged we're practically parked. Nothing to do so I slide my hand up her thighs just to steal a little warmth and bingo, first surprise of the night. My cold knuckles bump against a fluffy little tuft of hair.

"When did you stop wearing panties?" I ask, trying not to let the surprise trickle into my voice.

"Well, it's a long story," she begins, a little sheepishly. "I phoned Linda just before she went to the airport. She was busy. One of the last minute things she just had to do was, um, she had to get what she called a good 'clitting' from her husband because she's going to be away for almost a week and says she usually can't go that long without a 'monster come.' So I asked her about it and she started telling me how he did it, you know, exactly how his tongue would lap her and how he could make it flick her clit just right, faster and faster until she would just come and come. So while she's telling me all this in detail I got hot. Real hot. I was standing there in my panties and bra and just couldn't help but slide my hand in and frig myself good. Suddenly Linda's breathing gets all labored and pretty soon all I'm getting on my end is this sort of 'Nnng' sound and then she whispers hoarsely that her husband's just walked up and started fucking her from behind. Then she starts describing how big his cock is and how it's ramming her hot little cunt. I've never heard her talk like that, but her little explanation got me coming. It was a gusher. Got myself all soppy. Honestly, I think I could have wrung out my panties like a wet washrag."

"So you didn't wear panties tonight because those were the last ones . . ."

"Oh, heavens no. I had to take another shower. It was all matted— my pussy I mean—from the come. It felt so good when it was all clean and dry. I didn't want to spoil the feeling."

"Jesus." The glass is foggy and across the streaked windshield it's a wonderland of red brake lights all starry and glowing. I'm thinking I could fuck her right there in the car and nobody would notice. I'm wishing she'd at least suck me off and I'm thinking of requesting this but hell, I figure maybe the moment is past . . .

Then we start moving. On the verge there's a car spun around, its right flank streaked black from where a car grazed it.

We're late to the airport. Linda's waiting at the luggage place. Carrousel eighteen—sounds like the State Fair but much more dismal. No rotating horses, and the bearded lady is working the late shift at the Rent-a-Wreck. I'm still horny, thinking of what it would be like to lift Linda's skirt and slip my cock into her from behind, maybe while she's reaching for her bag as it thumps by. I imagine her saying "Oh, thanks very much. It's often very lonely and impersonal waiting for one's bag. Much better with a good, stiff cock in you."

But we get introduced in a more conventional manner. She extends a hand. I bend to kiss it, knowing she'll be thinking "how gallant" and I'll be able to sense if she's had to frig herself on the plane. I sniff softly but can't tell, really. More research is needed.

Then it's off for drinks to Jack's, a favorite joint of ours. Linda wraps her fingers around a short glass of straight bourbon. I'm fixating on those long, slender digits; they're the kind that gets me all hard and I don't know why. We exchange a few jokes, dirty ones, through the dark cigarette fog. We're shouting because of the noise. Then the booze hits and I rock back in the chair dreamily imagining those long fingers of hers stroking her slit, then my cock. It keeps me hard well past midnight.

After too many drinks we drive home. The next few days pass uneventfully; each morning Linda appearing at breakfast in a long, thick bathrobe. She's civil to me, that's all I can say. My wife has returned to wearing panties, at least far as I know. We don't fuck on the living room rug while there are guests so I'm still horny.

Then Friday my wife is called out of town on emergency. At midnight I drive her to the airport. I check; she's wearing panties. This seems to me like a good thing, but I can't fathom why.

The next morning is Saturday. Just past seven I hear Linda futzing in the kitchen—doors clattering shut, a liner bag of cereal ripping accompanied by that labored grunt you need to help you punch through the impenetrable plastic bladder, that sort of thing. I rise creakily out of the bed, throw on a bathrobe and go downstairs.

Surprise numero uno: She's not wearing that ratty bathrobe thing. She's in a tee shirt, her long legs completely exposed to my tortured gaze. I'm suddenly awake, hoping she'll reach up into one of the top cupboards so I can tell if the shirt is the only thing she's got on. I want to say something like, "nice legs" but I can't bring myself to. The words just stick in my throat. I worry about these things. I'm civil. I think I'm way too civil and that's why I'm horny all the time with no prospects, if you know what I mean.

She finally notices me standing there. She's looking at me with big brown doe eyes like she's expecting me to say something. When she turns away I notice her lips flicker into a kind of frown. As she settles in her seat I stroke myself just a little. They say you can generate some sexual aggressiveness that way. Something to do with testosterone. I don't know, I still can't find the courage or foolishness to say to her, "Geez, you got dynamite legs and those fingers . . ." Christ, what would she think if she knew I thought her fingers were sexy?

Then the phone in the living room rings. It's the wife. First thing she asks is, "How's Linda?" in a voice sort of dripping with innuendo. What kind of question is that right off? I figure a married man doesn't get so involved with a houseguest to answer a question asked that way, even though said houseguest happens to possess various appendages that send the blood coursing right to the married man's groin. Linda does what she does and I do what I do. We share the house. We're civil. And besides, if he was familiar with her, a guy wouldn't be blathering on about it to his wife. All this is going on in my head until it throbs and finally I get so angry I blurt out, "she's got on a tee shirt that barely covers her ass. In fact, I can see the cheeks of it sometimes." A chortle comes from Portland, or wherever she is.

Then it's, "How about her breasts?"

So now I'm getting mad. What is the world coming to when your wife asks you about the breasts of a casual acquaintance slurping Cheerios in the next room? It's not a time to be civil, so I muster enough anger to give her both barrels. "They're wonderful. Full and ripe and they stretch the cotton so that you can see the dark coloration of her aureole right through. A kind of mahogany color I believe. And those nipples! In the cool, morning air they tent the shirt quite nicely. I'm thinking of just going into the kitchen at this moment and clamping my mouth around one instead of having a bowl of cereal, you know?"

I suddenly realize that in my excitement I'm talking far too loudly. Confirmation of this fact comes in the form of a low moan from over my left shoulder. Linda. She comes around the front of me and bends to set her bowl down on the low coffee table. She is not wearing underwear.

"Oh, Jesus, she's heard!" I mumble into the receiver, almost dropping it.

Linda is smiling. My head's about to explode.

"You see her? Is she right in front of you?" comes the reply.

"Yes."

"Tell her 'hi.'"

"Uh, Mrs. Anderson says 'hello,'" I mumble.

Linda nods, smiling.

Then my sweet executive wife exhorts in my tender ear, "Tell her she's got a nice body and you like the way her breasts seem weighty but don't droop."

"I can't tell her that! Besides, how do you know?"

"We played racquetball in L.A. She'd just been fucked. The court reeked of sex—you know how they're all closed off—and pretty soon I had to tell her about the big wet spot I was seeing on the crotch of her shorts. One game and we had to hit the hot tub to wash the come off her. Great thighs too, by the way. So tell her. Now."

So I give up and tell Linda she's got a fantastic body. "Do you think so?" she coos while cupping her breasts.

"Tell her to show you her pussy."

"She won't do that! Not for me!"

"I'm her boss."

O.K., so I'm outta my mind with embarrassment and lust. I screw up as much courage as I can muster and blather, "Mrs. Anderson wants you to show me your pussy."

"It's she who wants it, huh? I always thought . . ." Linda says, her soft voice trailing off as she inches the hem of the tee shirt higher and higher until the soft pink of her pussy is visible, then an unshaven vee of curls.

"She did it!" I practically yell into the phone.

"Fine. Now have her stroke her clit. I'll do the same."

Linda seems to be going along with all this, so I feel O.K. about telling her to finger her clitoris. I use the clinical term to make me feel like I'm someone with a little status like maybe a doctor or researcher so that I can get the upper hand. Linda walks her feet apart and gently saws an index finger through her slit.

"She's doing it!" I whisper hoarsely into the phone. Linda's cunt is maybe three feet in front of my face and I've started to hear the smoosh-iness as her juices start to lubricate the furrowed groove her fingers are plowing through. I'm glad I'm sitting down and my cock is relatively free. I can't take my eyes off her pussy as her hand starts to blur and that smooth, pink skin is set to vibrating. I can hear her breathing. There's short puffs and some little snorts that tell me she's getting close.

"Tell her to stop for a minute."

Linda isn't happy. Her pout is cute though. I'm beginning to like this.

"Taste her."

I motion her to come forward. Her knees press gently against mine and I'm aware of the heat rolling off her body. When I look up I notice her eyes on my crotch; my cock seems to have snuck out from between the folds of my robe and she's looking at it like a lion eyeing a sirloin. I take her hand—meaning she has to bend over a little—and thrust three of her fingers into my mouth. Her face hovers dangerously near my cock. My cock strains to reach her lips. There's a tension here that's becoming dangerously unbearable.

"Sweet. A little musky," I announce. "Just musky enough to make me want to fuck her."

At that Linda bends forward and bites my earlobe, the one that doesn't have a phone plastered to it. "Please," she whispers.

"She wants me to fuck her."

"Not yet. Feel her."

I slide my finger through her slit. Then back over her clit. She leans into me, I feel her hot breath on my neck. My fingers circle her clit. I feel her thighs tighten, forcing my fingers to smash against the hard little nub.

"She's very wet. I can feel the wetness that's spreading itself all over her thighs. She's trying to help me get her off. You know, her ass is swaying back and forth. She's awful close to coming." All I hear back is heavy breathing. It's coming in both ears. Two women, hot as soup.

"It wants a cock. It's seething with want. If my fist gets close it'll suck it right in. Oozing quicksand . . ."

Her voice on the phone is hollow, hoarse, "Her what? You need to be specific."

"Her pussy. It's small outside. Inside it's huge; it's pumping musky oil; it's sucking, trying to take in everything in its range."

I slide my hand fast through the moist folds of her pussy until my finger brushes against the crinkly pucker of her ass. She gives a jerk like she's had an electrical shock. Her tongue slithers into my ear, plugging it wetly. Heavy moaning in the other.

"Sensitive ass," I manage to blurt out, gathering courage, "I think her husband bangs her back there. She can come anytime. She's a fucking machine. In fact, she comes on the bus frequently. Yeah, that's right, just after her husband's taken her in the ass she gets on the bus to go to work. She can still feel the soreness in her ass. It makes her squirm in the seat. Then when she looks up and sees a bulge in someone's pants and the hungry look in those dark stranger's eyes she clamps her thighs together and comes right then and there."

There's a thud on the other end of the phone like it's been dropped but still I hear every nuance of my wife's howling. She comes like a banshee sometimes. Now her cries are rhythmic, pounding. I hear the creak of springs and imagine her ass lifting off the cheap mattress to push her cunt against her flying fingers. Then a long sigh and silence.

"Oh, god, I'll need several towels to clean this up," she says finally.

"But what next?" I yell out for help. I'm keeping Linda on the brink. Strange she hasn't made a move toward my cock. Maybe she doesn't want it.

"O.K., so tell her to lick your balls." The voice is a bit shaky but welcome.

At my command Linda's tongue pops out of my ear like a champagne cork and she buries her head between my legs. After a few seconds I gently push her head back and inch my butt up to get my balls to hang off the edge of the chair. Once I let her at it she gets all ravenous—licking, brushing her nose against my hard cock, taking my balls into her mouth so gently it's like they're wrapped in soft forest moss. I could drive a nail with my cock.

"Tell her to walk over to the sofa and drape herself over the back. You're going to take her from behind. Give her the phone."

I obey. What can you do? Linda takes the phone and leans forward over the back of the couch, her beautiful ass thrust out and illuminated by the glowing light filtered through the lace curtains. I slide my cock into her pussy. It's like buttered velvet. I push against the throbbing pillow of her ass, burying my cock to the hilt. Her free hand slips between her legs and I can feel it bounce against my balls as she strums her clit. I feel my cock get harder still. I'm slamming into her as she's trying to talk on the phone.

"Yes. Yes. Thank you. Yes, he's quite good, although I think he could be more assertive sometimes. I've been oozing for a hard cock since the plane, and, well, you'll just have to excuse me now but I suspect my cunt's about to get filled and he hasn't let me have my orgasm yet. I'm going to come like you wouldn't believe."

I make sure she has a hard time holding the phone—I'm bucking her hard enough to inch the sofa toward the window. Suddenly she pushes away from the couch and starts frigging herself with the receiver. I'm thinking this is a very strange thing. But then I feel the little curls of that icy cord whipping against my slick cock and balls and it's all over. I'm filling her. I think it will never stop. I'm throbbing from my ass to the tip of my cock and she's yelling "yeah yeah yeah" like a cheerleader in a tight game and I can feel her thighs clamp together and a warmth pour over me. We collapse in a spasmmy heap in the dim shadows behind the enormous, overstuffed couch.

And when the panting's just about all over we hear a strangled and crackly voice. It's the phone, juicy and hanging off the back of the sofa. Tinny sounds waft over us like savage music from a far land. We listen intently, and when it's over and the silence comes we smile knowingly and Linda nestles her head in my lap and with the tip of her tongue begins a playful flicking on my shriveling cock.

"Hello," says the strangled voice from the receiver. "Hello?"

BOTTOMLESS ON BOURBON

Maxim Jakubowski

He had often promised to take Kathryn to New Orleans.

But it had never happened. They had spectacularly fallen apart long before the opportunity arose. In fact, the travel they had managed to do in between feverish fucks had proven rather prosaic. So much for promises. They hadn't even visited Paris, Amsterdam or New York either.

So, whenever he could, he now took other women to the Crescent City.

For sex.

And fantasised about Kathryn's face, and eyes, and pale breasts and cunt and more.

New Orleans was for him a city with two faces. Almost two different places, the aristocratic and slightly dishevelled languor of the Garden District on one hand and the hustle and bustle of the French Quarter on the other, contrasting like night and day. The touristic charms concealing darker, ever so venomous charms. The heavy placid flow of the Mississippi river zigzagging in a serpentine manner through the opposing twin shores of Jackson Square and Algiers. The gently alcoholic haze of New Orleans days and the enticing, dangerous attraction of fragrant New Orleans nights. Nights that smelled and tasted of sex.

He loved to see the women sweat as he made love to them, enjoyed the feel of bodies sliding against each other, in moist, clammy embraces as sheets tangled around them. He took unerring voyeuristic pleasure in watching them shower after, washing his seed away from their openings, cleaning away his bites, the saliva that still coated their nipples, neck or ear lobes which he had assaulted with military-like amorous precision.

Those were all memories he treasured. Stored away for all eternity in his mental bank vaults. The curve of a back, the soft blonde down slowly being submerged in a small pool of perspiration just inches away from her rump, highlighted by a solitary light bulb, as she kneeled on all fours on the bed and he breached the final defences of her sphincter and impaled himself in her bowels. The sound of a moan, of pleasure, of joy. Ohhh . . . AAAAHHH. . . . Chriiiiiist. . . . The tremor that coursed through the girl's taut body as he discharged inside her or she rode the ocean waves of her oncoming orgasm.

Yes, New Orleans, his city of sex.

Endless walks through the small streets between hotel room episodes. Invigorating breakfasts of beignets and coffee and ice-cold orange juice at the Cafe du Monde; oysters and thick, syrupy gumbo at The Pearl off Canal Street; loitering hand in hand in the markets full of the smell of spices and seafood, chewing on garlic-flavoured pistachio nuts; obscene mounds of boiled crawfish at Lemoyne's Landing; hunting for vintage paperbacks through the dusty shelves at Beckhams'; po'boys at the Napoleon House; zydeco rhythms at the House of Blues; a routine he could live on for days on end. Until he would tire of the woman, because she bored him once past the mechanics of fornication, never said the right thing or talked too much or simply because she wasn't the woman he really wanted to be with in New Orleans.

There had been Lisa, the software executive, Clare, a lawyer who looked like Anne Frank had she ever grown up and liked to be handled roughly, Pamela Jane, the investment banker he had met at the hotel bar who wanted to be a writer and Helene the biology teacher from Montreal. He didn't feel he was being promiscuous; four women in six years since Kathryn. Some he had found here, others he had brought.

But somehow none had fitted in with this strange city and, even though the sex had been loose and fun, and the company never less than pleasant, there had been something lacking. Even at midnight, buckling under his thrusts on bed or floor or sucking him off under the water streams of the shower, he knew they were creatures of the day, anonymous, predictable; they had no touch of night, no share of darkness. And the darkness was what he sought. In women. In New Orleans. What he knew he had once detected under Kathryn's fulsome exterior.

He had high hopes for Susi.

She was Austrian, in her late 20s, and worked in a managerial capacity for a travel agency in Vienna, which made it easier (and cheaper) for her to jump on a plane for purposes of pleasure.

They had met in New York some months earlier. It was Spring and the weather was appalling for the season. The rain poured down in buckets and all Manhattan was gridlocked like only New York can manage. He'd been in town promoting a book and negotiating the next contract with his publishers there (he never used an agent) and was booked on an evening flight back to London. He'd been staying, as usual at a hotel down by the Village, off Washington Square. He had booked a car to JFK and it was already half an hour late. They had checked at reception and found out that the driver was still blocked in traffic near Central Square and Columbus Circle. He had promptly cancelled the car and rushed with his suitcase to the hotel's front steps to hail a yellow cab. They were few and far between and he wasn't the only hotel guest heading for the airport. Both he and the tall, slim red-headed woman went for the same cab which declined the airport ride pretexting the conditions. They agreed to share the next cab to come along. She was even later than him, as her flight preceded his by twenty minutes.

"My name is Susanne, but my friends call me Susi with an i," she had introduced herself as the driver made his slow way towards the Midtown Tunnel.

Despite clever shortcuts through Queens, the journey took well over an hour and a quarter, so they had much opportunity to talk as they inched towards their planes. She had been in town for a week, visiting her parents who both worked as diplomats for one of the big international organisations.

She did miss her flight, while he caught his with a few minutes to spare. E-mail addresses were exchanged and they had remained in touch since.

They had quickly become intimate. He'd sent her one of his books and she had remarked on the sexual nature of many of his stories and confessed to some of her own sexual quirks. She was an exhibitionist. Would sometimes take the subway back in Vienna dressed in a particularly short skirt and without underwear and allow men to spy on her genitals. She was shaven, so they had a full view of her naked mound. She was also in the habit of masturbating in parks, where she could be seen by passers-by, actually encouraged voyeurs to do so and knew that, sometimes, men were jerking off watching her just a few meters away.

She would pretend her name was Lolita. He asked her why.

Because she had little in the way of breasts and her bare pubis evoked a child or a doll, she answered. She was submissive by nature, she told him.

She sent him a series of photographs taken by an ex-boyfriend she had broken up with shortly before the New York trip. He found them wonderfully provocative in a tender sort of way. In the first, her long, skinny frame stood in contrast to the sluttish, traditional black lingerie of embroidered knickers, suspender belt and stockings almost a size too big for her. Yes, she had no breasts, barely a hillock worth of elevation and no cleavage and, he imagined (the photographs were all black and white), pale pink nipples like a gentle stain in the landscape of her flesh. Her hair was a bit longer than when she had been in New York, her eyes dead to the world. In the second photograph—he could guess the sequence they had been taken in, pruriently imagined what the boyfriend in question had made her do, perform, submit to, after the camera had been set aside—she was now squatting only clad in suspender belt and stockings, her cunt in sharp focus, lips ever so ready to open, her head thrown back so you could barely recognise her features. Photograph number three saw her spread-eagled over a Persian carpet and parquet floor, one arm in the air, both legs straight, holding herself up by one arm, like a gymnast, her face in profile, a most elegant and beautiful vision of nudity with no hint of obscenity at all, her body like a fine-tuned machine, a sculpture. In the fourth, she was standing and the photographer had shot away from crotch level and her body was deformed like in a hall of mirrors by the skewed perspective, the focus on her enlarged midriff. The one thing that struck him as he kept on examining the photos on his laptop screen was how her sex lips didn't part and how he wished to see inside her. The final photograph she had sent him (were there more? more explicit or extreme? she answered that others were just out of focus but his imagination as ever played wildly on) was both the sexiest and the most vulgar. She was on all fours, her arse raised towards the camera in a fuck-me pose, long legs bent, rear a bit bony, the line of her cunt lips straight as a ruler and continued by her arse crack and darker hole. Every time he looked at this one, he couldn't help getting hard. And he knew that she enjoyed knowing that.

He told her about the delights of New Orleans and invited her to join him there one day.

To explore possibilities, he said.

Initially, she only said maybe.

But he persisted, courting her with a modicum of elegance and she agreed. It took a couple of months to find a week when both could free themselves from previous commitments (ah, the sheer logistics of lust!) and arrangements were made. Flights to New York were coordinated— her job came in useful—and they both arrived in Newark an hour or so apart. Neither flight was delayed.

Curiously enough, there are no direct flights between New York and New Orleans and their connection went via Raleigh-Durham.

As they emerged from the airport luggage area, Susi smelled the heat that now surrounded them like a blanket and turned towards him, kissed him gently on the cheek and said: "I just know I'm going to like it here . . . Thanks ever so much for bringing me."

By the time the taxi dropped them off at the small hotel he had booked on Burgundy it was already dark.

It was summer. Moist, no wind from the Gulf, the air heavy with the powers of the night, the remains of the day lingering in patchy clouds, they were both sweating, their bodies not yet acclimatised.

They dropped their bags and he switched the air-conditioning a notch higher and suggested a shower.

He undressed her. Now she was no longer black and white. The nipples were a darker pink, closer to red than he expected and darkened a shade further when he kissed them. Her pale body was like porcelain. Long, thin, exquisitely supple. Since Kathryn, none of the other women, here or elsewhere had been anywhere as tall.

He escorted Susi to the shower cubicle and switched the water on. She looked at his cock, growing slowly at the sheer sight of her nudity. He soaped her with infinite delicacy and tenderness and explored her body under guise of washing, refreshing her from the transatlantic journey and its grime and tiredness. He fell to his knees and wiped the suds away from her crotch. Her gash red against the mottled pinkness of her pubic mound. She hadn't shaved there for a week or so; they had agreed she would let him shave her clean. A delight he had long fantasised about. He parted her thin lips, like opening a rare flower and darted his tongue inside to taste her. Susi shuddered.

The first time was good.

They were shy, affectionate, slow, tentative, testing pleasure points and limits with great delicacy.

She was extremely self-conscious of her lack of opulence breast-wise and he lavished particular care on her there, sucking, licking, nibbling, fingering her with casual precision until he caught the precise pulse of her pleasure behind the gentle swell of her darkening nipples.

They came closely together. Silently.

The later days filled quickly between wet embraces and ever-more feverish fucks as they grew used to each other's quirks and secret desires. She had always wanted to take a riverboat down the Mississippi and they spent a day doing so, passing the civil war mansions and lawns and observing the rare crocodiles still lingering in the musty bayous. Just like tourists. Which they were. Sexual tourists with, so far, no taste for the local fare. Breezing down Magazine Street in mid-afternoon as the antique shops reopened for business. Taking a tram to the Garden District. Lingering, with verbose guides, in the atmospheric cemeteries, with their ornate crypts and walls of bones. Visiting the voodoo Museum trying to repress their unceremonious giggles. He covertly fingering signed first editions at the Faulkner House.

Susi never wore a bra—she had no need for one—and neither did she slip knickers on when they would go out walking. Long, flowing, thin skirts revealing the shape of her legs when she faced the sun, only he knowing how unfettered her cunt lips were beneath the fabric, sometimes even imagining he could smell her inner fragrance as they walked along hand in hand and conjuring up the thoughts of other, lubricious men passing by had they known of her naked vulnerability. It turned him on, this constant availability of hers, this exhibitionistic desire to provoke. Walking along Decatur, passing one of the horse-drawn carriages waiting there for tourists, a dog held in leash by a small black child wagged a tail frenetically and brushed against Susi's leg. He smiled. She asked him why.

"He could smell your cunt," he said.

"Do you think so?" she remarked, her eyes all wide.

"Yes," he told her. "You smell of sex. Strongly."

Her face went all red, approximating the shade of her short bob and he watched her as the flush spread to her chest and beneath the thin silk blouse.

"It turned him on," he said.

"Oh . . ."

"And me, knowing how naked you are under those thin, light clothes," he added.

She smiled.

Later, back in their hotel room, she insisted they keep the curtains open when they made love, knowing any passing maid or room-service staff might see them in the throws of sex as they walked past on the steps outside the window, and as he moved frantically inside her, he saw she kept her eyes open, was actually hoping they would be seen. The idea excited her.

The same night, a few blocks before Bourbon, she suddenly said:

"I have to pee."

They'd only left the hotel a hundred yards or so ago, so she must have known the need would arise. He offered to go back to the room.

"No," she said. "The side street there. That will do."

It was dark, no one around, although the risk of passers-by emerging off Toulouse was likely.

Susi pulled her long skirt upwards and bunched it around her waist, her thin, unending legs bursting into pale view, the plumpness of her cunt in full display under the light from the illuminated wrought iron balcony above them and squatted down. He watched, hypnotised, as the hot stream of urine burst through her labia and splashed onto the New Orleans pavement. Her eyes darted towards the main street, begging for someone to come by. None did. Her bladder empty, she rose to her feet, the skirt still held above her waist in insolent provocation.

"It's a bit wet," she said to him. "Would you dry me?"

He got down on his knees, wiped her cunt lips clean with the back of his hand then impulsively licked her briefly. Her clit was hard, swollen. Susi was in heat.

"Fuck me here," she asked him. "I don't mind if people see us."

"I can't," he said. "We've only just got out of bed. I don't think I could get hard enough again so quickly."

Susi glanced at him with disapproval.

She dropped the folds of her dress.

They began talking.

"Does it turn you on?" he asked.

"Yes."

"What is it? A feeling of control over people, men that they can see you but not touch?"

"I don't know," Susi remarked. "My body is nothing special, but I love to show myself. Gives me meaning. It's a bit confusing."

"Your body's great. You shouldn't underestimate yourself," he answered. "But you must be careful. On the nude beach outside Vienna, with your girlfriend along, there's an element of safety, but elsewhere it could be risky, you know."

"Yes."

"Some people could read other things in your need to exhibit yourself. You could get yourself raped."

"I know," Susi answered, with a slight sigh in her voice. "Sometimes, I even imagine what it would be like. Several men."

"Really?"

"Yes. Five of them. First they fuck my every hole, then I am made to kneel, still naked, at their feet and they all jerk off and come in my face and hair."

"A bit extreme . . ."

"I know . . ."

He tried to lighten the mood. Already anxious as the darkness neared.

"The ultimate facial treatment. Better than soap!"

Susi laughed and led the way back towards Bourbon Street.

*   *   *

He described to her how Bourbon Street would be when Mardi-Gras came. The noise, the coloured beads, the floats, the beer, the wonderfully hedonistic atmosphere that gripped the whole French Quarter, the fever that rose insidiously as the alcohol loosened inhibitions and the music from the bars on either side of the street grew in loudness, competing rhythms crisscrossing on every corner, clouding minds and bodies.

The revelers on the balconies would bait the walkers below, sprinkling them with drink, offering beads for the flash of a nipple or a quickly-bared backside to massive roars of approval from the wild crowds.

He could see Susi's eyes light up. Yes, she would enjoy Carnival here. No longer requiring an excuse to bare her parts to one and all and the more the merrier.

"And what happens behind doors?" she asked him.

He shuddered to think. He'd only ever stayed in New Orleans for the first night of Mardi-Gras. Had heard mad rumours of uncontrollable excess, of sex in the streets. He'd once come across a range of video cassettes in a 7th Avenue porn joint in New York documenting the sexual side of Mardi-Gras here year after year. But like with wine, he was unaware which were the good years or the bad years and had never sampled any of the cassettes in question.

His mind raced forward. To a clandestine video cassette in a white box and Polaroid cover shot of Susi's porcelain-white body, face covered with come, labelled "SUSANNE 'LOLITA' WIEN, MARDI-GRAS 1999." A vintage performance, no doubt.

Bourbon Street night deepened as the beer flowed ever more freely, spilling into the gutters from plastic cups being carried up and down the street by the Saturday night-revellers. The music surging from all around grew louder, the lights more aggressive and the crowds swayed uncertainly. Young kids tapped away for a few cents or break-danced outside the bars, the neon signs of the strip clubs entered battle, pitting male strippers against female ones, topless joints against bottomless ones. A row of mechanical legs danced a can can from the top of a bar window, advertising further displays of flesh inside.

Susi was curious.

"I've never been to a strip tease place before. Can we?"

"Why not?" he acquiesced.

They entered the dark bar. A woman down to a shining lame bikini was dancing around a metal pole at its centre. A few men sat by the stage desultorily sipping from half empty glasses. They ordered their drinks from a sultry waitress and watched the stripper shed her bra with a brief flourish. The performance was uninspiring and the most exciting thing about the dancer for him was her gold navel ring which shimmied in the fluctuating light. His mind went walkabout as he tried to recognise the rock and roll tune she was, badly, dancing to.

Several shimmies and swirls later, and a liberal shake of silicon-enhanced mammaries exposed, the song (some country and western standard given an electric and gloomy Americana twist) came to an end and the stripper quickly bowed, picking up a few stray dollar notes thrown onto the stage by the isolated punters on her way off.

"Is that all?" Susi turned to him, asking.

"I think so," he said.

"But it's not even bottomless. She didn't even show her cunt!"

"Maybe because it's a bar. I don't know," he said, "there must be some local bye-laws or something. Don't know much about the rules in American strip clubs," he continued, surprised by Susi's interest.

Another stripper, black, stocky, took to the stage and a soul number burst out of the speakers. The previous performer was on the other side of the dance area, soliciting tips from some of the men. One whispered in her ear as she accosted him. She nodded. The man rose and he followed the woman, who now wore a dressing gown, to a darker corner at the far end of the bar. Susi nudged him and they both peered in that direction.

They could just about see the stripper throw back her gown and squat over the lap of the man who had now seated himself.

"A private dance," he said to Susi.

"Wow! Cool!" she said, one of the more irritating mannerisms he had picked up on when they chatted online back in Europe.

There wasn't much to see. The stripper moved in silence. The man appeared to keep his hands to himself but the darkness engulfed the couple.

"I'm turned on," Susi said in his ears.

"Really?" he said, finding the atmosphere in the bar quite unerotic, the black stripper now strutting her square rump a few feet away from his face.

"Yes," Susi added. "I don't think I'd make a good stripper. No tits, as you well know. But I sure could lap or table dance. I'd like to do that for you . . ."

He grinned.

"Sure. Later in our hotel room, I'll look forward to your demonstration."

"No. Here," Susi said, a deep tone of excitement in her voice.

"Here?" he queried.

"Yes." He could see that her right hand was buried in the folds of her dress, that she was fingering herself through the material. "Can you arrange it? Please. See the guy at the bar, he appears to be in charge. Get him to agree. Please pretty please?"

He shrugged.

It cost him fifty bucks and some haggling.

He walked back toward the stage where Susi was downing the rest of her Jack Daniels.

He nodded.

"It's yes," he said.

She rose, a mischievous glint in her eye. She took him by the hand and led him to a chair, nowhere near the darkness that offered shelter further down the bar but in full view of all. She pointed a finger, indicating he should sit down, which he did. Sensing what was to happen now, the bar attendant stationed himself at the door to Bourbon Street to prevent further spectators and a possible loss of his license. Susi camped herself facing the chair he now sat on and pulled her dress above her head. You could hear a pin drop as the barman and the few spectators dotted around the stage witnessed her naked form emerge from the cocoon of the fabric, whiter than white, shaven mound plump, and so bare, like a magnet for their disbelieving eyes. A couple of the attendant strippers peered out from the dressing room on the side of the bar counter.

The music began and he had no clue what it was, his mind in such turmoil.

Susi began writhing a few inches away from him, knowing all too well how much she was the centre of attraction.

She danced, wriggled, swerved, bent, squatted, obscenely, indecently, her hands moving across her bare flesh in snake-like manner, her fingers grazing her by-now erect nipples, descending across the flatness of her pale stomach and even, although he hoped he was, because of his close proximity to her dance, the only one to notice, lingering in the region of her cunt and actually holding her lips open for a second or so.

He felt hot. Even though he by now knew every square inch of her skin, this was a new Susi, a creature he had only guessed at.

It was quickly over.

He held his breath.

A few people clapped in the background.

Susi's face was impassive but flushed.

She picked up her discarded dress and slipped into it.

"That was good," she said. "Can we go, now?"

On their way to the door and the muted sounds of Bourbon Street, the barman handed Susi a card.

"You're quite a gal," he said, as she brushed past him. "My name is Louis. If you're seeking more serious fun, just call me."

Susi slipped the card into her side pocket without even acknowledging him and emerged into the twilight.

"I'm hungry," she said.

One of the nearby hotels had an oyster bar. They shared a plateful each of oysters and clams. She smothered each with a generous helping of tomato flavoured horseradish as she gulped them down.

"One of your fantasies realised?" he asked her.

"You might say that," Susi answered. "But there are others."

"I have no doubt," he smirked, still uncertain of the path they had embarked upon.

"Don't look so glum," she smiled. "You did say we would come to New Orleans and explore possibilities, didn't you?"

"I suppose I did."

The rawness of their sex that night was compelling and savage. She sucked him with hungry determination and wouldn't allow him to withdraw from her mouth when he felt his excitement rise. Usually, he would hold back and penetrate her, which prolonged the pleasure. He came in her mouth. She let him go and he watched her tasting his come before she finally swallowed it.

"You taste sweet and sour," Susi said.

The following day, she insisted they visit a place called The Orgy Room. On Bourbon, of course. As pornographic films were projected on the walls, a group of people pressed together like sardines in a can were force fed into an exiguous room and allowed to jostle and play on pneumatic fun fair carpets or were they waterbeds? Most were drunk. The constant wall of sound was, he felt, somewhat unpleasant, and far from arousing. Soon, he was separated from Susi in the swaying crowd but could still see her at the other end of the room. She deliberately exaggerated her movements and rubbed herself against others, often pulling her short black leather mini skirt up her thighs so her genitals were fully visible to those closer to her. He observed as various men took note of her and soon congregated around her. He could see her face flush amongst the laughs and the human wave of bodies soon directed her against the back wall where she stood motionless, her skirt now bunched at her midriff and a couple of men frantically fingering her as she pretended to ignore them. He watched from afar, not quite knowing what he now felt. Eventually, the siren rang and the crowds thinned and made for the exit. As Susi reached him, trailed by the puzzled men she had snared in her net, she took his hand in hers. The men observed this and interrupted their progress towards her. Sweat poured down her forehead, her thin red hair plastered down against her scalp. They walked out. He looked up at the sky. There was a storm brewing.

"I came," she remarked. "Jesus . . ."

"Susi . . ."

"Take me back to the hotel," she ordered. "Tonight, I want you to fuck my arse."

The next morning, she expressed a desire for breakfast in bed. They had woken up too late for the hotel room service. He volunteered to fetch food from a nearby 24-hour deli. The night rain had swept away the heat momentarily and the cool air came as a welcome relief as he walked the few hundred meters to the shop and back.

When he returned to the room, Susi was speaking on the phone. She put the receiver down as he walked in.

Maybe he shouldn't have asked, but he did. Force of habit. He'd left the hotel number with a few friends back in London, in case of sudden business, magazine commissions.

"Was that for me?" he asked Susi.

"No," she replied. "It was Louis, from the bar."

"I see."

"I wanted to find out about the . . . secret places, the real New Orleans, so to speak . . ." she looked down as she spoke, the white sheet lowered down to the whirl of her navel. There were dark patches under her green eyes, from lack of sleep and the intensity of the sex. He'd never found her as attractive as now, he knew.

He set the bread, snacks and fruit juice bottles down on the bedside table.

"And?"

"And he's given me a few addresses. Said it's his night off, offered to show us around."

"We barely know him. Do you think it would be safe?"

"You always told me that New Orleans was a city of sex. Not vampires or voodoo. That it was constantly in the air, you used to say, remember."

"I did."

"Well, it would be silly not to find out more, wouldn't it?"

"I suppose not."

"He's picking us up from the hotel lobby around nine tonight. He'll show us beyond Bourbon."

They walked through the market at midday. Beyond the food area full of cajun spice mixtures, chicory blends, pralines, nuts and colourful fruit and fish, there was a flea market of sorts, stalls selling souvenirs, bric a brac, clothing, counterfeit tapes of zydeco music, hand-made bracelets and all the flotsam that brings people to a tourist town. On a previous visit on their second day here, Susi had spotted a black felt table where a long-haired superannuated hippy was selling fake body jewellery, which could be worn without the need for piercings. She selected several pieces.

Late afternoon, back in the room, she retreated to the bathroom for a shower. She emerged half an hour later, splendidly naked and scrubbed clean, her dark red hair still wet.

"Do you like it?" she asked him.

He looked up from his magazine.

She took his breath away. How could her body be so damn pale and so heartbreakingly beautiful? She had rouged her nipples a darker shade of scarlet and accentuated the bloody gash of her sex lips with the same lipstick. A courtesan adorned for sexual use.

She had also strategically placed the small rings and clips she had purchased in the market across her body. A ring hung from her lower lip, stainless steel clamps from her hardened nipples and a stud appeared to have been pierced into her clitoris from which a thin golden chain hung, which she had until now worn around her wrist.

"Like a creature from a dream," he said. "From a very dirty dream, may I add. You look great." He could feel his cock swell already inside his boxer shorts.

"Come here," he suggested.

"No," she said. "I have to dry my hair. Anyway I also want you to conserve your energy. Your seed . . ." she concluded with a smile.

"As you wish," he said, unable to keep his eyes away from her jewelled cunt.

"This is my fantasy night," she said.

It felt like a stab to his chest.

He already knew what she had arranged with Louis.

It was a very private club on Ramparts, at the other end of the Quarter. From outside, it looked like any other house, slightly run down and seedy. But the moment you passed the door, you could almost smell the familiar fragrances of money and sin.

"You sure you still want to?" Louis asked her as they walked in to the lobby.

"Yes," Susi said.

Louis guided them into a large room full of framed Audubon prints and a fake fire-place and asked them to make themselves comfortable. And left through another door after showing them the drinks cabinet.

Alone with her, he said nothing at first. Then, seeing his unease, Susi said:

"It's not quite the fantasy I told you about. Just the second part, really . . ."

"Oh. . . ."

"And I want you to be one of the men . . ."

"I'm not sure I. . . ."

"I'd feel more comfortable with you there," she interrupted him. "You'll enjoy it, you'll see. Anyway, you knew what I am, what I like, when you suggested we come here. You'll get a kick out of it. You like watching. I see it in you. Even when we fuck, your brain is like a machine, recording it all, storing every feeling, every tremor, every moan away. Memories that will last forever."

Before he could answer her, the door opened and Louis came through with three other men. Two of them were black, tall, built like football players, the other white man was middle-aged, stocky, silver-haired.

"Here we are, Susanne," he said, without introducing the others.

"You're in charge now . . ."

The thought occurred to him he had called her Susanne. "Friends call me Susi" she had said back all those months ago as they caught that New York cab. So Louis was not considered a friend!

Susi indicated the centre of the heavily carpeted room.

"A circle around here," there was something more Germanic than usual in her voice as she ordered them to clear the heavy chairs away from the room's epicenter.

The circle soon emerged, as the furniture was set aside.

Susi stationed herself there and undressed.

"You all stay dressed," she said to the five men. "Just cocks out, okay?"

She positioned herself and as the men's eyes followed her every movement she opened her legs and stuck a finger inside herself. She was visibly already very wet and there was an audible squishing sound as the finger penetrated her. Louis unzipped his jeans and pulled his cock out. The others followed his example. One of the black guys, he noticed, was enormous, at least 10 inches and thick as hell. He discreetly examined the other cocks, and was reassured that his was still reasonably sized in comparison. Joint second biggest, he reckoned, not without a wry thought.

Susi now introduced a second finger into her cunt, secretions now flooding out and dripping down the gold chain.

There was both a sense of the ceremonial and a sense of the absurd about them all. Six human beings masturbating frantically. Five men with their cocks out, fingers clenching their shafts, rubbing their coronas, teasing their glans, heavy balls shuddering below as the woman in white at their centre teased her cunt in a parody of lovemaking.

"Not yet," she warned. Had one of them intimated he was close to come?

Time felt as if it had come to a standstill, swallowing all their halting sounds of lust.

She adjusted her stance, now kneeling, her hand buried deep inside her crotch, almost like praying and indicated she was finally ready for her baptism of cum.

The men came, one by one, spurting their thick, white seed into her face, as she leaned forward to receive them. He was the third to orgasm and noticed the arc of his ejaculate strain in the air separating him from her body and the final drips landing in the thin valley between her muted breasts. Soon, she was covered with the men's seed, like syrup dribbling across her thin eyebrows and down her cheeks. He didn't think she herself had actually come, although all five men had.

There was a long silence as they all stood there, the men with their cocks shrivelling already, the drenched woman in quiet repose.

Finally, Louis spoke:

"Well, Susanne, just the way you wanted it?"

She nodded as the men began zipping up.

"Care to move on to your next fantasy?"

What next fantasy? he wondered. What else was she after?

"Yes," she said, rising to her feet and picking up the green towel Louis had previously left on a nearby chair and wiping her face clean.

"Good," Louis said. "There's quite a crowd out there waiting."

Still not bothering to put her clothes on again, Susi asked him:

"Can you give us a few minutes alone, before, please?"

"Sure, Susanne," he said and the four men trooped out of the room.

"So," he asked her the moment after they had closed the door. "What else have you planned for the menu, Susi? It must be a fantasy I am unaware of. You're full of surprises."

"I know," she answered. "I should have told you before. I'm sorry. It'll only happen once and then I shall return to my boring life, you know. Maybe the time will even come for me to settle down, marry some decent guy and even have kids. A nice *hausfrau*."

"What are you talking about, Susi?"

"I want to be fucked in public . . ."

"What?"

"Just one man, that's all. But I have to know what it feels like with people watching, you see. You said this was a city of sex, I'll never have the opportunity again. Just this once. We're miles away from home, no one knows us, we're not likely to come here again. Only you and I will know . . ."

"You mean with me?" he asked.

"Yes. If you wish to be the one."

"I . . ." He was at a loss for words.

"It's all arranged with Louis. We'll even get paid five hundred dollars."

"It's not the money. . . ."

"I know . . . I understand if you don't want to. Arrangements have also been made for another man, if you decline. But I do want you to watch . . . really . . ."

His thoughts were in turmoil. This had all gone too far. He had played with fire and the flames were now reaching all the way through to his gut. As they always did. He never learned the lessons, did he? Long before Kathryn, he'd been going out with a woman who was avowedly bisexual and it had planted a bad seed in his mind. Not for him the common fantasy of watching two women together, no. The idea of bisexuality had preyed on his mind for months and one day, curious to know what it must feel like to suck a man's cock, from the woman's point of view (after all, they never minded sucking his, did they?), he had agreed to an encounter with another man. He distressingly discovered he enjoyed sucking cock and had been irregularly doing so for years now, in secret, whenever a woman was not available and the tides of lust submerged him. He had never told any woman about this. Feared they would misunderstand. Blamed his insatiable sexual curiosity. Even Susi wouldn't understand, he knew. Not that this was the time to tell her. He always went that step too far. And paid for it. Emotionally.

"I just can't, Susi. I can't."

"But will you . . ."

"Yes, I will watch."

There was a crowd in the other room of the house on Ramparts. They had been drinking liberally for an hour or so, it appeared. There was a heavy air of expectation about them.

Louis led Susi in. Like a ritual, holding the thin gold chain secured to her clitoris, her eyes covered by a dark blue piece of cloth. This is how she had wanted it to happen. She didn't wish to see the audience. Just feel it and hear it around her as she was fucked.

They had cleared a low table in a corner of the room and Susi was taken to it, carefully installed across so that all the light was focused on her already gaping and wet red gash and positioned on all fours, her fake jewellery taken from her body and was helped to arch her back and raise her rump to the right level. The man who had won the quickly organised auction came forward. He looked quite ordinary, late 20s, an athlete's build, not very hairy, he had kept his shirt on but his cock already jutted forward as he approached Susi's receptive body. He was uncut and his foreskin bunched heavily below the mushroom cone of his glans. He was very big.

The man found his position at Susi's entrance and buckled forward and speared her. A few spectators applauded but most remained quite silent. From where he sat, he couldn't see Susi's face, only her white arse and the hypnotising sight of the dark, purple cock moving in and out her, faster and faster, every thrust echoed by a wave of movement on the periphery of her flesh, like a gentle wind caressing the surface of a sand dune.

It lasted an eternity—longer he knew that he would have ever managed. The guy was getting his money's worth. As was the audience, many of whom were blatantly playing with themselves in response to the spectacle unfolding before them. She would be very sore at the end of this. Sweat coated Susi's body like a thin shroud as the man dug deeper and deeper into her and he watched her opening enlarge obscenely under the pressure of that monstrous cock.

Shamefully, he couldn't keep his eyes away from the immediate perimeter of penetration, noting every anatomical feature with minute precision, the vein bulging on the side of the invading cock as it moved in and out of sight in and out of her, the very shade of crimson of her bruised labia as they were shoved aside by the thrusts, the thin stream of inner secretions pearling down her inner thigh, and neither could he help himself getting hard again watching the woman he knew he had fallen in love with getting fucked in public by a total stranger.

That night, she curled up against him in the slightly exiguous hotel room bed, drawing his warmth . . . and tearing him apart.

They had packed and waited in the hotel's lobby for the airport shuttle they had booked earlier that morning. One suitcase each, a Samsonite and a Pierre Cardin. They hadn't discussed yesterday night, acted as if nothing had happened. They had the same flight to Chicago where they would part. He on to London, she to Vienna. Now he knew, he would want to see her again, in Europe. It would be easier. They had come through this crazy experience and he realised how much she had touched his heart.

The blue mini-coach finally arrived, ten minutes late and he picked up the suitcases and carried them to the pavement. As he was about to give her case to the shuttle's driver, Susi put her hand on his arm.

"Yes?"

He had never realised how green her eyes were.

"I'm not coming," she calmly said. "There's nothing for me back home, I'm staying in New Orleans."

"But . . ."

She silenced him with a tender kiss to his cheek. When he tried to talk again, she just quietly put a finger to his lip indicating he should remain silent.

"No," she said. "No explanations. It's better like this."

The driver urged him to get on board.

As the shuttle moved down Burgundy, he looked out of the window and saw Susi walking to a parked car with her suitcase. Louis stood next to it. The shuttle turned the corner and he lost them from sight.

The short drive to Moisan was the loneliest and the longest he had taken in his life.

He would, in the following years, continue to write many stories. That was his job after all. In many of them, women had red hair, green eyes and bodies of porcelain white. And terrible things happened to them: rape, multiple sex, prostitution, drug addiction, even unnatural forced sexual relationships with domestic animals. But they all accepted their fate with a quiet detachment.

He would continue to occasionally meet up with strange men and take uncommon pleasure in sucking them off. This he did with serene indifference, because in his mind it didn't count. It was just sex, meat— it was devoid of feelings.

He never visited New Orleans or saw or heard of Susi again.

OPEN SPACES

Adhara Law

She liked to fuck in public places. In the elevator, she settled against him inconspicuously as the heat of seven bodies filled the car. His fingers toyed with the edge of her short skirt and brushed against the back of her thigh where the curve of her ass joined with her leg. A soft tickle of rough fingertips. Slowly now, he slipped the length of his index finger deeper into the warmth between her thighs. Seven people. Seven sets of eyes staring straight ahead into the dead reflection of smudged metal. Seven faces whose expressions never changed even when her own mirror image opened its mouth in a tiny, quick gasp to swallow the stifling air of the elevator.

His finger moved inside the soaked heat of her pussy and eased into her with excruciating slowness. The barely perceptible sway of her hips, back and forth, was hidden from the mirror of the elevator doors by a tallish, middle-aged man in a dark gray suit. She could smell his cologne as it wafted back to her, a spicy haze of sweat that meandered its way through the cramped elevator. Sixth floor. The odor did not belong to the man whose finger was now buried to the hilt between her legs, and that made her wetter. Seventh floor. A woman standing against the left wall shifted her weight and blew a stream of air between her lips. The woman's stare was solidly locked to the readout of steadily increasing floor numbers. Eighth floor. She ground her hips as invisibly as possible against his hand, which stayed as motionless as it could while his finger swirled and slid faster inside of her. She felt the tip of his thumb press lightly against the tiny flower of her ass, teasingly pushing but not entering. Her breath escaped in tiny, soundless whispers between her barely parted lips. Ninth floor. People shifted and fidgeted as they readied themselves for departure. A man to her right reached down and grabbed his briefcase off the floor, startling her momentarily and making her wonder if they'd been caught. Her legs trembled visibly now. Tenth floor. The doors opened, the passengers departed, the doors closed, and she clenched her teeth in a barely contained scream as she fell against him, the insides of her thighs soaked with her orgasm, her chest rising and falling in quick jumps.

He told her she was impenetrable.

She told him she wanted to fuck him in the American Museum of Natural History. He made a low sound in his throat, shook his head slightly, but let her lead him by the hand through the crowded hallways and into the shadows of man's evolution. Stragglers passed them by as they hurried to the exits a half-hour before closing. In the corner next to *Australopithecus*, she pressed her body against his, shoving the small of his back almost painfully against the cold metal of the rail. A young man and woman passed by them on the other side of the room, too occupied with each other to notice them. Her hands worked furiously to pull down the zipper of his pants. There was a shakiness in his breath and a hesitation in his hands as he ran them down the back of her soft sweater. He kissed her, he gripped her wrists in a futile attempt to slow her down.

But there was no slowing down. With a single pull, she opened his zipper and hiked her skirt up at the same time. Pressing her mouth against his, she snaked her tongue past his lips and pulled the top of his cotton boxers down. She cupped the length of his cock in her hand and gripped the shaft. A smile shimmered around the corners of her mouth as she ran the palm of her hand over the silk skin of his cock and tickled its base with her long, painted fingernails. His teeth clenched to keep his voice down. After a quick glance around the empty room, she locked her hips with his and slipped the full length of his cock inside of her in one smooth, orchestrated move.

The thin echo of disjointed footfalls from the hallways of the massive museum drifted in and surrounded them. Her eyes darted every so often toward the doorway of the room, and with every glance she bucked her hips harder against his. He moved down and sucked the softness of her earlobe into his mouth.

"Don't fuck me," he whispered.

With a startled expression—her mouth hung open and her eyes stretched wide, showing their full, glaring whites even in the shadowy alcove of the museum—she turned her face up toward him. Her hips missed a beat. The muscles of her jaw stretched taut under her skin as she threw herself back into the rhythm. She grabbed his hips with her hands and pulled him hard into her. He resisted. Every rock of her pelvis brought out a tight, constricted moan that seeped through the spaces of her teeth and skittered off into the echoes of the room. When he closed his eyes and placed his hands delicately on her cheeks, she grabbed his wrists and brought them down to his hips, locking his hands against his legs as his breaths came faster. She watched him shake his head from side to side as he struggled against her and clenched his own teeth. As her hips crashed into his, he pulled his body back away from her and at the same time, rested his forehead against hers. With a shudder, he spilled into her as they both came, her nails digging deep into his forearms and leaving etched, bloody half-moons in their pale and clammy flesh.

She pushed back away from him, smoothed down her skirt, and walked away, the echoes of her high heels reverberating through the room as she left him standing alone with the inanimate stares of distant relatives.

There was dinner at one of the more expensive restaurants in town the next evening. She sipped her red wine slowly, never taking her dark eyes off of him. He shifted in his seat. The fork in his hand stabbed at a medallion of beef, but it missed. He drew a breath.

"Why?" He asked her.

The black holes of her eyes bored through him. "It excites me."

"It's not normal."

"I'm not normal."

He set his fork down with a tinny chime onto his plate. "I love you. Marry me."

A thin current of air brought the mixed scents of her perfume and asparagus with béarnaise sauce under his nose as she leaned forward over her plate. "Fuck me," she breathed. "Right now." She leaned closer to him over the small round table. Her warm, moist breath raised the tiny hairs on his cheek. "Fuck me." Her gaze drifted to the couple at the table nearest them.

"Please," he began. "Can't we, just once?"

After a good, long stare, she dropped her eyes to her plate. "All right."

He got a room that night in the best hotel possible. Twenty stories high, she stood naked at the window, surveying the lights of the city below them. Venus' glimmer peeked over the roof of the skyscraper, the only beacon visible in the sodium-washed city sky. The penetrating coldness of the glass seeped deep into her skin as she pressed her body against the window. It slid into the warm spaces between the lips of her pussy, leaving its mark in a small, uneven circle of condensation on the glass. Did they watch? She wondered. Did they strain to see the tan haloes of her nipples as they etched the windowpane? Her fingers traced a tiny O in the forever-indelible moisture of her pussy heat. She turned and walked to the bed where he lay.

He kissed her. Hands, fingers, lips, eyelashes. She felt them flutter over her skin in a delicate ballet. She hated ballet. She hated pink silk slippers and the fragile desperation of girls in white leotards. He kept dancing over her in slow motion, roses in his eyes and lips. She hated roses and embraced the thorns. She wanted to prick his thumbs on their jagged beauty and show him what she was really like. Instead, she let him make love to her on the bed, the feel of his cock as it nestled into her cunt like the feel of worn and weary thorns too dull to sting. She pulled at his hips with sharp nails in a futile attempt to make him fuck her.

As she leaned her head back off the edge of the bed, she stared out through the smudged glass of the nearby window. She saw the yellow face of Venus as it sank beneath the other rooftop, and she saw the blurred silhouettes of strangers pass by the windows of distant offices. As he crushed his hips down into hers a last time, she reached back behind her for Venus and the silhouettes, touching only the last dots of the breath that escaped from between her legs on the icy windowpane.

NADIR

Harry Tasker

The salt air smells clean, purged. The trembling beam from my torch barely reaches the edge, but I don't need to see to know where I'm going. I can hear the surf tearing into the base of the cliff two hundred feet below me.

I've left the car keys dangling in the Lotus' ignition. The briefest smile plays across my lips at the thought that Jeremy will inherit it. He's always wanted the damned thing. Now my brother will have everything. Full house.

What a winner.

I catch myself shuffling, and resolve to be more purposeful. Each stride I take makes me shiver. With fear? With anticipation? Part of me still questions my motives, my reasoning. But there's no other way. I've been to the other side of the world to forget her, and twelve thousand miles wasn't enough. There's only one place left to try.

I remember the very first time I met her, nearly three decades ago. There was no attraction then. How could there have been? I was five years old, she was eighteen. Laura, the woman who finally captured big brother's heart, who pointed his life in the right direction.

Not that she received credit for transforming him from sponging son to shrewd capitalist. No, that was attributed to Jeremy himself. One of the fringe benefits of being first born in my family is that you receive an exaggeration of favourable press, while bad items rarely stick.

Unfortunately, Teflon was in short supply by the time I arrived.

If you listened to my parents talking about Jeremy, something they do often, you'd probably conclude nothing was beyond him. There must be family friends who actually believe he conceived his children by himself. Perhaps that's why it happened. Perhaps Laura finally got tired of existing within her husband's embellished shadow. She never said so, but you can't suppress a personality like hers forever. Eventually, something has to give. It's just the physics of the soul.

For me, there was no such decision to make. My motives were much less complex than hers. I'd been in love with Laura since my teens.

She was everything you could desire. An abundance of adjectives applied to her: vivacious, intelligent, beautiful, considerate, spirited, radiant. On countless sleepless nights I've tried to put them together in the most appropriate combination, and I've always fallen short.

Fantasies about Laura became tangible, physical, once I reached fifteen. By then my body was ripe with hormones, my cock an enthusiastic marionette that danced beneath every vaguely erotic thought. Girls had kissed me, teased me, but when my brother insisted I accompany him, Laura, and my two nieces to the sun-kissed Aegean, I was still a virgin.

The sea's spray is vague against my face as I near the cliff edge. I close my eyes, and see Laura on the first day of that long ago holiday, striding through the hotel lobby. I'd assumed her bikini top was damp, the way it adhered so completely to her voluptuous flesh. With each step she took, the flowing halves of her wrap-around skirt tantalised me with glimpses of creamy thighs. As she passed me, I inhaled jasmine and warm coconut.

On our second day's beach lazing, Laura casually reached up to release the fastening of her bikini. Jeremy huffed, a customary sign of his disapproval. Laura turned to me. "You don't mind if I go topless, do you John?" There was no taunting edge to her voice.

"Er, no," I mumbled, desperate to sound casual, failing effortlessly.

Hers were the first real breasts I ever saw. A woman's breasts. They filled my mind. Together with her green eyes and her full lips and the tender flesh of her slightly prominent belly and the mystery of her closed thighs.

That night in my narrow hotel bed, I stroked myself into a frenzy. As I did for the rest of the holiday.

The next ten years saw lots of women trip through my life. I decided not to be exclusive with my body. Blonde, red, brunette. White, black, yellow. I drew few lines. Some were beautiful, some intelligent. Some even managed to show consideration. But none measured up to Laura.

Not that I consciously compared them to her. Laura remained my vain fantasy, one I guarded carefully, terrified lest I jade it. Whenever we met, I kept the longing from reaching my eyes. She was my brother's wife.

I swear I could have left it at that.

Straining my ears, I can hear the ringing of a five year old phone call above the crashing waves. I was in bed the night she rang, and, fortunately or unfortunately, I was alone.

"Hello?"

"John!" The line waxed and waned. There was a note in her voice I had never heard before. It took a few seconds for me to recognise it as desperation.

"Laura? Are you alright?"

"I'm stuck. The Range Rover's got a flat tyre. Can you come and help me?"

"Where's Jeremy?"

There was a significant pause. "Forget Jeremy."

"But . . ."

"Will you help me or do I phone for a garage?"

"Of course I'll help, it's just . . ."

"Thank you," she said, ending my inquiry. She gave me directions to find her, and hung up.

It was a longish drive, and my mind overflowed with questions. Laura dodged them all. The October wind blew sharp, so I gave her my jacket to put on over her thin evening dress. Black was definitely her colour. The framed, ivory cleavage, the slender legs sheathed in silk, the high-heeled shoes. Every inch of her demanded attention. It was difficult not to succumb. I found myself back on that Greek beach, loins ablaze, desperate to stare at the woman, ashamed because she had bought me a football when I was ten.

I started to loosen the wheel nuts before I used the jack. Three turned readily, but the fourth defied me.

"What's wrong?" Laura asked. Even with a glance, I couldn't miss the racoon rings of mascara, the bloodshot eyes.

"It's seized." I set my muscles against the wheel brace with greater determination.

"Can you undo it?"

"Yes. I think."

Her smile lit up her face.

"What's wrong, Laura?"

For an instant her eyes locked with mine, and then flickered away. "There's no point talking about it."

It began to rain. The black membrane above tore apart, releasing a million gallons of icy water. My shirt plastered itself against my back in an instant.

"Get inside," I shouted, wrestling with the wheel brace.

"You'll get soaked staying out here."

"Only one of us has to."

Reluctantly, Laura slipped into the driver's seat. The rain numbed my fingers quickly. I thought the nut was beginning to turn when my grip on the brace slipped. A burst of exquisite pain erupted as my hand crashed against the wheel hub. I raised my bleeding knuckles to my mouth. My flesh was like marble, but my blood tasted hot.

Laura was suddenly beside me. "Let me see."

"It's nothing," I mumbled.

She pulled my hand down to inspect the damage, and when she touched me, a bolt of static shorted through my frame. Laura's eyes found mine, and when she spoke, I was glad to know I had not been alone in the moment.

"Let's get in the dry," she said.

The windows fogged quickly once we were inside. The Range Rover echoed hollowly to the rain's barrage. Laura slipped my jacket from her shoulders and draped it across the back seat. There were no words for either of us as we sat shivering. Her hair hung limply about her face, enhancing her vulnerability. A drop of water slipped from one damp curl, and my eyes followed as it trickled down between her breasts. When I looked back at her face, we both knew.

Laura wrapped a handkerchief around my hand. Then she reached for my face with cold, trembling fingers, brushing the raindrops from my cheek. "Darling John," she said.

Her lips felt tight as they pressed against mine. I drew her to me, my embrace clumsy in my desire to return her kiss. Her lips slowly warmed and melded with mine. After a few moments I felt her tongue for the first time, and I met its questing tip with my own.

The rustling of her dress was the sound of provocation. I slipped my hand up from her waist, and Laura arched her breast, soft and full, to meet it. The hard nipple pressed against the centre of my palm, making me ache for her. Her mouth slid a fraction from mine, allowing a small groan to escape.

Part of me needed to ask if she wanted this, wanted me, but I was too afraid to give her the chance to say no. Instead I stitched kisses along the side of her neck, as I eased the straps of her dress from her shoulders.

The inadequacy of my fantasies became apparent before the reality of her breasts. I cupped them reverently in my hands, marvelling at their supple weight, their taut texture. I bowed to capture a rose-pink nipple between my lips, worshipped it endlessly with my tongue. Laura gripped my hair as I gently ate of her flesh.

Time was limited. Laura lifted my mouth back to hers, her hand slipping from my thigh to my loins. Her palm touched the hidden hardness, and she gasped, groping for the openings to my trousers. I lifted myself up to help her. Her hand plunged inside my briefs, and I groaned helplessly into her mouth as her fingers enveloped me.

Her fingertips aroused me with a thoroughness that belied the fervour of her kisses. One hand caressed me with long, languid strokes as the other fondled the laden sac between my thighs. I shivered violently as her nails grazed the thin flesh. My hands, idle through my own pleasure, rediscovered her breasts; I took her nipples between my fingers and squeezed.

"Harder," she breathed.

Our hands shuddered over our bodies as our mouths became ever more frenzied. I caressed the inside of her thighs in wild sweeps, my nails drawing furrows across her stockings. Laura clutched for my hand and urged it against her.

The slow heat radiating from her dazed me. Precious seconds were lost as I struggled with the edge of her panties. She whimpered as my fingers slipped between her labia. I was beyond subtlety and finesse. I eased two fingers inside her, and fucked her to the pace of her hand on my cock.

"I want you inside me," Laura gasped between kisses. I helped her slide into the passenger seat as she tugged the hem of her dress towards her waist. The taut suspender straps along her thighs whipped at my senses.

Laura grasped me in her hand, guiding me towards her. I was ecstatic to be taken. She pulled her panties to one side, and pulled my cock forwards to face her fever. A drop of lustful dew smeared between our flesh. I could almost hear it sizzle.

"Take me, John," she said. Just as she had in a thousand fantasies she knew nothing about.

I eased forward, delighting in her wail as I entered her to the hilt. I paused, revelling in sensation. Finally I started to move within her. The veiled ridges of her sex gripped me, controlling, exploiting each stroke. Her panties chafed me, but I didn't care. I kissed her deeply as my fingers snaked between our bellies, searching for her clitoris.

"Oh, that's lovely," she groaned, encircling my hips with her thighs. The heels of her shoes were spurs against my legs, urging me on. I moved slowly, trying to ignore her demands, to make it last. But being inside her was too much. Soon I was thrusting without restraint, my hands clutching feverishly at her breasts as her nails sank into my buttocks.

Laura's head tossed wildly. "That's it," she moaned. "Hard. Fuck me hard!" She pulled my mouth back to hers.

I tried to tell her what I felt, how it was so much more for me than she might think. Laura silenced me with a finger. Then she closed her eyes, abandoning herself to the rhythm of our flesh. Her groans became cries became screams. "Oh, I'm coming!"

An unmistakable shudder rippled through me as my own orgasm built. Laura felt it too.

"You . . . mustn't . . . come . . . inside me!" she gasped.

Reluctantly, I started to part my flesh from hers. A dark voice inside my head urged me to brand her, to spill my seed across her skin. And then Laura locked her thighs around me, holding me in place. My groan of satisfaction had a note of bewilderment, as I emptied myself inside her.

"Why?" I asked her as we dressed afterwards.

"Inspiration," she said, after a moment.

That was as much of an answer as I ever got.

Laura never told me how she'd ended up alone that night. She never revealed what event had sent a responsible wife veering into me. Whatever problems existed between her and Jeremy, she obviously found a way to live with them. "We've never been happier," my brother beamed to the family's regular Christmas Eve partygoers.

I begged Laura to see me again, more times than my ego allows me to recall. At first her refusals were sweet, almost remorseful. Soon they began to sound irritable, and finally angry. She'd made her choice. Couldn't I see that?

I couldn't. For the briefest moment, I'd glimpsed a chance of the life I'd searched for, longed for. Each encounter with Laura was another barbed reminder of what I'd won and lost in a fraction of one night. I could not face her being denied to me.

I left for Australia on New Year's Day. I stayed out of touch.

For five years, a rainbow assortment of women filtered through my sterile days and empty nights. Each failed miserably to close my mind to Laura. The alcohol and the drugs I ingested only made her face clearer, my loss more lucid.

If Australia was an experiment, then its conclusion was inescapable. I merely existed. I could only live with Laura.

So five years later I came home to reclaim her. My brother met me at Heathrow. He'd brought a son to see the aeroplanes, and to meet his new uncle.

"When was Ian born?" I asked my beaming Mother at the inevitable celebration.

"The July after you left, dear."

And finally I realised: I'd been an infusion of strength for Laura, a boost to get her through the next ten years. Nothing more.

So here I am, perched like a gull, waiting for a favourable breeze to carry me away. The sea's rush is soft, welcoming.

Laura won't entertain the idea I can't get out of my head. Now the two most important people in my world are denied to me.

Where's left to go when you've reached your nadir?

NIGHT IN PHILADELPHIA

Gin Smith

It was cold outside, many months from the balmy summer night she sought to recapture and release. The city stretched out before her, its colors more vivid beneath the gray winter sky than she remembered.

She smiled as she walked by the fountain, now dry and silent. In front of her, the museum rose, towering like some fabled Greek temple. She mounted the steps, reached the top and held her breath, then turned and gasped as the city opened up and the night flooded back.

"That's Logan's Square at the end of the Parkway," Kino said as they walked hand in hand. It was late, just past 1 A.M. The night was warm, the air stirred occasionally by a tepid breeze blowing in off the Schuylkill River. The air invaded the flowing length of Rachel's long skirt, stealing beneath to caress her naked flesh.

"Come, I want to show you something," Kino said, pulling Rachel along. Ahead of them a colossal rampart of steps raised skyward toward the face of a huge columned building. Hand in hand, they scampered up the steps. Rachel hurried to keep pace with Kino, feeling slightly breathless as she neared the top. She cleared the last step and came to a stop directly in front of him, her back to the stairs she had just traversed. Kino smiled.

"Turn around," he said, his hand guiding to her waist. Rachel turned and felt her heart race in her chest. Philadelphia opened up before her, its skyline illuminate in the summer night.

"It's beautiful," Rachel said. They stood for a few moments, absorbing the light and heat then Kino grabbed her hand and pulled her away. They walked toward a large fountain, its watery jets splashing among the prisms of city lights. Kino let go of Rachel's hand and sat down on a concrete bench. Rachel walked to the water's edge and dipped her fingers in—it was cool and inviting to the touch. She momentarily thought of kicking off her shoes and leaping into the water, to splash around like a small frivolous child. Instead she turned and walked back to stand before Kino. She placed her hands on his shoulders as he looked up at her; his arms encircled her waist and pulled her close. Rachel ran her fingers through Kino's dark close-cropped hair as he leaned toward her and rested the side of his face against her stomach. Neither of them spoke, although there was little doubt of what thoughts coursed through their minds. They were here, incredibly, together, in this place, tempting a life that could never be—seeking something, somehow to remember each other by.

Rachel let her hands linger at the back of Kino's neck, in his hair, along the sides of his bronzed face. She looked down at this exquisite young man before her and for a moment tried to fathom, as she had a thousand times before, how what they shared had come to be. Kino was 8 years her junior. Rachel remembered vividly the first time they had met. In a room full of introductions his dark eyes had swept her quickly from head to toe making her flesh feel so incredibly alive. "I'm Joaquin, call me Kino," he said, followed quickly by a warm smile that radiated over his entire face. From the outset the attraction had been near instantaneous and Rachel knew that it would be the innocence of circumstance laced with passion that would inevitably bring them together.

And so it had begun just as she knew it would. At first, it was purely the slaking of sexual needs that drove them. For Rachel, it was the attention and aggressiveness of a younger man; for Joaquin, the excitement and discovery to be found with an older woman; and it was unmistakably the danger and thrill of an affair that fueled them both. But now, Rachel knew they were flirting with something much more dangerous, that they had moved beyond the straightforward satisfaction of mutual needs and now their hearts were becoming entangled, becoming involved.

Rachel felt the steady heartbeat in her chest, she tipped her head back and gazed skyward, looking at the myriad stars receding into the heavens. Kino turned his face toward her midriff, his mouth kissing her skin through the gauzy white film of her blouse. Rachel let her hand slide down to caress the side of Kino's face, her thumb brushing over his lower lip as he pulled away and looked up at her. Silence reigned between them. Kino stood, his body sliding full up against Rachel's as he did so. His hands traveled from her waist up the flanks of her body and then cupped the sides of her face. Kino looked at Rachel for a long moment and then kissed her, a soft languid kiss that quickly dissolved into something much more urgent. Kino let one of his hands slide around the back of Rachel's neck, his fingers wrapping in her hair, his other hand slid to her waist crushing her hard up against him. Kino's lips moved over hers, his tongue penetrating her mouth. Rachel felt her body instantly ignite as she reveled in the taste of him.

Without warning Kino pulled away, his eyes searching Rachel's face as she sought to catch her breath. Rachel suddenly became aware of another couple walking a short distance away and then the shadowy form of a homeless man appeared shuffling along close to the museum wall. Kino grabbed Rachel's hand and walked quickly toward another shorter set of stairs that led up to the colonnade just outside the museum entrance. They walked hurriedly up the stairs, Rachel hesitated for a moment, wanting to look back into the courtyard and the fountain in its midst, but Kino quickly pulled her away and behind one of the ribbed columns, backing her up against it.

He kissed her again, hard, insistent, one hand behind her neck again, the other running down the front of her body, cupping her breasts, pinching her erect nipples through the sheer cotton blouse. Rachel felt her body cleave to his, a moan escaped her as Kino pressed his hips hard up against hers. His hand slid down to her waist and gathered up the loose filmy peasant skirt, then slipped beneath and between her thighs. Rachel gasped as she felt Kino's fingers slide across her mons, his index finger slipping easily between the wet folds of her cunt. Kino withdrew his hand and placed the moistened finger in Rachel's open mouth. She closed her lips, sucking on it, caressing it with her tongue. Kino kissed her, pulling his finger away from her mouth, and quickly unzipped the fly of his khaki shorts. He grabbed Rachel's right leg and hooked it around his waist as Rachel gathered her skirt out of the way. Kino pulled his hard cock out into the open and nuzzled it against Rachel's soaked pussy. Rachel draped her arms around Kino's neck, their eyes locked and then Kino slid himself inside. Rachel was unable to stifle a soft moan as his body penetrated hers.

"Put your other leg around me," Kino demanded. Rachel held tight to Kino's neck and lifted her other leg off the ground, wrapping both her legs securely around his waist. Kino's hands slipped down and grabbed the rounded curves of her ass. He thrust himself deep inside of her, then pushed her hips back slightly, fully controlling the limited movement before stroking into her again. Kino fucked her this way for a short time and Rachel felt herself quickly becoming lost in the strength and power of him—fucking her while her body clung so desperately to him, her weight completely supported by his. This was what she craved, what Kino met and satisfied in her—the simplicity of sex—of wanting to be wanted. Kino's intensity intoxicated Rachel, the depth of his passion, the rawness of his desire. The way he looked at her when she walked into a room, his eyes devouring her from head to toe, then meeting her gaze with his own to convey his thirst, to convey his hunger and desire for her. At such moments Rachel knew a power and need unlike anything she had ever experienced. It was an attraction of lust that was, even now, unraveling into trust and the tangled realm of something much more complicated than either of them had ever bargained for.

Kino sunk himself fully into her again and then shifted her weight, his hands hooking under her thighs as he stepped out from behind the column and carried her over to a waist high cement wall at the end of the colonnade. He seated Rachel upon it, his cock still buried deep within her. Rachel shifted back slightly and let her legs relax, letting them slip from around Kino's waist and instead twine around the backs of his thighs. She let go of Kino's neck, putting her hands behind her on the cement and leaned back. Kino grabbed her hips again and pulled her forward, hard onto his cock. Rachel groaned and tipped her head back, her blonde hair cascading down her back. Above, the stars glittered in the sky. Kino thrust into her slowly, deliberately, leaning his body over hers. He nuzzled her neck, his lips kissing her ear.

"Is this what you want Rachel?" he whispered sliding deep into her again.

Rachel lifted her head, turning her face to the side, her lips capturing his.

"Yes," she breathed reveling in the feel of his hips pressing hard against her clit, the sweet taste of his saliva on her tongue. Rachel could feel the heat building between her thighs, like the rushing waters of a whirlpool racing toward an inescapable void.

"Are you sure," Kino asked, his tongue sliding into her mouth, his hips taunting her with short shallow thrusts as he kissed her.

"Yes."

"Do you want me to come inside of you?" Kino's strokes deepened, then receded, then deepened again. Rachel pushed her hips forward, feeling herself poised on the precipice of ecstasy, her body demanding the full measure of his.

"Yes," she whispered.

Kino slid his cock deep inside of her, withdrew almost completely and then shoved deep inside again, he began driving completely and steadily into her.

"I'm gonna lose it Rach," Kino soon breathed.

"Lose yourself in me baby," said Rachel watching his face, feeling her own orgasm tumbling forward.

Kino's dark eyes captured hers, "I already did that a long time ago," he whispered as he thrust hard once more and with a groan emptied himself into her.

The sound of him and the feeling of heat splashing within her put Rachel over the edge and her own orgasm rushed forth. She collapsed back onto the cement, her back arching off the surface, the back of one hand flying to her mouth as she bit down softly, stifling a cry that threatened to penetrate the night.

Rachel drifted, momentarily convinced that time no longer existed, her body shuddered with residual aftershocks. She felt the cement beneath her, felt the heat of Kino's body lean over and gather her limp form in his arms, pulling her back up into a sitting position, her legs still draped loosely around his thighs. Rachel leaned her head on Kino's shoulder, turning her face to nuzzle his neck. She kept her eyes closed, her arms tucked into her chest as Kino wrapped her in his embrace. Rachel felt like a fragile, beautiful animal in his grasp. She kissed his neck letting her lips linger, drinking in the musky deep scent of him, wanting the moment to never end, knowing that it was already slipping away.

They remained wrapped together silently for a short time. Rachel lifted her head and pulled back slightly, her eyes scanning Kino's face. He looked at her, his face masking emotions she could only dare try and discern. He kissed her forehead and then tucked her head back into his shoulder, his hands rubbing absently up and down her back. They gazed out onto the city, watching the play of lights upon the fountain, the occasional car traversing Eakin's Oval, the shadowy forms of other lovers meandering on the museum steps—the moon sinking low on the Philadelphia horizon.

"Rocky, be careful on the steps."

A mother calling to her child disrupted Rachel's thoughts. She watched the tow-haired boy scampering toward her. The chill of the October afternoon made Rachel wrap her coat more tightly around her. The cement at the end of the colonnade where she sat felt suddenly cold and she stood, looking back momentarily at where she had been seated. A sad smile curved her lips as the memory enveloped her once more.

"I miss you Kino," Rachel said aloud to no one. She smiled again thinking back to the many moments they had shared, to the passion, the intensity—to the raw desire that had ruled them. Her face flushed and warmth rushed through her. She felt the pall of sadness move strangely away, perhaps not deserting her completely, but momentarily leaving her to contemplate without remorse, without regret.

Rachel tossed her blonde head and quickly descended the museum steps. A young man with incredible blue eyes flashed her a wide smile as he passed her by. Rachel laughed and smiled in return. At the bottom of the stairs she stopped and gazed back up at the museum, the dormant fountain, the rising columns—she closed her eyes for a moment, then turned and walked quickly to her car.

OPENING CEREMONY

Jean Roberta

Pru's tall, slim body was coiled elegantly on the leather sofa in her new shop. Her grand opening was scheduled for the next day, but for now we were alone, like two actors on a stage before the curtain goes up. I couldn't help admiring the glow on my friend's dark lively face, or her elaborate hairdo. She had learned from a Nigerian woman how to wrap dozens of tiny braids in black thread that caught the light from different angles whenever she moved her head.

"Well, what do you think?" she asked.

"It looks good, Pru," I assured her.

Pru's clothing store was decorated to look like a forest, and the effect of the murals on the walls and the indirect lighting was surprisingly convincing, despite the full racks of dresses, suits, blouses and pants that seemed to be blooming in the unexplored wilderness. The furnishings were in earthy shades of green, gold and brown. "It looks like a sacred grove," I ventured, running the risk of offending her.

Pru rolled her eyes, as I knew she would. She leaned toward me, and I caught a whiff of her musky perfume. Her blouse gapped to show the gentle rise of a small brown breast.

"Beth," she laughed, "you know I'm not superstitious, but I want this place to be blessed. I know what my mother would say. Pru-dence, you must trust in de Lord." I knew that Pru and her mother had moved to the city from their native island of St. Lucia years before. I knew that Pru's mother and aunts practiced a combination of pious Christianity and kitchen voodoo that seemed very odd to me, and that Pru had rejected prayers and spells of every kind when she was a rebellious teenager with a quick mind and a burning desire for upward mobility.

All the same, she knew that the success of her store would somewhat depend on luck.

I caught sight of us in one of the mirrors that reflected gleams of light around the room. My skin, tanned to a light peach color, and my reddish-gold hair contrasted with Pru's. I was wearing an old T-shirt and a pair of jeans that had both shrunk, so that my shapely breasts (of which I was vain) and my hips and ass were gripped by the fabric. I wondered if Pru thought I looked tacky, and if she thought I had dressed this way to show off. I wondered if she might be right.

As if reading my thoughts, Pru uncoiled and stood up, then casually reached for my hands and pulled me to my feet. "I want to see my merchandise on you," she chuckled. There was something strangely shy behind her outer confidence, as if she wanted more from me than she could put into words.

Without asking my size, she smoothly pulled a draped turquoise silk dress from the rack and handed it to me. "Try this," she ordered. *She wants to change my image*, I thought with amusement.

I gasped when she handed me a pale blue lace bra in my size, 36C (but how did she know?), a matching pair of panties, a cream satin garter belt and a package of stockings. The shoes to go with the ensemble were a pair of turquoise satin pumps, simple in design but too high in the heel to allow for easy walking. I felt a hot blush spreading all through me.

I had wondered for months whether Pru wanted anything more than friendship from me. After nights of fantasizing hopelessly (or so I thought), I wasn't sure I could handle her obvious intentions.

"You know I don't wear dresses, Pru," I mumbled. In spite of everything, I wanted to feel the silk on my skin and the skirt swinging against my legs. For Pru.

"Just go try it on," she laughed, pushing me with surprising strength. "Unless you want me to dress you like a baby."

Alone in the cream-and-gold fitting room, I could feel Pru's presence nearby, as if she could see through the curtain as I peeled off my everyday clothes and stood naked before the mirror. It was near the end of summer, and my body was clearly marked where shorts, swimsuits and halter-tops had protected my white breasts and belly from the sun.

Feeling self-conscious but increasingly excited, I put on the clothes Pru had provided. Reaching over my shoulders to fasten the tiny blue buttons up the back of the dress, I watched the silk pull at my lace-covered breasts. Smoothing down the skirt and running a hand through my shoulder-length hair, I felt strangely proud of my ladylike appearance. I had worn clothes like this before, but never for another woman.

Her eyes were sparkling when I wobbled out of the fitting room on the killer heels. "This is ridiculous, Pru," I muttered under my breath.

She replied by grasping me by the shoulders and pulling me close to her for a long, soft kiss. Thanks to my shoes, she didn't have to bend her head much to find my lips, and the warmth of her mouth on mine complemented my eagerness. Her skin felt as soft and comfortable as old denim. When her persistent tongue found its way between my teeth, I moaned.

I wrapped my arms around her long, slim back and felt the hard edges of ribs under a thin layer of flesh. Her body was like her spirit: vulnerable but determined. *May the Goddess forgive me my past*, I thought, *and may this decent woman never find out*. A faintly spicy smell rose from her skin, mixing with the musk of her perfume. "Pru, I want you," I murmured in her ear.

Her ribs heaved in a silent laugh. "Then why didn't you ask me before now?" she teased. " 'Stead of always giving me those hungry looks?"

I was mortified. I had known Pru casually during the years we had both been going to the same bars and even some of the same parties. I could name her last three lovers, but I had never believed I could get close to her until I had forced myself to join the conversation when I overheard her telling two friends about the store she was planning to open. My knowledge of design had attracted her attention and she had asked for my advice. My ego had expanded, but I had never guessed that she was watching me watching her. "I didn't think I had a chance with you," I confessed, burying my nose in her warm neck.

Her long, probing fingers slid over my silk-covered breasts, making my nipples hard. Dipping her tongue into one of my ears, she grasped my bursting tits and began squeezing and playing with them. Hot moisture oozed into my panties.

We were standing in front of a wall mirror, and I could tell by her sudden change of position that Pru was watching her reflection over her shoulder. "My mother used to say something about seeing an albino woman over your left shoulder," she sighed, as if to herself. "It's supposed to be good luck." She pulled back and looked in my eyes to see how I was taking her remark.

"I hope I'm good luck for you, Pru," I chuckled, "though I suppose an ordinary white person is less exotic than an albino."

"Everyone is exotic to someone else, girl," she said, running one hand gently through my hair.

I realized that she knew how it felt to be a coconut among apples, or a swan in a world run by geese, but my feelings stopped me from pursuing this thought. "Let's use the sofa," she purred.

I watched Pru's firm, high ass in a pair of loose pants as she led me by the hand to the leather sofa. She unbuttoned the back of my dress, and we reached for each other almost simultaneously.

The sight of her willowy brown body with the two black nipples on her tight little breasts made me eager to touch her all over—but first I wanted the satisfaction she could give me. She gently pushed me onto my back as her deep brown eyes burned into mine.

"What do you want?" Pru asked me in a low voice. She looked embarrassed, and I saw with surprise that she was nervous. "Do you want me to be the butch and you'll be my woman? Or you want us to be equals and take turns? Do you want my tongue or what do you like?" The look of strain on her face showed me how hard it was for her to ask such honest questions. Her courage and her respect for me were breaking my heart.

"Pru," I told her, "I want us to take turns doing everything. I want you to suck my tits and my pussy and I want to learn your whole body by heart." I stopped talking to kiss her, and this time I gave her my tongue. I felt slightly nauseous with guilt and fear, but I was not going to back down. Like her, I wanted to change my life.

Suddenly Pru slid down my body until her head was level with the soaking hair of my crotch. Parting my lower lips, she spread something smooth over my inflamed clit, then darted a pointed tongue over and around everything she could reach. Lightly holding my folds of tense flesh with her teeth, Pru began diligently sucking my pearl toward surrender.

She was teasing me out of my mind, and I wanted more. Just when I thought I would have to settle for what I could get, she touched me where I was hungriest. One, then two gloved fingers slid into my slick, steaming entrance, stroking and teasing me to frenzy. I didn't believe I deserved so much pleasure, but she was giving it to me and I didn't feel as if I had a choice.

I came as though a bomb had exploded in my clit. I clutched Pru in relief and amazement as she slid up my body to give me a long, deep, possessive kiss. "Honey, you're so good," I sighed. She laughed and ruffled my wavy hair.

Slowly, almost lazily, I pressed my hands down the round curve of her buttocks and across her smooth, flat belly to the springy black hair below. I was delighted to find her almost as wet as I was, and squirming with impatience.

"Elizabeth," she breathed into my hair, which was now trailing across her breasts and hard torso as I moved downward. "Kiss me down there."

When I arrived at the swamp between her legs, I gently pushed them farther apart and savored the sight and the smell in front of me. Her hips were rocking in a restrained but definite rhythm that pushed her hard clit in my face to a regular beat. Her hunger for me was like her hunger for beauty, wealth and space of her own. At that moment, I wished I could give her everything she wanted.

Her downy cleft was like a ripe fruit waiting to be picked. Much as I wanted to taste her, I knew it was too dangerous. I grabbed a dental dam from a pocket of my jeans on the floor, and shielded her swollen clit with it. I began flicking her with my tongue, then fastened my mouth on her and sucked. The motion in Pru's hips changed to hard thrusting.

Something more was needed, and I managed to pull on gloves, one at a time, to explore her more thoroughly. After some searching, I found the small, wrinkled entrance to her back passage and massaged it with one finger. In a few minutes, my woman was bucking and clutching my head as if she was afraid she might explode.

As the tension in her body subsided, I pulled off the gloves and ran my hands down her long thighs. Sliding upwards, I sucked each of her shiny black nipples, then paused to admire the contented look on her face. "Beth, you're a born lover," she cooed.

I couldn't stand it. "You could say that," I muttered, tasting the salt in my own saliva. "I've even been called a professional."

Her dark eyes flew open. "You a ho?" she demanded. "You sell it to men?" I wanted to cry.

"Not now!" I assured her. "Not any more. I never did that while I was going with a woman. I wouldn't." *I'm so honorable*, I thought to myself sarcastically.

"Do cocks turn you on?" she inquired coolly. "Or couldn't you find a job doing something else? You really like earning money on your back, girl?" Tears were stinging my eyes, and I wished I could disappear.

"I don't love it, Pru," I said. "I did what I had to do, that's all. I worked for two escort agencies for about five years, between regular jobs and my classes. Sometimes I pounded the pavement looking for real work but I couldn't find anything, and welfare always screwed me up one way or another." I paused for breath, and switched to the present tense.

"My degree in Fine Arts just makes most employers think I'm over-qualified or too flaky for an ordinary job, and I can't get any more student loans until I pay back the ones I've already had. What would you do?" I wanted her forgiveness, but I was beginning to hate her for making me defend what I wanted to forget.

"Last time a man mistake me for a ho, I slap him," she spat at me. "I would rather scrub floors than sell pussy." She gathered breath.

I felt dizzy, as though she had thrown me against the wall and beaten me up. I didn't want to hear whatever she might have to say about my sleazy life. I felt an overwhelming urge to fight back.

"How do I know about you, Pru-dence?" I hissed in her face. "What all have you done, and who with?" Her long, hard fingers were still grasping one of my breasts, unwilling to let go.

Pru began to speak, but I didn't really want to hear a roll call of her past lovers. Not now.

"Woman," I interrupted her, "there's still a lot we don't know about each other, but I want to find out everything about you. I'm sick of the lies men always want to hear, and I don't want to play that game with women. Especially with you. That's why I told you the truth." My eyes were starting to overflow, leaving embarrassing wet tracks on my cheeks to match the wet patch on the leather of Pru's new sofa.

The look in her deep brown eyes revealed an uneasy mixture of anger and compassion. "Are you ashamed, 'Lizbeth?" she asked thoughtfully. "Are you sorry you let those men use you as a thing?"

Oh shit, I thought. *Fuck this.* "I'm sorry there aren't more serious jobs for a person of my abilities, Pru," I said aloud. "I'm sorry the men who paid for the use of my body wouldn't hire me to work in their offices. I'm really sorry this world is mostly run by stupid men who don't know that women are human beings. But I did what I had to do, that's all. Don't tell me you've never had to sell yourself in any way to pay the rent."

Pru's eyes clouded over briefly, as though she were remembering something.

Suddenly she wrapped both arms around me and pushed me down underneath her. The hurt she felt was beginning to show in her eyes.

"How did you do it, Beth?" she asked quietly. "Did the johns come pick you up, or did you find them somewhere? What did you wear?"

My face was burning. "They liked me to wear garter belts, split panties, lacy bras—you know. Under sexy dresses. They liked colors like red and black, or anything that contrasted with my skin. And spike heels. You know the kind of thing, Pru. We never did anything in the office except make the arrangements. The men liked to think they were taking me out on a date."

The look on Pru's opaque face was hard to read, though her softly stroking fingers sent a message of need and promise into my skin. I could feel a warm current of anger still humming through hers. She was also stiff with embarrassment at her own confused feelings.

"Baby," she begged, "do you still have the lingerie and jewelry you used to wear for men? Would you wear them for me? Would you let me take you out for a drink and then take you home? Just me and no one else?"

"Oh yes, Pru," I breathed into one of her small ears. "I'll wear anything you like. Just—don't—blame me," I panted. "Or condescend. Or deny my feelings."

Pru kissed me in a way that somehow felt fierce and gentle at the same time.

"I don't want to hurt you, Beth," she mumbled almost inaudibly. She stroked my back persistently. "I not one of the assholes who wants to use you." Her shame seemed to be stuck in her throat. Her eyes pleaded with me. "I scared for myself, Elizabeth. I got loans up to my eyeballs and they all got to be paid back sometime. If this store doesn't make money, I'm screwed." She sighed in my arms. "I guess we're all scared of ending up on the street, angel woman."

In the crazy flashes of light that bounced off the mirrors, I shifted her until I was lying on top. "Mmm," I hummed, grinding my crotch into hers. "You'll be all right, Prudence," I soothed her.

I kneaded her shoulders, her arms, her breasts and her belly while the scent from her crotch and her armpits rose to greet me. "Show it to me, Pru," I whispered. Her long dark fingers obediently reached down to spread her pussy lips in a classic gesture, exposing her tender purplish interior.

Spreading a square of latex over her delicious flesh, I wondered if I could get the response I wanted. When I fastened my lips on her clit and began flicking it with my tongue, she jerked. Soon I had to withdraw to pull on my gloves, and I felt grateful when she chuckled good-naturedly.

I reached into her with two fingers. I could feel her holding back, afraid of being overwhelmed. Like me, she was terrified of the pit of hunger identified as the irrational slut in every woman.

"I want it, Pru," I insisted. "I won't stop until I get it. I'll just keep going until you give it to me, honey." I slid up to suck her hard nipples.

"You want to let go," I whispered. "You know you can't hide anything from me. Trust me, baby."

She seized my head, crying out when her inner muscles rippled around my fingers. I continued to stroke her as she squeezed again and again, greedily wringing sensation from my hand.

"It's all right, honey," I murmured. "I'll hold you. Just don't ever tell me I'm a ho and you're a virgin saint." She stared into my eyes until I slid up to kiss her, plunging my tongue into her mouth.

Her eyes slowly opened. She breathed heavily before speaking. Her words, of course, were about the store. "You could work for me for a salary," she suggested quietly, looking at the painted trees on the walls and the jiggling lights from the mirrors. "You know how clothes are made, even though your taste is in the gutter." I rose on my elbows in indignation, and she pushed me back down, laughing. "Girl, you'd have to work," she went on. "It's hard to get a new business off the ground and I can't afford any lazy woman in my life." I laughed with her.

"I can work, honey. I love your store and I want it to be here a long time." The smell of our satisfied bodies seemed to fill the space.

I could feel Pru's nervous exhaustion. "But can you mix business with pleasure by working with me all day is what I'm asking, sweet woman? I don't know if you want to be my employee. I don't know if I could handle being your boss. You could be my partner, but you'd have to buy into the store. This a serious entanglement we're discussing."

I caressed her troubled face. "Pru," I told her, "don't worry about it. I won't know whether I can take orders from you until I try it. If it works out, I could become your partner. If we can't work together, I still want to give you what you need. Let's see how much of our lives we want to share."

Pru relaxed with a deep sigh, lazily running a hand down my back. "I'm not sure I can keep my hands off you," she chuckled.

"I bet you'll love helping women in the fitting rooms," I joked.

She laughed and slapped my behind so that my cheeks quivered. "You naughty girl," she scolded. "You need a good spanking. I don't intend to molest my customers."

"No, honey," I protested, sliding against her skin. "I don't believe in molesting anybody. I just want to help women get what they want whether men like it or not."

"Mmm," she agreed, squeezing the back of my neck. I suddenly felt tired, and wanted to fall asleep in her arms. "Hey," she snickered, stroking my face. "Don't close your eyes, woman. You want the customers to find you here like this tomorrow?" I laughed, forcing my eyes open. "Let's go eat something."

Reluctantly I pulled myself off her and stood up, stretching. "Well, we broke in the store," I told her, reaching for my jeans.

"Uggh," she protested. "Baby, no. If you're dining with me, you can't wear those things. Wear the dress I gave you." Trying to wipe the smile off my face, I retrieved the lingerie and the dress.

"That's better," she said.

"Just one thing, Pru," I said humbly, looking into her eyes.

"What's that, sweetheart?" she urged me.

"I can't walk in heels like this. They'll ruin my feet." I didn't like the look of disappointment on her face, but the pain in my feet was worse. "Could I save them for special occasions? With you?"

Pru laughed with delight and wrapped her long arms around me, pulling me close to her. "Sure, Beth," she breathed into my hair. As soon as she let go, I found a more sensible pair of low heels in the shoe display. I loved the look of admiration on her face as her eyes traveled from my shining hair to my neatly shod feet and back up my body. When we turned out the light and locked the door, we knew we had started a new phase of our lives.

THE PIZZA GUY

Eve Feral

August 17

Dear Becky,

You won't believe what happened to me Saturday night. Well, maybe you will. I don't surprise myself too much anymore, but I'm never sure about others' tolerance for the unexpected things I do.

I figure there are two kinds of people in the world, Becky—those who have fantasies, and those who decide to live out their fantasies. I slipped into the latter category Saturday night. It wasn't planned. It just happened.

I had called for a pizza delivery after Jeff said he might drop by to see me and watch some movies (yeah, dirty movies!). I decided to have pizza and beer on hand, just in case. When the pizza guy rang the doorbell, I smiled a greeting and stepped partly onto the porch, propping open the glass storm door with my body. As I handed him the twenty-dollar bill our hands touched, and I felt a spark of electricity. I glanced up at his face to see whether he'd noticed. He was gazing at me intently. Smiles flickered across our faces. He dug in his pocket for change and handed me some bills.

"Thanks, darlin'," I said, a common enough expression here in the south, and one I toss around indiscriminately. I don't know whether that's what did it or whether it was the "Sublime" perfume I bought last week or whether it was something else. I'm still trying to figure out what happened.

"You're very welcome, honey," he replied. And his index finger barely grazed along mine. I remembered my friend Michael telling me that's one way he always tested a woman back in the 1970s, to see whether she'd go home with him. If she didn't mind his touching her like that, he knew he had her. But I digress.

Our eyes locked for what seemed like hours, though it was more likely only five seconds. His gaze broke first, and he turned and walked away. I let the storm door shut and was pushing the wooden door closed when I noticed he'd stopped and was looking back at me.

"Did you need something?" I asked, opening the storm door again and holding it wide open. It was a pivotal moment, Becky. It felt like a metaphor, as though I were opening my legs wide instead of the door.

He came near again. His words were hesitant. His voice was low, strangled. "I'd like to . . . call you . . . get together . . . if you'd like to."

Our eyes held each other's once more, and his long middle finger traced along the palm of my hand where it was propped against the glass door. I held the boxed pizza in my other hand. I couldn't speak. I felt paralyzed. I wanted to fuck him.

Flashes of my fantasies about sex with a stranger raced through my mind, Becky, crowding out all the rules I'd absorbed in my lifetime about "proper" behavior. He tested my silence, bending down slightly to place a wet kiss on the tip of my middle finger. I think I had stopped breathing by this time. I know I felt lightheaded. When he met no resistance he kissed my lips—lightly at first, then harder, his tongue slipping inside my mouth.

I knew that the next move was up to me. I pressed my body against his and kissed him back. Hard. Wet.

I know, Becky, I can't believe it either! Even as I write about it now, I wonder whether I'm dreaming.

"I want to put my arms around you," he whispered. I stepped backwards into the house and laid the pizza box on the table in the foyer. He followed. I was keenly aware that any neighbors who might be looking toward my house could easily have observed what happened next.

And what happened next is that the pizza guy—a total stranger, probably 10 years my junior, good-looking, well built—stood in front of the glass door next to me and reached under my denim dress. He registered only momentary surprise to find that I wasn't wearing panties (I never do anymore; I don't know whether I've told you that). His hand parted my legs and he stuck his middle finger and then two fingers deep in me. We never quit staring into each other's eyes, Becky, not even when he began to pump his fingers in and out of me in a furious finger fuck that left me quivering. I was moaning and holding onto his shoulders; and he then bent low to massage my clit. I leaned against the table and spread my legs as wide as I could while still standing up. He was kneeling in front of me, staring intently into my red curls as he kneaded and stroked with his thumb.

"I want to taste you," he murmured in a choked voice as he buried his tongue in me. The stubble on his chin was pleasantly rough. I grasped his forearm and, tossing the last remnants of caution aside, pulled him toward my bedroom. "I'm such a slut," I thought, and just mouthing the words inwardly made me even more ravenous for him. I fell backwards onto the bed and threw my glasses aside. (After he left, it took me an hour to find them in the tossed bed sheets.) He pushed my dress up above my bra and ran his eyes and his hands over my bare tummy. I held my breath, waiting to see his reaction to the big, beautiful woman splayed out before him. Out of the corner of my eye I saw the cats perched on the far corner of the bed, watching. I sighed with relief and pleasure when he knelt on the carpet, pulled me to the edge of the bed, spread my legs wide, stuck his tongue in the cleft and began to lick and suck noisily. Once again his fingers rammed into me, and this time he found my G-spot. His exquisite massage of that vaginal treasure (isn't that a funny term? I read it in a book or magazine somewhere) resulted in a climax of a kind I'd experienced only twice before, when I was masturbating. Now, with this nameless stranger between my legs, I came hard, screaming, my body arching and convulsing as I ejaculated hot wet come all over his hand. The cats ran.

Hang on, Becky. It doesn't stop here.

"Take off your dress."

The urgent need in his voice banished the lazy satiety that wanted to settle over me. I whipped the denim dress over my head in seconds.

"Take off your bra."

I tossed it across the room after fumbling for precious seconds with the hook-and-eye fasteners.

"God, your breasts are beautiful," he moaned, kneading them with his hands in a motion that was somehow both rough and tender. He squeezed them together, sucked them, jiggled them.

"Suck your nipples." He was breathing hard. "I love to see a woman suck her own nipples."

I complied with his request, astonished at the eroticism of tasting my own nipples. As he watched me, he slipped off his own shirt and pants. I noticed that he too was wearing no underwear. (Later, Becky, we laughed together about that, wondering whether there's some signal that bare-bottomed people send each other.) And as I sucked my nipples he stroked his erect cock, rubbing the glistening, puffed-up head across my breasts, into my cleavage. And he began finger fucking me again. God, Becky, it was wonderful!

"Get on your knees." His voice was softly demanding. I thrilled at the slightly stern tone. "I want to fuck you."

I crawled to the edge of the bed and grabbed for the condoms on the wicker table. As I fumbled with the foil packet I felt his hesitation and once again held my breath. Gazing into his eyes I began to stroke his beautiful purple glans. He rocked back and forth, fucking my hand, little moans escaping his throat. Then, trembling, I opened the packet and unrolled the sheath over his engorged cock. It was like dropping the green flag at a NASCAR race. Everything accelerated. He flipped me over on all fours and began ramming into me from behind with a wildness that was exhilarating.

"Beautiful . . . gorgeous," he kept repeating as he ran his broad hands over my ass, slapping lightly, rubbing, kneading the fleshy cheeks. "God, what a great ass you have." And all the while he banged into me. Hard. My arms extended across the wide expanse of the king-size bed; I clawed at the sheets, writhing and moaning with delight. My face and breasts were pressed flat into the mattress. My ass waved and undulated as he pounded against me, balls flapping and smacking in a delightful percussion. His shouts joined mine as he exploded in a screaming climax, thrusting violently, shuddering from head to toe.

"Can I clean up in your bathroom?" He was draped across my back, his lips so close to my ear that the words tickled. "I have to get going: they're going to wonder what happened to me."

Utterly exhausted, I could only nod and murmur, "Uh-huh."

"Come in here," he called out, his words riding on the sounds of water splashing in the basin. "Let me look at you while I wash up. I want to see those gorgeous big tits." I felt like a puppet, my limbs attached to his words.

I walked into the bathroom and watched his face in the mirror as he stared at me and grinned. "This is like a fantasy come true," he said. "Fuckin' amazin'." And we both started laughing. Uproariously. Holding onto each other. Slapping our thighs kind of laughing.

"Can I come back?" he asked suddenly. The intensity of his gaze extinguished the laughter. "We don't close till one o'clock. But I want to come back."

"Sure," I replied, my heart pounding, the wild unreality of this beginning to sink in. But it never occurred to me to say no, Becky.

"What's your name?" he asked, running his hands lightly over my breasts and tummy.

"Eve," I answered. "And yours?" Without waiting for his response I turned and walked back into my bedroom. I heard the zipper as he closed his pants.

"Greg." He was standing behind me suddenly, pressing his still-bare chest against my back.

"Will you lie down on the bed again, face down?"

I looked over my shoulder at him, wordlessly questioning his request.

"Please, lie down," he repeated.

I stretched out on the bed and luxuriated in the feel of his hands on my butt, kneading, smacking, pushing my cheeks together, probing the creases and folds of flesh with his strong fingers. I felt like clay in the hands of a sculptor. Lovely words tumbled out of his mouth as his hands glided across my bottom. "Yes. Oh yes. Beautiful. Oooh. Gorgeous. Oooh. Mmmmmm."

A few moments later we walked to the front door. Our laughter erupted again when we saw that my pizza had fallen to the floor and that his insulated bag was propped in the storm door, holding it partly open. I wondered whether the cats had escaped.

"I'll see you later," he said, and left.

It had been only twenty minutes since he'd rung the doorbell.

Jeff never did drop by the house for his pizza and beer and dirty movies, by the way. Never even called.

Well, Becky, you can imagine what the next few hours were like. Or maybe you can't. I relived that twenty minutes over and over, alternating between being aroused at the memory of it and being shocked at my wanton behavior . . . at my fantasy come true. I kept wondering what had made us click, what had caused the unmistakable chemistry. I'm still wondering.

At 2 A.M. I walked through the house, turning off lamps and the CD player. Obviously Greg wasn't coming back. At 2:07 the phone rang.

"Which house is it? The second on the right?"

"Yes. I thought you'd changed your mind."

"We closed late. I'm sorry. Is it still okay for me to come?"

"Yes. Hurry."

Greg stepped into the foyer ten minutes later. Neither of us spoke. He kissed me hard, then knelt in front of me and pushed up the silky gown I'd put on earlier in the evening. His hands parted my thighs and I reveled in his finger fucking, which was as wild and exciting as I'd recalled in the hours since his first visit. Shaking and moaning, I came in mere minutes, in a standing position, shuddering against his hand as I shouted my release.

He stood up then and stripped, tossing his pants and T-shirt on top of a small canvas bag he'd brought in with him.

"If it weren't against the law I'd go naked all the time," he said. "I will while I'm here. I wish you would too."

I didn't protest as he pulled my gown over my head and grinned appreciatively, running his hands over my breasts, kissing them, nibbling and pulling at my nipples. He looked carefully at me, all over, and caressed my big tummy, my big ass.

"You're beautiful . . . you're beautiful," he kept repeating.

I suggested he take a shower. While the water splashed over him I stood in the doorway of my bathroom and watched admiringly through the transparent shower curtain.

After he dried off, we went to the kitchen and he selected one of the Beck's Dark beers still in my refrigerator, left over from last weekend's party. I refilled my wineglass with the deep, rich Merlot I'd been sipping all evening for courage. As we wandered back to the living room, he commented on the shelves of books there, noting that playing football is what had kept him from flunking out of high school two decades earlier.

"You obviously went to college," he said. "Does it bother you that I didn't?"

It doesn't.

When ZZ Top's *One Foot in the Blues* came on we danced for a while. You know how much I love to dance, Becky. He does too. We smiled at the discovery.

With another beer and another glass of wine in hand we sat on the sofa, our bodies turned so that we faced each other. I pulled my knees up and spread my legs. God, Becky, I am shameless! While his finger languidly teased and tortured my pussy, he talked. For nearly thirty minutes he filled me in on his life as a construction worker who delivered pizzas and did other odd jobs between construction gigs to pay the bills. He'd sold his Harley a few years before, but not before touring all over the United States, camping along the way. He likes to hunt and fish. He has three dogs. He's part Native American, and spiritually connected to that aspect of his heritage.

"You've probably never been with anyone like me," he said.

He's right about that.

So, dear Becky, I've been thoroughly and exhaustingly fucked and sucked and licked and spanked by a biker dude. Christ, he's even a member of the NRA! He is confident, self-assured, comfortable with himself. Sexually he's roughly tender and naughtily sensitive, and he has staying power. His cock is long and thick, and it felt so good pummeling into me. Over the next few hours he rolled me all over my bed. He turned me every which way, entered me from the front, the back. We were upside down and right side up. Our grunts and groans and screams filled my house. Every inch of my body—inside and out—was felt, kissed, licked, fucked, examined, admired.

He stayed till 5:30 A.M.

I loved it.

He'll be back, by the way. He left a message on the answering machine today while I was at the office. I'm expecting him tonight when his shift ends.

Love,
Eve

VERONIQUE

Lybbe

eronique is the perfect wife for me. Let me explain. She is totally without, how you say, "inhibition." A creature of comfort. Catlike. She always gets what she wants.

I have been lucky in my life. I was born to a wealthy family and I will never want for anything. My father used to say to me, "Jules, you have a responsibility to society. You have advantages. You must never abuse them." My father was a very wise man, but he worked too hard all his life. He wanted me to follow in his footsteps. To enter the family business. To be a drone. Why would I want a life like that? I have no need to work. Life is short. I want to enjoy it.

When I was a much younger man I was considered to be a "play-boy." I could have any woman I wanted. Women are strange creatures. So many of them are excited by wealth. They hang around the casinos waiting for the chance to pounce. They will offer anything to spend a night with money. Back in those days I would have a woman suck my cock under the dinner table, just because I knew she would. They were so disposable. They were so boring. None of them had any real enthusiasm for life.

Then I met Veronique. I will never forget that day. I was strolling along the esplanade by the yacht basin. She was seated at one of those tiny tables constructed of wrought iron. She looked out over the sea as though she hadn't a care in the world. The thing that caught my attention was not so much where she was sitting, or even how she looked. What caught my eye was her obliviousness to her surroundings. She was in her own world.

She was wearing one of those sundresses that were so en vogue back then. Designed to be worn without a brassiere, the top was held up by some kind of wiring. There were no straps; the shoulders were bare. Veronique held a book in one hand, and was lazily rolling a nipple between the fingers of the other. She had dropped one side of the top of her dress to reveal an exquisite breast. It was this perfect globe that she stroked so boldly.

It wasn't unusual to see bare breasts on the beaches in the south of France, even in those days. I travelled to Southern California on business once, and I was astonished at the amount of clothing I saw at oceanside resorts. *Les Americaines* are so modest. However, Veronique wasn't on the beach. She was at a small café, and her display of flesh was out of place. I felt I had to approach her. She was like a magnet, drawing me to her.

"*Je m'excuse mademoiselle*, may I join you?"

Veronique looked at me from beneath her sweeping lashes. She seemed to be processing information, carefully studying, and only when she was satisfied with the results did she speak.

"Yes. Of course. Sit down."

She made no move to cover herself. She was totally without guile, and seemed unaware that her breast was still bare.

"May I ask what you are reading? The book seems to have captured your attention. Is it something I might like?"

"I'm not sure Monsieur. I know nothing of your taste. This book has been banned in many countries. It is not easy to obtain a copy."

"Banned? For what reason if I may be so bold."

"It is a story of sexual domination. Sexual submission. Sexual freedom."

"Ah. I believe I read something about that in one of the papers. A French woman, *n'est-ce pas?*"

"*Oui*. The book has won the Prix Deux-Magots, but still you can not buy it in any store."

"How is it that you have a copy?"

"It was given to me by a good friend."

We talked for hours that day. Veronique explained to me that she wanted to live the book. She wanted to experience everything the character in the book experienced. But she also made it clear that the experiences would be her choices, not the choice of a partner.

"For instance Monsieur. I am sitting here on a public esplanade. I am reading a book that excites me. I want to feel the pleasure in a physical way. Should I leave my place in the sun to do that? I think not. I do what I have to do. I know I am being watched, and that excites me further. You see?"

I was indeed beginning to see.

Veronique and I became inseparable. There was nothing she would not do to experience sexual nirvana. I asked her to marry me when we had been together only two months. There was no question for me. I had to own this woman. I loved her beyond explanation.

Most people think I control Veronique. This is not so. She controls me. She knows exactly what I need to be happy, and she gives that to me. I do not doubt for an instant that she can remove that happiness whenever the mood happens to strike.

We spend most of the winter on the yacht. Sometimes we anchor at Monte Carlo, sometimes we cruise the blue waters of the Mediterranean. Veronique once read a book about the French Aristocracy. She was intrigued by the depictions of nipple piercing and she demanded that I find a place where we could pierce hers. We shopped together for the gold rings that would be inserted behind each lovely breast-berry. My cock was bulging within my trousers as we stood at the counter trying to decide which pieces would be best. The old man who waited on us could not conceal his shock when Veronique opened her blouse to expose herself to him.

"Which do you think Monsieur? Which will look best? Perhaps you could hold the rings against the nipples while my husband decides which he likes."

The old man hesitated only for a moment. We were alone in the shop, and he could smell a large sale. He was not about to pass up the opportunity to touch the perfect fruit my wife was offering.

I suggested that he stand behind her. That way he could reach around and display the rings against her nipples without interference. Veronique shrugged the blouse from her shoulders, leaving herself bare from the waist up. The old man stood behind her and tried his best to display the rings on her nipples.

"Wait my good man. The rings are not being shown to advantage. I am not sure if you know about nipple piercing, but the idea is for the nipple to be constantly erect once the ring is inserted. My wife doesn't seem to be quite erect enough to show the rings properly. Could you help her along a little? Pinch each nipple. Twist a bit. She likes that. It is important for me to know I am purchasing the perfect pair."

Veronique looked at me with pure lust in her eyes. I love her best when she gets like this. I know she pleases herself, but I like to think that she wants to please me too. For her the pleasure intensifies when she brings someone else into the game. She does have limits though. She will not fuck another man. That is her only limitation. Her cunt belongs to me, and we both know that.

I saw Veronique squirming against the old man. She was pushing her ass against him, encouraging him. Her nipples were swollen and red. I pushed the old man's hands away so I could suck each beautiful tit into my mouth in turn. My saliva left each one to glisten in the subdued overhead light.

"*Oui ma petite*. The rings are perfect. I cannot wait to see them installed."

The old man was flushed, and tiny beads of sweat were visible on his wrinkled brow. He wrote a bill of sale while I paid him from the stack of bills in my gold money clip.

Veronique was buttoning her blouse. She leaned to me and kissed my ear.

"*Merci, cherie*. I cannot wait to wear these rings."

We left the shop and stepped into the bright afternoon sun. Veronique grabbed my hand and pulled me into the alley beside the store. Piles of boxes were stacked up against one wall, and the height of the next building cast a dark shadow, making it difficult to see.

Veronique bent herself over the pile of boxes and flipped her skirt up from behind. It was summer. She was naked beneath the skirt.

"Fuck me Jules. Fuck my ass. I want you now!"

I fumbled with the opening of my trousers. I was afraid we might be visible from the street, but that is what Veronique wanted. I clutched at her cunt. She was wet and ready for me. I pushed the head of my cock into her.

"No! My ass! Fuck my ass!"

Her own fingers were busy strumming the oily ball of her clit. She already had her own rhythm going. I was merely a player in her game. I moistened the entrance to her ass with a few drops of spittle and inserted the tip of my finger.

"For god's sake Jules! Your cock! I want your cock in my ass! Fuck me Jules. Fuck me now!"

I pushed into the resentful opening. I was afraid of hurting her. She pushed herself back on me hard. I was in and trapped by her strong muscles. Veronique was like an animal, grunting her passion into the cardboard boxes. I loved this woman so. My knees grew weak as I felt my orgasm build. I could feel her sucking me into her. There was no way I could escape, even if I wanted to.

My eyes were adjusting to the light. A sudden chill crossed my body as I realized we were not alone. A bum sat huddled at the end of the alley. He cradled a bottle of wine between his legs. I heard him mutter, "*Mon dieu*" as I saw him release his cock from the confines of his ragged trousers. He was stroking in time with us. I knew Veronique saw him. I knew she was looking at him. My orgasm was over quickly.

The Greeks knew about the exquisite feelings to be found in a tight anus. Veronique was particularly fond of this type of fucking.

Veronique was never quiet with her enjoyment of sex. If it is possible to scream a moan, that is what she does when she comes. The walls of the alley reverberated with the echoes of her voice. I withdrew and she pulled herself away from me, straightening her skirt and returning to a sense of normalcy. The bum at the end of the alley was still stroking himself to erection. I don't think he even realized that we were gone.

Veronique linked her arm through mine as we strolled down the boulevard.

"*Maintenant cherie*, we look for the old woman who said she will pierce me. Yes?"

"*Oui mon ange*. Whatever makes you happy."

WHAT ARE YOU WEARING?

Thomas S. Roche

"What are you wearing?" the guy asked my wife, and she told him. I was sitting across the living room, my hand covering the receiver of the portable phone. Legs spread, Jen sprawled on the big white chair that faced the open window.

I was more turned on than I had been in months.

I wondered if I was invading the guy's privacy—but Jen didn't see it that way; she felt that as long as her phone partner was getting what he wanted, there was no harm in letting her husband listen in. It was the first time I'd done this; the first time I'd been an audio voyeur listening to my wife cheat on me.

It wasn't cheating, of course—the whole thing had been my idea. And my pounding heart was accompanied by a seething, throbbing hard-on, a flush to my skin, an excitement and arousal I hadn't felt for a long time.

"My name's Rick," the guy said quickly, as if in afterthought to his previous question—as if he'd realized it was rude to demand to know what she was wearing without introducing himself. That out of the way, he repeated hastily, "What are you wearing? Tell me what you're wearing—Jen, was it?"

"That's right. My name's Jen."

Jen is who she is, and she never lies. Well, almost never. No imagined see-through teddies for her, no thigh-high black fishnets with their lace tops clipped to garters fastened to a garter belt. No G-string or merrywidow for my wife—with her personality, and her simple, unobtrusive sexiness, such accoutrements would have been, well, gauche.

"I'm wearing sweats," she told the guy. "Sweat pants and a tank top."

"Oh God," the guy moaned. "I love sweat pants. Are they tight?"

"Pretty tight," laughed Jen. "I've lost a little weight, so. . . ."

"I love them when they're tight," said the guy.

"Yeah, they're tight," said Jen. (See? Almost never.) "So tight I kind of want to slip them off."

"Are you wearing anything underneath?"

"Just a pair of panties," said Jen innocently. "A really small pair. Not much to them."

"And a bra?"

"Nope," she said. "No bra. I don't wear one around the house. I'm just an A-cup . . . no need."

"I love small tits!" So did I, and as I watched Jen running her hands over her breasts, stroking them through the sweaty material of her white tank top, I pulled down my own sweat pants and took out my hard cock. I began to stroke it, and Jen made eye contact with me, licking her lips slowly to let me know she was getting turned on.

"I almost never wear a bra, in fact," said Jen. "I like my nipples to show, whatever I'm wearing."

"Oh my fucking God, I love women who don't wear bras," the guy moaned. "I'm getting hard thinking about you. Take off your sweat pants," said the guy. "Take them off and tell me about the rest of your body. Tell me what you look like."

"Well, let's see . . . I'm 32-22-32," said Jen, cupping the phone against her shoulder as she squirmed out of her sweat pants, exposing her slender, pale legs. "I'm not very curvy . . . sort of boyish, slender, I guess."

"Oh my God," said the guy. "I think that's so fucking hot. Are you getting turned on?"

"That all depends," she giggled. "Are you getting turned on?"

"Fuck yeah," the guy said. "I'm so fucking hard already I can't stand it."

"Your cock's nice and hard?" she said breathlessly, staring at mine and licking her lips.

"Yeah, big and hard."

"Are you stroking it?"

"Yeah, I'm stroking it. I'm jerking it off, nice and slow."

"Mmmm," moaned Jen. "Then yeah, I'm turned on, too. In fact, I think I might be getting wet."

Jen was—I could tell from the way she had her eyes locked on my erection as I pumped it. Her cunt was dripping inside those panties.

"God, that's so fucking hot . . . your pussy all nice and wet. . . ."

The guy was moaning and gasping into the phone. "Why don't you take your panties off and see if you're wet? Slip your finger in there. . . ."

"Yeah," sighed Jen, "I'd like to." She whimpered softly, pulling her tank top up with one hand to expose her small, firm tits while, with the other hand, she yanked her panties down to her knees. She squirmed some more and kicked them off of her feet, spreading her legs to expose her freshly shaved pussy and her swollen, erect clit hood with its small, silver piercing. "I just shaved my pussy, so I can feel every bit of flesh. . . ." She began stroking her bare slit up and down. "God, I'm dripping," she moaned. "I'm fucking juicing everywhere."

"Why don't I stick my cock in there, then," the guy growled. "Since it's nice and big and hard."

"Oh yeah," Jen moaned. "Fuck yeah. I'm spreading my legs. I'm sliding my lips apart. God, I'm so wet and ready for you."

I was up and across the room in an instant, my sweat pants shucked and my hard cock in my hand.

"God I want it in my cunt," she moaned. "Shove it into me. Shove it hard!" Jen was always so fond of the word "shove" in instances like this.

She reached out and eagerly took my cock in her hand, leaning forward so she could get her mouth around it. "But first I want to suck it," she moaned quickly, just as my cockhead entered her mouth. She sucked it down, pumping it into her mouth and then gulping it eagerly down her well-trained throat.

I muttered soft encouragements to Jennie as the guy moaned "Yeah, yeah, suck it first, suck that hard cock . . ."

She came up for air long enough to whisper "Yeah, I'm sucking it, I'm deep-throating it, it tastes so good," and to make unsavory slurping noises into the phone, which brought a groan from Rick. Obviously he found such sounds more savory than I—but then again, they seemed, to me, superfluous—because I was getting my dick sucked.

Jen rubbed my cock over her face and then leaned back into the chair again, spreading her legs wide.

"Put it in," she moaned softly into the phone.

Rick growled back at her, "Yeah, yeah, I'm climbing on top of you. I'm shoving it in. I'm pounding your cunt!"

Falling on Jen hungrily, I kissed her deeply, my tongue teasing its way into her mouth and exploring it. With my hand, I guided my cockhead to Jen's entrance, and leaned back just enough so she could reach her clit. I started fucking her rapidly, knowing she was as close to climax as I was. I held silent so as not to interrupt Rick as he groaned and whimpered, shouting obscenities as he came. Then Jen was coming as she rubbed her pierced clit in little circles, and I felt the spasms of her vagina milk the orgasm out of my cock—and I came inside her, pumping and gasping as Rick and Jen finished.

"Yeah . . . yeah . . ." sighed Jen. "Call me again?" she begged.

"I sure will," said Rick. "And tell your boyfriend I hope he enjoyed it, too."

Jen giggled as I reddened. "My husband. That obvious?" she asked.

"I'm afraid so," said Rick.

"Well . . . he listens in on every conversation I have," she said.

"I'm not complaining," said Rick. "Talk to you, say, next weekend?"

"It's a date," said Jen.

Rick hung up. Jen kissed me and smiled.

"We'll make it a threesome," she said, as if to Rick, and cradled the phone.

JOHNNY'S STORY

Mary Anne Mohanraj

It was the summer before I started college. I was working in the factory and living with my family, saving up the money to buy my books and pay my rent, 'cause even if I *had* gotten a partial scholarship, it wasn't going to be near enough by itself, and my poppa didn't have anything to spare. Though he was proud, I think. None of the men in our line had ever even finished high school before. Just my momma's sister, who married the doctor, and Cassie, of course. Though it's not like Cassie's really my sister. She's just the daughter of the woman my poppa married after my momma took off. She doesn't look anything like me; she's little, y'know? Little like a bird, a little chocolate stick of a thing.

The guys in our family, the women too—they're all big-boned. Big-boned with some flesh on 'em, momma and poppa types, "generous" as my momma used to say before she took off with that rich guy. That's what my poppa says she did, anyway. I don't remember her saying that. I remember the day she left, though. Jamie and Jase had started up another one of their hollering fights, which had progressed to whaling on each other with their fists and making an unholy noise, and I was all ready for momma to turn around from the sinkful of last night's dishes and lay into both of them.

Instead, she just turned and stared, stared at those boys until they froze stock still. She stood there in the kitchen with her hands on her broad, heavy hips, with a dishcloth on her shoulder and this look on her face. This look like if she had to put up with me and Jamie and Jase for one more moment, she was gonna strangle us all the way she wished she'd done when we were born. She'd say that sometimes, y'know? "Sweet Lord Jesus forgive me, I should have strangled you at birth." In that flat voice, that said she was gonna crack, just split wide open like a bean pod, spilling out green bits. She didn't say anything that time, though. Just picked up her purse and walked out, with the blue striped dishcloth on her shoulder, and she didn't come back.

Cassie's momma is a lot like my momma. She moved out here from the big city, moved into the old Manelli house down the road and took a job at the plant, working right next to my poppa in the assembly line. That woman was so angry, so bone-deep angry, she told everyone she met that she had had it up to here with *that man*, and she wasn't going to put up with that kinda crap no more. That man had cheated on her for seven years. That man hadn't been able to keep his hands off any woman over eighteen excepting maybe his own daughter. That man had given her no peace. What Cassie's momma wanted more than anything else was some simple peace and quiet. Why she married my poppa then, I don't know, considering. Maybe just 'cause they were both lonely. Them getting together caused a lot of talk in the town for a while, 'cause some people here don't like white folks and black folks mixing together. I about thought my friend Pete's momma was gonna have herself a stroke, but that's mostly quieted down now.

Cassie isn't like either her momma or mine. Cassie wouldn't put up and put up and put up until the day she cracked. You say one word, look at her wrong, maybe pinch her butt as she walks by and she'll be on you so fast. "Fucking bastard!" She'll whip around and she'll be sticking one long brown finger in your face, hissing like a snake, promising to get her homeboys from the old neighborhood to come kick your face in if you push her one more time. And it's scary for a second, that fury exploding out at you, bright colored sparks flashing and screeching and you maybe take a step back. Hell, Jase'd take off running. Jamie'd blush bright red and look like he wanted to run and then he'd stand his ground. What else could he do—she's nineteen, older'n any of us, but she's so tiny, we could stomp her into the ground. He's gonna admit he's scared of that two-bit little girl? So they'd hiss at each other, and you could practically see the hair rising on their necks, their tails swishing as they turned and walked away. And me? Me the eighteen, me the should-know-better? Me who can't help grabbing a bit of that skinny butt as it walks by?

I just laugh when she explodes. I always step back for a sec, but she's so funny-looking, like an angry baby bird, and besides, I can tell she's bluffing. Just making this shit up, about homeboys and the 'hood, trying to make herself sound all city and tough. I can't help but laugh. A strangled chuckle and she's still shaking that finger, and then my mouth opens and a big belly laugh comes up from my big belly, and she's looking like all the brown's gonna wash away to white she's so mad . . . Most times, that's how it ends. Cassie looks like she'll explode, and my poppa hollers, "What're you doing to Cassie?!" I catch my breath and say I'm sorry, very calm, like a gentleman. And she can't do anything but take it.

Only one time, it didn't happen that way. I was sitting on the front room couch, that old cream-colored thing with the wide arms so comfy to lean against. I was sitting there reading so quiet, reading this book about kings and elves and rings, liking it a lot more than I'd expected I would, when Cassie came walking by. Cassie's mom had gone off to church, and poppa had said he was taking the boys to baseball, and maybe Cassie had thought he meant me too, and she'd have the house to herself. But I'd twisted my ankle coming down the stairs that morning, and so I couldn't go, and she'd maybe forgotten. 'Cause here she was walking down the hallway past the front room wrapped in nothing but a white towel, with those skinny long arms and legs sticking out of it so I whistled, 'cause what else is a brother to do if his sister walks by dressed like that, even if she isn't any kind of blood relation and he's only known her for a few months now? She'd been so careful around us boys that I'd never seen above her knees or even above her elbows before this. Nice.

So she whips around the way she always does and storms into the room, almost tripping over all the kids' junk on the floor but catching herself. She starts shaking that finger in my face. And I'm feeling a little guilty already so I hold back the laugh and let her harass me, let her holler in my face about her homeboys and how they'd kick my ass from here to next Sunday, and she's shaking like crazy with all that energy . . . and that towel starts slipping.

I can't help it, I laugh as she grabs at it and you can tell she's gonna explode like a grenade or a firework, and I'm clutching my stomach and laughing and knowing I'm gonna feel just rotten about this later. Cassie gets this look on her face, all twisted, screwed up tight and she reaches back with her fist and then slams it at my face, and if that had landed it would have hurt like hell. I may be big, but I'm not slow and I grab that fist and hold it. Her hand just disappears into mine with a thump and oh, this is the worst thing to do but I swear I can't help it; I'm still laughing as I hold her hand inside mine, our hands shaking together with the force of it—and then she starts laughing. I'm serious. The laughter just bursts, sunshine across her face and we laugh and laugh until we've got sore stomachs and damp eyes and when we're done laughing there's such a good feeling, such a warm fellow-feeling in that room, like nothing I've known, like this is gonna be a friend for life smiling at me with her eyes.

Her hand's dropped down but it's still in mine, the other one still holding up that damn towel. Her hand so warm, practically vibrating with the energy in her, and I want to open it up, open that fist gently and squeeze her hand tight. Maybe drop a kiss into her palm, and I'm looking in her eyes and I know that she can see my wanting in them. I can't read her though. Her hand twists in mine, uncurling and squeezing for one brief moment and I think maybe she's feeling what I'm feeling. Maybe Cassie's feeling that warmth uncurling in the belly. But instead of hanging on, she lets go. Lets go of my hand, which is feeling so cold and empty in that moment, like something's missing, like I've lost a limb that's supposed to be part of me.

It's then that she takes this one step back, slow and careful. That might have been it, she might have just walked away right then, but Jase'd left his backpack on the floor, and she steps right onto it, losing her balance and sticking a hand out, catching the edge of the doorframe and almost falling but not quite. And the towel slips. Just a little, and then she catches it up again, leaning against the doorframe, steadying herself. Then she stands up straight, her eyes locked on mine, on me sitting there, on the edge of jumping up to catch her. Cassie gets this look. There's this big grin on her face as she slowly takes both top edges of the white towel and pulls it open, open like a wall of white and she's posed against it. Small dark breasts with almost black nipples, surprisingly large. A flat stomach, and a mound shaved bare, a triangle between her thighs. I want to feed her. I want to put some meat on those skinny bones and then kiss my way along them. I want to drag her into bed and screw her 'til we're both sore and screaming. But she takes another step back, still smiling, and so I sit there on that cream-colored couch, thinking of how she'd look lying on it, arms stretched up above her head, legs bent and waiting. Sitting still has never been so hard.

"It's their house," she says, and I know what she means. She's not really my sister, not really . . . but poppa'd never understand. And I am despairing in that moment, despairing until I realize what she's saying.

"I start school in October," I offer. A long silence, waiting to hear her reply. She slowly wraps the towel back around her, hiding those slight curves.

"Maybe I'll come visit." She tilts her head, considering, and then nods, once, as if she's made a decision. Then she turns and walks down the hall.

I go back to reading, but even hours later, when the kids are back and the house is shouting again, I can still feel her smile warming the room.

ABOUT THE AUTHORS

ROBERT BUCKLEY is a Boston native, whose work has been published on the Web at the *Erotica Readers & Writers Association*, *Ophelia's Muse*, *Clean Sheets*, *Amoret*, *Solomon's Refuge* and *Adult Story Corner*, and in the British erotic-horror magazine *Peep Show*.

M. CHRISTIAN is the author of well over 100 published stories, the editor of over ten anthologies (including *Best S/M Erotica*, *The Burning Pen*, and *Guilty Pleasures*), the author of two collections, *Dirty Words*, and *Speaking Parts* (from Alyson Books) and having the honor of being not only in *Friction*, *Best of Friction*, *Best Gay Erotica*, *Best of Best Gay Erotica*, *Best American Erotica*, *Best Transgendered Erotica*, and *Best Lesbian Erotica*. Visit M. Christian at his website: mchristian.com.

PORTIA DA COSTA wrote her first erotic story, just for fun, way back in 1984. Since then, she hasn't really stopped writing. Her first story, "The Man in Black" appeared in the British magazine *Forum*. In the intervening years, she's had over 70 stories in various magazines, and fourteen books published under numerous pseudonyms. Her best known books are eight Black Lace novels; *The Stranger*, was voted "Best Erotic Novel of the Year" in 1998 by the Guild of Erotic Writers. If you want to know more about her, visit her website at wendywootton.co.uk—where you'll discover that her real name is Wendy!

WILLIAM DEAN is Associate Editor for *CleanSheets.com*. He is a Featured Writer for *MindCaviar.com*, and writes the monthly column Into the Erotik for the *Erotica Readers & Writers Association* (erotica-readers.com). He also has a weekly column, Erotik Journeys, at

Adult backwash.com. His non-erotic writings have appeared in *Slow-Trains.com* and SoMa Literary Review. His fiction and poetry is included in three published anthologies. He lives in California.

EVE FERAL is a communications professional who claimed her bisexuality and discovered her gift for writing erotic short stories and poetry only after leaving a 25-year marriage. She is the mother of one young adult daughter and two cats and lives happily and lustily in the southeastern U.S., where she doesn't let the prevailing Bible Belt mentality keep her down.

ROD HARDEN, also known as James V. Emanuel, lives in Northeast Ohio with his wife, two teenage sons, and three cats. He began writing erotica on a whim. His stories have appeared on numerous locations on the web, including *Erotica Readers & Writers Association, Jane's Guide, Mind Caviar, Slow Trains, Dare Magazine, Adult Story Corner,* and, of course, his own web site (rodharden.com). In addition, two collections of Mr. Harden's stories have been published by Renaissance E-Books. A novella is currently available from Olympia Press, and his novel, *Bound in Pleasure*, will be the featured selection for January 2002 from Venus Book Club. When Mr. Harden is not writing titillating tales, he enjoys playing classical guitar, trombone, and piano.

CLAYTON HOLIDAY is a native of St. Louis, currently living in Oklahoma. He has traveled extensively in Ireland and Mexico. Holiday's travels will next take him to the Mideast, where he plans to live for an undetermined time.

DEBRA HYDE is a busy writer whose erotica has appeared in a number of major anthologies and webzines. You can find her most current work in *Erotic Travel Tales, Zaftig: Well Rounded Erotica,* and *Of the Flesh: Dangerous New Fiction*. Upcoming work will appear in *Herotica 7, Noirotica 4,* and *Body Check*. When she's not writing erotica, Debra tracks sexuality news at her online weblog, *Pursed Lips* (pursedlips.com). Failing that, she's out getting some.

MAXIM JAKUBOWSKI was born in Barnet but brought up in Paris. He followed a career in publishing by opening the Murder One bookshop in London in 1988. He writes, edits and publishes in many areas of genre fiction, including SF and fantasy, mystery and erotica. He has published over forty books of his own, including *On Tenderness Express* and *Kiss Me Sadly* (June 2002), and is editor of five best-selling volumes in the *Mammoth Books* series including *The Mammoth Book of Best New Erotica* and the newly released *Mammoth Book of Illustrated Erotica.*

MIKE KIMERA is fascinated by the way sex and lust shape people's lives. His stories, which range from the tender and intimate to the dark and dangerous, have been posted widely on the web, and recently in the anthology *From Porn to Poetry: Clean Sheets Celebrates the Erotic Mind.* He is a member of the *Erotica Readers & Writers Association* (erotica-readers.com) where like-minded souls help him to improve his writing. Mike works as a management consultant (it's an easy job and someone has to do it) and lives in England and Switzerland.

ADHARA LAW has been writing fiction since she was a little girl, but really got going when she fell into erotica. Now 29 years old, her work has been featured both in print and online, in places such as *Clean Sheets, Scarlet Letters,* and in *Desires.* Her corner of the Internet, adharalaw.com, contains her fiction, non-fiction, and more. She lives in California with her husband but calls Wyoming her home.

MARILYN JAYE LEWIS' short stories and novellas have been widely anthologized in the US and UK. Editions Blanche, Paris, published the French language edition of her critically acclaimed collection of novellas, *Neptune & Surf,* in Fall 2001. She is co-editor of *The Mammoth Book of Erotic Photography* and recently won Best Erotic Writer of the Year in the UK for 2001. Her upcoming novel, *The Curse of Our Profound Disorder,* was a finalist for The Evans Harrington Award in the William Faulkner Writing Competition in New Orleans. As webmistress, her erotic multi-media sites have won numerous awards. Visit Marilyn's homepage at: marilynjayelewis.com.

LYBBE is a Canadian woman who has had a long time love affair with words. She writes erotica for the thrill that comes from knowing somebody else might be turned on by her words.

MARCI McDONALD (Desires' cover artist) was born in Kansas City, Missouri, and lived in Montana, California, and Nebraska before moving to Pennsylvania in 1971. She studied Fine Art at Montana State College and the University of Nebraska at Omaha. Her artistic career began with the challenging medium of woodcuts. Her remarkable prints have won numerous awards in juried shows and competitions throughout the United States. Now she has turned her attention to painting, Her inter-

208 *About the Authors*

pretations of figures and nature are wonderfully imaginative with a fluidity of line suggesting Art Nouveau. Marci has been featured in more than forty one-person shows and her work is included in many private and public collections. View Marci's art at: marcimcdonald.com.

JAMES MARTIN is no stranger to desire. He lives in a constant state of bafflement over the fact that extraordinarily ordinary people can waltz into his stories at the most erotic moments to have experiences he can only dream of.

MARY ANNE MOHANRAJ (mamohanraj.com) is the author of *Torn Shapes Of Desire*, editor of *Aqua Erotica* and *Wet* (forthcoming 2002), and consulting editor for *Herotica 7*. She has been published in a multitude of anthologies and magazines, including *Herotica 6*, *Best American Erotica 1999*, and *Best Women's Erotica* 2000 and 2001. Mohanraj founded the erotic webzine, *Clean Sheets* (cleansheets.com) and serves as editor-in-chief for the speculative fiction webzine *Strange Horizons* (strangehorizons.com). She also moderates the EROS Workshop and is a graduate of Clarion West '97. She has received degrees in Writing and English from Mills College and the University of Chicago, and is currently a doctoral student in Fiction and Literature at the University of Utah. She received the Scowcroft Award for fiction in Spring 2001.

D. E. RIDER, born in 1951, grew up in eastern Virginia. After college study in a number of fields, Rider made a career in computers, which, among other things, gave Rider a chance to enjoy the Internet before it became a household word. Now residing in New York State with spouse and children, Rider maintains a long-standing interest in writing science fiction, fantasy, and other fictional genres, but to this point it is only erotica that has inspired Rider to any significant output. Rider has written widely for Internet consumption under pseudonyms but this is Rider's first published story.

JEAN ROBERTA is a woman of a certain age who can pass for White Anglo-Saxon Protestant. She has dual citizenship (American and Canadian), a half-Nigerian daughter, a Latina partner, an academic job and an interesting past which must sometimes be discussed with others. She has had erotic fiction published in anthologies such as the *Best Lesbian* and *Best Women*, *Wicked Words*, *Best Bisexual Erotica 2*, and *Herotica 7* and in print journals and websites, including the erotica galleries of the *Erotica Readers & Writers Association*, to which she is grateful.

Her lesbian novel, *Prairie Gothic*, will soon be available as an e-book from Amatory Ink.

THOMAS S. ROCHE has written over 100 published short stories and 200 published articles. His books include the *Noirotica* series of erotic crime-noir anthologies, the short story collection *Dark Matter*, and the forthcoming crime novel *Violent Angel*.

NATASHA ROSTOVA (hyperlinx.net/~blue) is the author of four Black Lace novels, including the best-selling *Captivation* and *The Naked Truth* as well as *Tea and Spices* (Carroll and Graf). Her work has appeared in several anthologies, and she is working on a compilation of short stories. She lives in Montreal, where she is studying art history.

JASON RUBIS lives in Washington, DC. His erotic fiction has appeared in *Leg Show*, *Variations*, *High-Heeled Women*, *Tales from the Asylum*, a number of adult websites, and the anthologies *Fetish Fantastic* and *Guilty Pleasures*. He is the author of several erotic novels, including *Guilt* and *Paying for the Prodigal*, from Pink Flamingo Publications and *Operation Tickell*, from MTJ Publications.

ROBERT SCHAFFER is a photographer/writer who lives in Manhattan. He loves rubber stamps, cats, fake fish, Hawaiian shirts, and photographing dominatrixes. Interested parties can check out his website: home.earthlink.net/~photo824.

SHIVAJI SENGUPTA is a scholar and an author; he is a professor of English in a liberal arts college and a senior academic administrator. His work has appeared in *Clean Sheets*, *Hoterotica*, and various other websites and anthologies.

HELENA SETTIMANA lives in Toronto. Her short fiction, poetry, and essays have appeared on the web at the *Erotica Readers & Writers Association*, *Scarlet Letters*, *Clean Sheets*, and *Dare*. In print, she has been featured in *Best Women's Erotica* 2001 and 2002, *Erotic Travel Tales*, *Best Bisexual Women's Erotica*, and *From Porn to Poetry: Clean Sheets Celebrates the Erotic*. Contributions to *Herotica 7*, and *Shameless*, will be released in the spring of 2002. Helena moonlights as Features Editor at the *Erotica Readers & Writers Association* (erotica-readers.com).

GIN SMITH is the pseudonym of a writer living east of Eden somewhere in the southern United States. An editor by night (don't ask her what her day job is), her erotica has previously appeared on the Internet in *Sauce*Box* and *Dare* (daremag.com), and in The Gallery of the *Erotica Readers & Writers Association*. This is her first anthologized erotic short story.

CECILIA TAN is the author of *The Velderet, Black Feathers,* and *Telepaths Don't Need Safewords.* Her erotic fiction has appeared everywhere from *Ms. magazine* to *Penthouse, Best American Erotica* to *Nerve.com.* She is the founder and editor of Circlet Press, publishers of erotic science fiction and fantasy. Many juicy details about her life and work can be found at: ceciliatan.com.

HARRY TASKER is a writer fascinated by the darker shades of the human soul. He has been published in (amongst other places) *Clean Sheets, Blue Food, Amoret, Blowfish, Blood Moon Zine,* and *JaneZine.* Some of his work is available to read on his website "Perdition's Flames" (harry.tasker.btinternet.co.uk). He hails from Cornwall, England.

ELANA WHITE is a graphic artist and production manager living in Ottawa Canada. Besides appearing in *Desires,* her erotic poems and a story have been published in *Blue Food,* a quarterly literary journal.

ABOUT THE EDITOR

ADRIENNE BENEDICKS founded the *Erotica Readers & Writers Association* in 1996, and is still a bit surprised to find herself administrator of a community that dwells in the sensual and the erotic. She never expected all those dogged-eared naughty books residing under her bed would lead her to editing her own *Desires*. She finds it liberating to realize the only dirty things under her bed are dust bunnies; that her passion for things erotic is simply a healthy interest in sexuality. There's nothing quite like a community of like-minded people to light the way. Adrienne graduated from Florida State University with a degree in Anthropology, has three kids away at college and lives with her professor husband in Florida. However, the New Yorker in her is still alive and kicking.